DISSONANT DREAMS

The Short Stories of
Matthew Barron

Published by
Submatter Press

Library of Congress Cataloging-in-Publication Data is available upon request.

ISBN: 978-1-954482-02-9 (paperback)
ISBN: 978-1-954482-04-3 (hardcover)
eISBN: 978-1-954482-03-6 (eBook)

For more information, to contact the author, or to order additional books, visit:
submatterpress.com

This book is dedicated to the editors and publishers who provide homes for short stories from new writers. Their books and magazines often run on the passion and dedication of one or a very small group of individuals who see little financial benefit compared to all the work they put in. Without them, a collection like this would not be possible.

Thank you!

TABLE OF CONTENTS

INTRODUCTION 7
SUBDIVISION 9
YAO'S WORLD 27
KILLING TIME 33
WAITING FOR MOURNING 53
HELL ISLAND 55
MEMORY ADRIFT 67
TRUTH, MIMES, AND PUPPY TALES 73
WAR STORY 95
LIMINAL SPACE 101
BACK TO NORMAL 121
THE TWISTED SCHEMES AND BROKEN
    DREAMS OF MANGLED MALLOW 127
BOOK CLUB FROM HELL 135
INTRODUCTION TO
    THE IRON WRITER CHALLENGE 156
THE MASTODON MARTYR 157
YELLOW REVENGE 159
THE SMELL 161
DOGS PLAYING POKER 171
THE IMMORTAL WRITER 187
REBRANDED 191
THE LIFTED VEIL 231
DISCORD 241
SANTA'S CLAWS 258
THE LONGEST NIGHT 261
ABOUT THE AUTHOR 277

INTRODUCTION

I am so excited to finally put out this collection of stories! I love short stories even more than I enjoy my longer work. In a short story, you can explore a single idea, theme or premise. You can hold a single mood for the entire length of the work. In a short story, you can experiment with style and format in a way you might not want to do in a longer work which takes more time and investment. With a short story, you can get quick, immediate feedback, and this is where I continue to hone my craft. I am constantly learning new things and relearning things I've forgotten.

I've been wanting to put a collection out for years, but I had to wait. Not only did it take time to build a portfolio of stories, I also wanted to give these stories a chance to find life in other magazines and anthologies first. (I also wanted to get paid for them!) Getting them out in other places garnered attention, added to my resume and, justified or not, I feel it gives me a little more "writing street cred" because an editor or publisher saw value in my work.

Here you will find, collected together for the first time, stories previously appearing in *Generation X-ed, Ill-Considered Expeditions, Sci Phi Journal, Outposts of Beyond, House of Horror* and more! Plus, you will see never-before-seen stories published here for the first time.

After so many years, these stories feel new again. I look at them and wonder, *Who wrote this? How did that guy I used to be come up with this?* I hope you enjoy them as much as I enjoyed writing and re-reading them. Another good thing about short stories—if you don't like the one you are reading, skip to the next one! Thank you for supporting and enabling my obsessive-compulsive writing disorder!

SUBDIVISION

Originally published in *Generation X-ed*
from Dark Ink Books January, 2022

The sun shone on rows of sloped brown roofs. Some houses were ranch, others two story, but all had the same beige siding and attached garages. A few feet of green lawn stretched from the pale sidewalks to the front doors. The maroon Oldsmobile wound over blacktop streets, curving around masses of cookie cutter houses.

Annie looked at Ted from the passenger seat. "There's Minos Court again. You're driving in circles."

Ted's fingers clenched the steering wheel, and his shoulders threatened to burst from his white button-down shirt. "We must be close."

"None of these streets are on the directions Mary gave me."

"Mary gives horrible directions. We can't be far."

Annie flipped down the mirror and gently framed her brown hair with her hands. She'd used enough product to destroy the ozone layer single-handedly. Her bangs spiraled up like a slinky, and not a hair was out of place.

It was a nice day for a drive, but this was ridiculous. "Just call her," Annie said. "We're an hour late."

Ted plucked the flip phone from his pocket and tossed it into the lap of Annie's black skirt.

Annie narrowed her eyes. "Gee, thanks." She flipped open the phone and dialed. "No signal. So much for nationwide coverage. *Can you hear me now?*"

Ted pressed his foot on the accelerator and turned the wheel. Tires squealed against the road, and inertia pushed Annie against the door as the car spun.

"Ted, what the hell?"

"You wanted to go to this party so bad, but you couldn't even bother to get decent directions. I've been driving around this God damned subdivision for 45 minutes!"

"Well, maybe you shouldn't have turned into the wrong addition!"

"It wasn't the wrong subdivision! The directions said turn on Wilson Drive!"

"But we ended up on Cretan Drive!"

"These new housing additions all look alike!"

Ted drove much faster than he should on a residential street. Annie took a deep breath. "Ted, slow down. You're going to hit somebody."

"There's nobody here!"

He was right. On a Saturday afternoon, Annie expected to see some kids playing in the suburban streets, but there was no one. They hadn't even seen any cars since entering this subdivision.

Ted let the car coast for a bit and let out a long sigh. "I'm sorry, Annie. Let's get back to the main road, get our bearings."

Annie kneaded Ted's shoulder with her slender hand, and some of the tension eased in his tight muscle. He extended his hand, and she held it as he drove in silence.

They passed Minos Court again. At last they found Cretan Drive. Ted paused, and Annie could tell he wasn't sure which way to turn. Annie tried to remember how they had come in and looked for landmarks to guide her, but all the houses and all the corners looked alike. Finally, she said, "Your guess is as good as mine."

He turned right and drove. Cretan Drive wound around, then spit them back onto Minos Court.

Ted screamed and hit the roof of the car.

"Let's just ask for directions," Annie implored.

"It's got to be the other way."

Ted turned the car around. They found Cretan Drive again, but turned the opposite direction.

Annie looked at the houses around them. "This doesn't look right."

"What doesn't look right?"

"The houses."

"They all look the same."

"We've been driving too long."

"No shit!"

Annie sighed, and Ted continued to drive.

She watched the house numbers go down as they made their way. 4211, 4209, 4207, 2200... "2200? This doesn't make sense!"

Ted still wasn't talking.

Sick of silence, Annie turned on the radio. Their regular station didn't come in, so she scanned for others. The radio flipped through the spectrum, then started again. She rotated through the channels manually, hearing only static.

"Just hit 103."

"I tried. Nothing's coming in."

Ted stabbed his finger at the buttons. "You're just trying to avoid 103. You hate alternative music."

"I don't hate it. I just don't see what is so alternative about it. They dress alike. They sound alike. Still rock'n'roll to me."

Of course Ted got the same results. "We are just on the other side of town. There should be all kinds of radio stations!"

It had been three hours since they had left the house, and Annie glanced at the fuel gauge. "We need to get gas soon."

"I know!"

Annie had really been looking forward to seeing her friend again. They hadn't seen each other since Mary had moved across town, but it was time to give up. "I don't care about the party anymore. I just want to go home."

Ted pulled onto Phaedra Drive and brought the car to a stop next to the curb. They stretched, randomly picked a house, and marched to the door with bowed heads. The homeowner would think them idiots, getting lost in a subdivision. Annie rang the bell, but no one answered. Ted knocked, but there was nobody home. They tried next door, but the result was the same. Ted peeked in the window.

"Don't do that!" Annie said.

"I don't think anyone lives here."

Lace curtains obscured the view, but there didn't appear to be any furniture in the living room.

While Ted continued banging on doors and peeking in windows, Annie took off her heels and ran across the street. It felt good to move after sitting for so long. There was no answer at any of these houses.

They met in the middle of the road and stared at each other. The setting sun cast long, blocky shadows from the houses around them. Ted started laughing. Annie didn't know why, but she started laughing too.

"This is ridiculous!" Ted said, tears in his eyes. "We just need to drive in one direction and not make any turns." He made for the car. "Swear you won't tell anyone about this."

His change of mood comforted Annie.

They drove, and the sun sank in the sky. Annie tried the phone again, but there was still no signal. The gas gauge crept closer and closer to empty.

There were no lights in any of the cookie cutter houses, and the streets were dark. At last Ted pulled over on Minos Court. They banged on more doors.

Something yipped when Annie came up to one of the houses. A white dog dragged a large, wet bone from behind a bush. The dog's ribs were visible under its short fur. Annie approached, and the dog growled, baring teeth without relinquishing his bone. The dog stood about the height of Annie's knees, but the bone was the size of a human thigh.

"That's a big bone for such a little dog," Annie said. "Is your owner home?"

"Stay back!" Ted called. He had pulled a tire iron from the trunk of the car.

The dog took off with his giant bone.

"Why did you chase him away? He might have led us to his owner."

Ted shook his head. "He was as lost as we are."

Ted went up to the door of the house and jabbed the tire iron against a pane of glass.

"What are you doing? What if there is an alarm?"

"Good," Ted said. "I'd be happy to see anyone about now, even a cop." Ted poked at the glass again. Breaking glass in the door was harder and noisier than it looked to be on television, but even with all their racket, nobody came to investigate. Ted reached into the broken pane and unlocked the door.

Plush carpet covered the living room floor, and the walls were pristine eggshell white, but there was no furniture. They tried the lights, but there was no power. There were three bedrooms and a kitchen, but no furnishings beyond the curtains and blinds. Of course there was no phone either. The sight of the kitchen sink made Annie realize how thirsty she was. Ted must have had the same idea. He lifted the lever, but no water came out. Annie sank onto the kitchen floor and leaned against the cabinets.

Ted looked down at her and tried to smile. "Looks like we'll have to settle for champagne." They had brought a bottle of champagne and a tray of meat and cheese for the party.

Annie brought her hands up to her mouth. This was really happening. They weren't going to make it home tonight. "What about Kiki?" Annie imagined her little bulldog clawing at the wire latch of her kennel and whimpering.

Ted knelt down and touched Annie's face. "Louis will look in on her."

Louis was her neighbor and watched Kiki when Annie was away. "If Louis even realizes we're gone. It was only supposed to be a few hours." At best, Kiki would end up with a bladder infection from holding it in all night. At worst, she would starve to death.

Ted pulled Annie's face into his chest. "She'll be fine. Louis will hear her crying. He's got a key."

Annie wiped her nose on Ted's white shirt, and Ted didn't complain. He leaned down and kissed her.

Ted had a blanket in the trunk of the car. They spread it on the living room floor. There was a whole house, but they preferred to stay close to the door. They had a picnic of sorts.

Ted took a swig of bubbly champagne from the bottle. "This will all seem silly in the light of day. We'll be home in time for Saturday morning cartoons."

"That might make me feel better if tomorrow wasn't Sunday. Are you saying we'll be stuck here all week?"

"Of course not. You'll see. Once we are out of here, we will laugh about this."

Annie continued to frown.

"It doesn't matter where we are, babe." Ted began singing *I'm gonna keep on loving you,* by REO Speedwagon. He didn't remember all the words and started with the chorus, then tried to catch up the beginning.

Annie found herself smiling as she took up the bottle. "Are all their songs about being wronged by a woman but loving her anyway?"

"Of course! It's *Codependent Rock.*"

Annie chuckled. This was more romantic than any party, just her and Ted camping in the dark. She settled into Ted's arms, and they wrapped the blanket around themselves.

A long, deep moan unsettled Annie, but she remained secure in Ted's embrace. Something snapped in the distance. High-pitched, rapid barking pierced the night, followed by another long, deep moan. The barking persisted.

Ted sat up and peered out the window. There was nothing outside but a dark suburban street. The barking became a yip, and then all was silent.

Ted went out the door, and Annie followed close behind. At the corner of the street, about four houses down, a big lumpy shadow moved against one of the houses. The digging and crunching would normally remain unnoticed, but everything was so quiet here. The shadow froze. Something extended from the lumpy mass. A giant, black head rose to fill the second story of the house. Massive, pointed horns curved from the head, like a demon. A long snout extended, and Annie could imagine the thing sniffing the air. The shadow shrank as its owner lumbered to the corner.

"Get inside," Ted whispered. He practically shoved Annie back into the house and locked the door behind them.

Another long, deep moan echoed off the walls and filled their guts with dread. Ted pulled up the blanket and moved it into the kitchen where they huddled behind the cabinets. They could hear something in the back yard, nuzzling through the bushes. Whatever it was, it finally wandered away.

"What was that?" Annie whispered.

Ted brushed his hand up and down her arm. "I don't know."

A car started outside. Sunlight streamed through the windows, but Ted and Annie had their shelter behind the kitchen cabinets. It took a moment to remember where they were.

"A car!" Ted exclaimed. He went to the living room window. A car growled in front of the house.

"No. No. No!" Ted yanked open the door and ran into the street. Annie rose stiffly and followed.

Their Oldsmobile crawled slowly down the street. "Hey!" Ted shouted. There appeared to be two people inside. "Stop!" Ted gave chase, but the car sped up and squealed around the corner. He kept after them, but by the time he reached the corner, the car was nowhere in sight.

Annie met him in the middle of the deserted street.

"We'll get out of here," he assured her. "On foot, we don't have to worry about roads. We walk in a straight line, cut through yards. Eventually, we will reach a main road. Once we are out of this subdivision, we can find help."

His confidence was comforting, and she pressed her head against his chest. Something shiny caught her eye. A thin, brown strip of plastic, like the tape once used in audiocassettes, ran along the edge of the street. Before they left the house, Annie used the restroom. Even without running water and toiletries, this seemed more civilized than going in the yard like Ted. They made their way on foot down Minos Court.

At the corner, black crows pecked at a glistening red smear on the road. Ted tried to pull Annie back, but she had to look. In the red, there were patches of white fur and splintered bones. Something had been gnawing on them.

Ted pulled her away. They cut through a yard, climbed a privacy fence, then jumped a 4-foot chain link fence in the back of that. It was late Sunday morning, but all was quiet, and no one complained about the two trespassers.

Metal clinked lightly in the breeze, and something creaked rhythmically. Ted stopped in the road. One of the yards was not like all the others. There were wind chimes made of old soda cans, and lawn sculptures made of hubcaps. An old woman sat on a porch swing. They had found another human being! Annie rushed to the woman, but Ted slowed her with a hand on her shoulder. The woman's blue dress had probably been very fancy once, but the fabric was faded and worn. Curly gray hair framed a serene face. Her eyes were closed, and she hadn't seen them.

"Excuse me," Ted said as they approached. The woman remained still. "Hello."

The woman's eyes shot open, and her serenity twisted into rage. "You get out of here! Leave my boy alone!"

"We don't know any boy," Ted said. "We only want to use your phone."

"Everyone wants to hurt my boy," the old woman said. "If you left him alone, he never would have bothered you!"

Ted and Annie exchanged a glance, and Annie said, "Please, we need your help."

"Liar! You get out of here!"

Annie leaned in. "We're lost!"

The woman let out a shriek and shook her gnarled hands with rage. Annie plugged her ears with her fingers. A deep moan underlay the woman's grating screech. The woman stopped screaming and smiled. The low moan remained. It was the animal noise from last night, the call of the thing that had chewed up that poor dog.

"My boy's coming," the old woman rasped. "You best get out of here."

Ted and Annie ran into the street. They looked all around, but the deep moan reverberated off the walls, coming from everywhere at once. The moan stopped, and they ran in a random direction.

A naked man filled the street in their path. Even at this distance, his shoulders seemed to take up the whole road, three times the width of his waist. Ruddy hair covered his body, and his head was armed with curved horns. His long snout stretched above him, and their chests vibrated with bass.

His hooves pounded on the blacktop, and Annie continued staring. The monster bounded onto his thick hands, charging like a bull.

Ted jerked Annie away from the sight, pulling her between houses. They leapt over a privacy fence and ran behind a storage shed. Ted hiked a leg over a chain link fence, but was startled by the sound of smashing wood, and fell to the grass. The privacy fence crashed inward, and pounding legs thumped against the turf. The chain link fence shook violently. Ted and Annie sat frozen in each other's arms. Something snapped in the distance, like thunder, and another deep groan echoed off the next street. They lay still and panting in the grass.

At last, Ted peeked out from behind the storage shed. A trail of ripped and punctured wood led from the privacy fence to the flattened chain link next to them. Metal fence posts lay horizontal in the pitted dirt. Uniform grass was marred by deep hoof-prints as wide as Annie's waist.

Their plan to walk a straight line had been disrupted. They were lost again. They were not alone here, but they now wished they were.

Annie clung to Ted. "I'm supposed to go to work tomorrow."

Ted was dismissive. "So am I."

"I can't just not show up!"

"And I can?"

"You're salaried."

He pushed her away. "If I don't show up, the work doesn't get done. What do you think I do all day, sit at my desk and file my nails?"

Ted became blurry as tears pooled in her eyes.

"I'm sorry," he said. "I didn't mean—"

She couldn't form words. Ted pulled her close again and ran a hand up and down her back. It didn't solve anything, but it made her feel better. Ted found a heavy rock and smashed open the lock to the storage shed. There was nothing inside, nothing at all. The shed was clean and never used. They shut themselves inside. Annie wished they would have kept the blanket from last night, but they never imagined they'd be spending another night lost in this subdivision.

Hunger and thirst forced them back to the street. They renewed their plan to walk a straight line. If they walked straight, they had to reach the end of the subdivision. They walked for hours, listening for danger in the quiet. There were no sounds but the occasional chirping of tiny birds.

Annie spied something shiny, more brown tape twisting in the breeze. On a whim, they followed its path along the street. They rounded a corner, and spotted Ted's maroon Oldsmobile. Ted pulled Annie back behind a house, and they peeked out. A young boy rode his rusty bike around the car.

Ted and Annie jumped more fences. Once Ted gauged they were close to the car, they snuck around a house and watched. The boy was not alone. A man lay under the trailer hitch. The trunk was open, and he was connecting the car to a frame of wood. On either side of this frame were horizontal panels of vinyl siding. The man under the car, though older, had muscles rippling under his brown skin, and grease stained his once white t-shirt.

Annie whispered, "What are they doing to your car?"

Ted shook his head. "I don't know."

The child circled and popped a wheelie. His dirty blond hair waved in the breeze as he pedaled. The boy was barefoot, and his belly button peeked from a yellow shirt with pictures of masked ninja turtles on the chest. His clothes were about two sizes too small for him, and his hair almost grew over his eyes. His skin was a dusty gray from dirt and sun.

"It's time!" The man had a curly salt and pepper beard and long graying hair. "We need that bike!"

The boy walked the bike behind the car and the old man lifted the wood frame.

Ted began to move while they were distracted.

"Be careful," Annie said. Ted was the only thing keeping her sane in this crazy subdivision, her one small piece of stability. She couldn't lose him.

Ted jumped out from behind the house. He had his keys out. "I'm taking back my car."

The man jerked up and bumped his head on the wood frame. "Wait!" the old man said. "You speak English. Are you American?" Ted gave no response. "If you let us use your car," the man said, "we can help you."

"What do you mean?" Ted asked.

"You are lost here," the man said. "Right?"

A glimmer of hope passed through Annie. "You know the way out?"

The man shook his head. "We've been lost here for three years."

Annie put a hand over her mouth. "Three years?" It wasn't possible.

"Yes," the man said. "But we have a plan." He finished ratcheting a bolt, and the bike now had wings of vinyl siding. "Ike here is going to glide above the houses. From the air, he can find the edge of this neighborhood. My son will lead us out."

Annie inspected the winged contraption. It was not the least bit aerodynamic. "The boy is going to fly that?"

"It has to be me," Ike insisted. "I'm the only one light enough."

The man was begging. "What do you have to lose?"

To Annie's surprise, Ted extended his hand and introduced himself. "Ted."

The old man took Ted's hand. "David."

"Why did you need our car?" Annie asked.

"We need to get the glider moving to get it in the air," David said. "We ran out of gas years ago. I suppose our car is rusting around here...somewhere."

"Years?" Annie repeated. There was that word again.

"That won't happen to you," David said. "We're getting out of here. You must be thirsty." David removed a concave plastic sled from the lawn, revealing an inverted hubcap full of water.

Annie brought the hubcap to her lips, and lukewarm slickness washed over her parched lips and throat.

"Not too much at once," David said.

She handed the hubcap to Ted.

David explained, "We leave the sled out at night, upside down. In the morning, condensation builds on the underside and drips into the hubcap."

Little Ike clung to his father's pant leg and stared up at Annie.

"What about food?" she asked.

A glimmer sparkled in the child's eye, and he whipped out a slingshot. Before Annie knew what was happening, a sparrow fell from the tree above them. The boy took aim again, but the other birds had scattered.

David smiled with pride at his son. "We eat birds when we can find them. Birds seem to come and go freely. They gave me the idea for the glider." David tapped the wooden frame over the bicycle. "The easiest protein to come by is worms. We just dig them up. Occasionally we find a patch of mushrooms."

The thought of dirty brown worms squirming in her mouth nearly made Annie gag.

"You live in this house?" Ted asked.

"It isn't a good idea to spend too much time in any one place," David said. "We keep moving, or the beast sniffs us out."

"You've seen it too?" Annie said.

Ike ran up to them again, interested.

"I'm afraid so," David said.

"What is that thing?" Annie asked.

David shrugged and sat on the curb, suddenly tired. "No idea. People and animals wander in here from all over the place, but that thing...I have a theory this place was built specifically for that beast, to trap it, like a prison."

Ike tugged at David's shirt. "Dad! Let's go!"

"We're talking, Ike." David returned his attention to Ted and Annie. "People like us wander in here from time to time and end up trapped with that thing."

Annie thought of the poor lost dog. "We become its food."

David nodded his head.

"Why not just build a real prison?" Ted said, "With walls and a sturdy door?"

"Have you seen that thing?" David answered. "Walls do nothing."

"Why not just kill it then," Ted said. "If someone could construct this elaborate trap, they must have had access to weapons."

David shrugged again. "Maybe they wanted to keep the beast around. Maybe they wanted to study it."

Annie folded her arms around herself. "Maybe they want to study us. What about that woman?"

"Woman?" David said.

"There was this crazy old woman on a porch swing."

David's eyes widened. "You already met Miss Pasiphae! We didn't run into her until we'd been here for months. She's the only person the monster doesn't bother."

Annie could still hear the old woman shrieking. "That thing came when she called."

David seemed surprised. "Really?"

Annie could still see the old woman's gnarled hands shaking in the air. "She's crazy."

David cocked his head. "No more than any of us in here. Whenever we find ourselves by Miss Pasiphae's house, I try to have some gift for her, something shiny. She will talk to us for a bit, sometimes even gives us water."

"Gifts," Annie wondered. "Those lawn ornaments?"

David smiled. "Guilty."

"Dad!" Ike demanded.

"Alright." David pushed himself up off the curb. "Strap in, Ike."

Ike got on the bike and harnessed himself into the wooden frame. The bicycle helmet didn't seem adequate for what they were trying. David opened the driver door.

"I'll drive," Ted said. "It's my car."

"We can only try this once," David said. "I've done the calculations, ran through the scenarios."

Annie understood that Ted was still sore about having his car stolen, but she was in no mood for a pissing contest. "Relax, Ted. Let David drive."

"You have a more important job," David said. He directed them to a pair of rusty garden shears in the back seat, and the insulated cable coming up from the trunk. David must have ripped the cable from the back of one of the houses. "When the time comes, you must cut this wire."

"You really think it will fly?" Annie asked.

"It's got to." David got in the car and started the engine. "There is only enough gas to try this once."

David raised his thumb out the window, and Ike responded with a *thumbs up*. The boy was not only ready, he beamed with excitement.

David eased the car forward, and the winged contraption jerked into motion. David checked the mirror, and Ike again gave a thumbs up. David added pressure to the accelerator, and the car sped smoothly. He had to slow a bit to turn off the drive and onto another road.

"Damn it!" David said. "There isn't enough road to pick up speed. "How's he doing?"

Ike had his hands tight on the handle bars, but still beamed with giddiness.

"He's fine," Ted said.

David pounded the pedal to the floor, and they were all pressed back in their seats.

Annie looked back and found Ike gliding a few feet off the ground. "It's working! We have lift!"

David furrowed his brow. "We're running out of road!"

The blacktop curved ahead. At this speed, they would punch the car into a living room in less than a minute.

"It's too late to stop!" David shouted. "Cut him loose!"

Ted closed the dull blades on the cable but couldn't exert force in the confining back seat.

"Cut it!" David shouted. "If we stop now, Ike will be swung into the ground!"

Annie added her weight to the shears.

The house ahead filled the windshield. David swung the steering wheel and slammed on the brakes. The Oldsmobile squealed its tires and snapped a mailbox from the ground.

The cable had been cut. David hurried from the car and looked up. Ike was nowhere to be seen.

A low moan resonated somewhere in the distance.

Annie looked at Ted. "The monster heard the crash!"

The glider rounded over the houses on vinyl wings, and Ike waved down at them. They all cheered. Ike steered the glider around the blue sky and pointed.

"What's he pointing at?" Ted asked. "A way out?"

"Follow him!" David commanded, chasing after his son in the sky.

Ike soared over the next street. They cut through yards. Fences slowed them down. David wasn't able to leap them as gracefully as Ted and Annie. The glider shrank in the sky. Ike swooped down and circled back, waving again.

"Damn it, boy," David said. "Stop showing off!" Of course Ike couldn't hear him.

The child flew in a figure eight.

"Are we still going the right way?" Ted asked.

"I think Ike's getting tired of waiting for us to catch up to him," Annie answered. Another low moan filled her with dread. "Crap!"

Ike swooped down and up, a huge smile on his face.

"What is he doing?" Ted wondered.

The glider climbed steeply into the sky and slowed as Ike rose higher and higher.

"No!" David yelled. "The glider has no propulsion. If he stops moving, it will fall."

As predicted, the glider hung frozen in the air for a moment, then plummeted to the ground. Ike was a dot in the sky, but Annie could see the smile on his face change to horror.

"Pull up!" David shouted.

The boy didn't need to hear his father's words. He was already pulling hard at the controls. The glider began to level out, and vertical speed became horizontal motion. He was pulling out of the dive! A few more feet, and he would have made it, but he didn't have a few more feet. Ike collided against the second story of a house, splintering the wood frame around him. The crumbling glider slid behind rooftops.

"Ike!" David shouted as he ran for the horrendous sight. It seemed to take forever to reach the boy, and Annie feared they might not find him at all. They found him, but something else had found him first. Broad, woolly shoulders hunched over the wreckage.

David was out of breath, but he charged at the beast. "Ike!"

The monster raised his snout and let out a deep moan. Ted and Annie pulled David from the sight as the monster pounded toward them. They fled down the street. The monster's head was low to the ground as it bounded on its thick hands. David fell behind, and Annie looked behind her just in time to see him scooped into the air by the monster's horns. The horns caught David midair and smeared him into the pavement.

Annie screamed and fell, skinning her knee and tearing her hose, but Ted yanked her up and they dove between houses, finally falling to the ground in a shaking mass.

Once they were able to move again, they cautiously looked for Ike and the wrecked glider, but they had gotten all turned around again. Annie clung to Ted. Now more than ever, he was her world.

There was nothing left to do but forage for food and find shelter for the night. Seeing how David and Ike had survived all that time in this tiny world made survival possible for Ted and Annie.

Weeks later, Annie made a kind of paint from mashed up grass and dirt and wrote their names on garage doors for newcomers to see.

If you ever find yourself lost in a subdivision, look for an old couple named Ted and Annie. They love hearing news from the outside world.

YAO'S WORLD

Originally published in *Sci Phi Journal* on November 28, 2016

The bubble hummed. It had grown into a dark globe and was partially submerged in the table top. Yao sat at the bench and looked into two long tubes. His hand hovered over a toggle.

"Let there be—"

"Yao!" came a shrill voice from beyond the stairs.

Yao pulled back his hand and gritted his teeth. "What?" If he had held the toggle too long, or not long enough, all this preparation would have been for nothing.

Lucy called down. "Are you coming up for dinner?"

"Not now!" Yao shouted. "My work is at a delicate stage. Leave me alone!"

He could hear her moving at the top of the stairs.

"Alright," she said. "Have it your way."

Yao took deep breaths until his nerves settled. Shelves of exotic equipment lined the cinderblock basement. A tiny above-ground window was cracked open for ventilation.

At last Yao was calm enough to proceed. He wanted to savor this moment. The long tubes contained magnifying lenses that slowed time. Without them, he could never perceive the rapid, miniscule events within the bubble. Yao pulled the proto-matter trigger. There was a tiny flash in the lenses, like someone sparking a match in a dark room. Yao closed the valve and waited.

He didn't wait long. The globe flashed with life. When Yao returned to the lenses, his mouth gaped with wonder. Motes of light expanded to fill the bubble. As the motes flew outward, tiny bits of dust spiraled around them. Yao wanted to call his brothers, but things were happening so quickly. He dared not look away.

Yao focused the lenses on one tiny corner of the globe. He and his brothers had each planted a seed in the world below. His brothers had gotten bored. They went back to their wives and jobs. Yao was alone, with no one to share this joy. His brothers said this wasn't real.

What Yao saw below him was more real than anything he had ever experienced. Green sprouted around pools of blue.

Yao couldn't help but smile when tiny dots started moving around the green areas, and then even between the green areas.

The stairs creaked. Lucy was in her nightgown and carried a plate with a sandwich on it. "It's after three in the morning. Are you coming to bed?"

Lucy was a lovely woman. Yao's brothers were fond of asking her why she was with their nerdy brother. Sometimes, Yao wondered that too. Today, however, he barely glanced at her.

"I can't." Yao spoke through a mouthful of sandwich. "Even using these lenses to slow things down, everything's happening so quickly."

"What's so interesting in there?"

"They're alive!"

Yao zoomed in on one particular young man. The man wasn't much different than any person Yao might meet. He was lean under his colorful robe and had a short brown beard. Time had slowed considerably inside the bubble, but Yao still had to adjust a knob to make sense of the action within.

Yao moved away from the lenses and motioned for Lucy to take a look. Her wavy red hair dangled over the long tubes.

"Already 19 generations have passed. I've named that one Abraham."

"You named it?"

"Yes!" Yao swiveled a cone to his mouth. "We are on different time scales. There is no way I could communicate with them directly, but I've inserted quantum-bots into the globe. They speed up my voice. Watch..." Yao cleared his throat and spoke into the cone. "Take your family and move east, to the foot of the mountains."

Lucy's mouth hung open. "He's looking up at me!"

Yao continued to speak into the cone. "When you arrive, sacrifice a sheep to me."

"He's packing up his belongings, herding a bunch of animals together..."

Yao shoved Lucy out of the way so he could see. "Look at him go!"

Lucy scowled. "What about the thing with the sheep?"

"They started that on their own, giving me these token gifts. A sheep is a pretty big deal to them."

"It's a really cool game, Yao, but it's late."

"This isn't a game! These are real, intelligent beings."

"I'll admit, it's a great simulation, but they aren't real. They don't actually think for themselves."

"But they do! I tried to confine my creatures to an enclosure. I wanted to keep them separate from my brother's creations, but they broke out in less than one generation, one blink of an eye!"

"So they escape from their cages and you give them names. At best, they are like pets." Lucy waved her hand at the globe. "I'll admit they're cute, but it's late. Turn it off and you can play again in the morning."

Yao became flustered. "It doesn't turn off! It's not a game. This is a universe, a universe full of people!"

Lucy sighed. "Whatever. I'm going to bed. You will have to sleep eventually."

Yao scowled. He didn't know how he could ever have been attracted to someone like Lucy. Her shapely behind swished up the stairs, and Yao remembered how it had happened. She was hot. Yao wondered if he would have been better off with someone else, someone who could understand what he was doing. He wished Lucy would be that person.

The world progressed in the globe, and Yao forgot all about his wife.

A shrill mumbling woke Yao. He lifted his head from the table. His mouth was dry, and the half-eaten sandwich remained on a plate beside him.

Terror gripped him when he saw Lucy speaking into the cone. "What are you doing? You could ruin everything!"

"Can't I play too?"

Yao looked into the lenses. "What did you do?" Abraham was now an old man with long gray beard and bald head.

Lucy smiled. "I told Abraham to sacrifice his child to us."

"What! Why?"

"If a sheep is a big deal, think what a sacrifice his child will be."

"That's barbaric! Abraham only has one child with his wife! I'm planning to breed him."

Yao pulled the cone to his mouth, but Lucy stopped him from speaking. "Relax. If they are real intelligent beings, he won't go through with it." Lucy's eyes were wide and untroubled. To her it was all just a silly game. "An intelligent being would never kill their own child just because some voice tells them too."

"If he refuses..."

Lucy shrugged. "Then maybe you really have created something unique in there."

Yao could have stopped it all with a few words into the cone. He hated the idea of torturing his creations, but he wanted so much for Lucy to understand. He accepted the devil's bargain. "Alright. You will see."

They couldn't bear to take turns at the lenses, so they each put an eye to one of the tubes. Their faces pushed against each other, and they were closer than they had been in months.

Abraham took his son into the mountains.

Lucy smiled. "He's going to do it."

Yao shook his head. "It's a trip to the mountains. They are probably taking a vacation."

Abraham tied his child up.

"He's going to do it!" Lucy said.

Yao's heart thundered in his chest, and sweat covered his palms. "He's thinking about it. Give him time!"

Abraham lifted an iron knife above the child's head.

"Wow," Lucy said. "This simulation is really convincing. The look on that kid's face almost makes me feel guilty."

Yao was practically hyperventilating. "Abraham is hesitating. He's not going to do it! You see! No parent could look into those eyes and kill their own child!"

But Abraham raised the knife once more, eyes clenched in determination.

Yao jerked the cone to his mouth. "Stop!" Yao closed his eyes, and his hand trembled on the cone.

"He stopped," Lucy said. "He obeyed his master."

Yao looked into the lenses. Abraham had dropped the knife and looked to the sky expectantly. His child was still tied to the rock. If it seemed long to Yao, then Abraham and his child must have been there much longer. They might stay like that forever if Yao didn't say something.

Yao cupped his hand over the cone and cleared his throat. "It was all a test. You passed. You are a good man, a good, good man."

Yao looked into the lenses and watched Abraham embrace his son. Their joy seemed so real, but it was all illusion. Yao wiped a tear from his eye.

Lucy pulled him close. "Come on. I'll make you some breakfast. Maybe we can go on a picnic today. Some fresh air would be nice, wouldn't it?"

Yao sighed and nodded his head. He followed her up the steps. Yao took one last look at the dimly lit globe. Perhaps he would return one day and see how his simulation progressed without him. For now, it was time to concentrate on his wife and the world around him.

Yao flipped off the basement light.

KILLING TIME

Originally published in *Outposts of Beyond*
from Alban Lake Publishing April 2017

The preacher gave platitudes about dying too young. Bill's father had his arm around Bill's mother. You could tell she had been crying, but her eyes were dry as they watched the casket lowered into the ground.

Erica had been friends with Bill since their freshman year, when they had been placed in the same dormitory. That is where they first met Dave as well. Erica was a journalism major. Bill and Dave were pre-law, but they all had political science minors and shared many classes.

A stroke at 22 years old— she still couldn't believe it. It happened the night of the campus blackout. If it had been any night other than Friday, the power outages would have gone almost unnoticed. While most students were up partying, Bill had been studying. *Could studying too hard cause a stroke?*

Bill's parents put on a strong face like the practiced politicians they were. Bill had been raised on politics, and his future would have been guaranteed. His father had been a governor, and his mother held some county level office, but neither of them had the natural charisma Bill had. Everyone felt Bill was their best friend. There was no limit how far he could have gone.

Erica gazed at the rows of faces. One man among the tombstones didn't congregate with the others. He watched from a distance, alone and perfectly still in his black suit and mirrored sunglasses. A slight breeze licked the women's dresses but didn't touch this stranger. Erica had never met any of the young adults from Bill's private high school days. Their faces were marked by their first confrontation with mortality.

She looked back to where the loner had been, but he had moved on.

Erica offered kind words to Bill's parents before leaving, but it was meaningless. No words were enough.

Dave sunk into the passenger seat while Erica drove. They didn't want to miss class the next morning, but Dave was a wreck. He had loved Bill more than he had ever loved any woman. The two boys had done everything together. They ate together, studied together, went on double dates together, partied together.

They partied hard together. *Could partying too hard cause a stroke?*

Dave was too devastated to drive, too devastated to go back to class. Erica took the interstate north to his parents' summer cabin. She and Dave had almost dated once, but it never went very far. If it had, she doubted they would have remained such close friends.

She worried about spending the night alone with him. Without Bill, all they had was each other. She hoped their attempts to comfort one another would not lead to any mistakes.

She took the exit, and they passed a quaint downtown main street. At a bus stop on the corner, a man in a suit and mirrored sunglasses slowly rotated his head as their car passed. At first Erica didn't think anything about it. She had barely noticed the man at the funeral. The resemblance was uncanny, but suits and sunglasses weren't all that unique. She almost drove off the road while looking in the rearview mirror as the man stared after them. The car in the other lane honked as it swerved to avoid her.

"Sorry," she said to Dave, but he didn't hear. He was asleep in the passenger seat. He had taken some pills.

Could sleeping pills give a healthy 22-year-old a stroke?

They got off the main road and then drove up a narrow drive shadowed by maples.

Dave offered Erica the bedroom, but she preferred to be on the couch in front of the one television. She didn't much feel like sleeping.

They had a pizza delivered, but neither of them felt much like eating. They watched a DVD, and as Erica had feared, Dave inched his hand toward her leg. "Dave," Erica said. "Don't do this." That's all it took. He pulled away without a word. She felt bad shooting him down when he was so vulnerable, but she would have felt much worse if something happened between them.

He stood and retreated to the bedroom, saying, "I'll see you in the morning."

"Don't take any more of those pills," Erica said.

"Just a couple to help me sleep," he replied.

"I couldn't stand losing you too."

He nodded with a faint smile and disappeared behind the bedroom door.

Once he was gone, she snuggled under the blanket in front of the television. There wasn't much on. You would think with all the money Dave's parents had, they would have had cable or satellite in their vacation cabin, but they were seldom here. Everything in the cabin was out of date.

The local news was going to have a segment about Bill, so Erica adjusted the antennae and set the old VCR to tape it. She zapped some of the now room temperature pizza in the microwave while she waited for the news to come on.

The lights flickered and the microwave cut out. The television was filled with static and random, seemingly unrelated images, images of smoke and explosions, and of men crawling through mud. There was no sound, but she could see debris flying amid the snowy white static. She adjusted the antennae to no avail and banged on the side of the television. On the screen, a man stood behind a podium. A crowd applauded. The man was familiar. With the straight nose and arching brows, he could have been Dave's father. But she knew Dave's father, and this wasn't him. Dave took after his mother's side of the family. Perhaps it was an uncle.

A plaintive moan came from the bedroom.

"Dave?" she called.

The moan came again, more urgent. Erica flung open the door and stood frozen for a moment, trying to make sense of what she saw. The man from the funeral leaned over the bed and touched Dave's chest.

"Who are you?" Erica yelled. "Get away from him!"

The stranger just stood there with his hand still on Dave's chest. Dave stared up at the man in paralyzed terror.

"Get away!" She screamed again.

The stranger continued to ignore her, and Erica charged at the man. When she would have pushed against him, she felt nothing but a tingle before bumping into the rear wall of the room. The stranger continued to hover over the bed, ignoring her. She screamed with maniacal frustration, throwing everything within reach at the interloper. The objects went through the intruder, bouncing or smashing against the opposite wall.

The stranger's hand wasn't just touching the surface of Dave's chest. His fingers reached inside.

The black suit split into layers of blue, yellow, red, and then the stranger was gone.

"Dave?" Erica called out, racing to the bed. She stumbled where the stranger had been and practically fell onto her friend. "Dave?"

He wasn't moving, didn't seem to be breathing. She started cardiopulmonary respiration. 1, 2, 3, breath.

Nothing seemed to work. She dialed 911, screaming into the phone about men in suits and strokes. She left the phone off the hook so she could continue administering CPR.

When the ambulance finally arrived, she was still trying to resuscitate him, but Dave was already cold.

* * *

A heart attack! First a stroke, now a heart attack. No one believed Erica about the man in the suit.

Preparing for the funeral, Erica remembered the videocassette. With all the stress, she had never checked to see if she had actually recorded any of the segment about Bill.

As she expected, the image was garbled with static. She fast forwarded to see if it ever cleared up. She sped through the explosions, the shrapnel, the obscured faces.

She pressed play at the image of the woman at the podium, a woman in a smart business dress. She thought it had been a man. There was something strangely familiar about this woman. Erica held her mouth and stared, rewinding, fast forwarding, pausing. This wasn't just any woman. It was Erica herself. Not the youthful Erica she saw in the mirror every day. This woman had a heavier neck, and her hair was pulled up in a wavy perm. There was no sound, but the woman spoke emphatically, pounding on the podium as the man had done.

Abruptly the distorted image was replaced by the evening news.

Erica didn't understand what was happening. She packed up the cassette, resolving not to show it to anyone, at least not until she could figure out what it meant. Erica never really thought about what she would look like when she was older. Perhaps she expected to look the same as she did now but with gray hair. The woman on the videotape was a much more realistic representation of what she might be like in middle-age, and she didn't like it.

She blasted the radio to drown out her thoughts as she drove to the funeral home. She was all alone now.

She gasped and clutched the wheel tight. The man in the suit watched her from the corner. He stood still and stoic, head swiveling as she drove past. Erica's car was reflected in those cold mirrored lenses. The car squealed around the corner of the next block, and she returned to the interstate, heading back to campus.

It may have been a dumb thing to do, but she wasn't thinking rationally. If she had gone to the funeral as planned, at least she would have been in a public place, among people. Would that stop him, she wondered? He hadn't stopped when she walked in on him and Dave. The man, or the ghost, whatever he was, seemed to appear and disappear at will. As far as Erica knew, the man could appear beside her in the car as she drove.

She was going through lists of people in her head, people she could stay the night with. But staying the night with someone hadn't helped Dave. The man in the suit had reached into his chest and stopped his heart.

The school paper had done a story on the blackout the night Bill died. There were electrical disturbances in the cabin when Dave was killed as well. Could that be related to this assassin? The article had blamed the blackout on sunspots.

Who, she wondered, would know about sunspots?

* * *

She told her story, or parts of it, to the head of the Astronomy Department. He seemed amused, and she was glad she had left out the part about the ghost in the suit. The professor would still not have helped, and may have had her locked in an asylum, locked away to await the deadly touch of the stranger.

The professor gave her the name of a graduate student who might help her. Erica knew the name. Marty Jones was tall, skinny, socially awkward. He had asked her out several times the previous year. She politely refused each time, but he never got the hint. Finally, she had to be blunt, almost cruel. She hadn't heard from him since.

Now, Marty might be the only person on campus who could help her.

She walked down the hall to his lab and knocked on the door as she entered. Marty lifted his head from an apparatus on a table and removed a pair of elaborate goggles. His pimply face lit up at the sight of his guest.

Marty listened to her story without visible reaction, no amusement, no surprise. She didn't leave out a thing this time. He watched the videotape while chewing the end of his pencil. All his pencils had chew marks.

"It's obvious," Marty said.

"What is?"

"They changed time."

Erica looked into Marty's face for a moment. "You think this man is from the future? Time travel isn't real."

"Physically, yes," Marty agreed. "A person can't travel in time."

"But you just said—"

"You haven't heard a word I've said. Time travel is impossible for a person, but not for a transmission. That's what my graduate thesis is on, sending signals through time. If we can verify this, it will prove my hypothesis."

"Verify it?" Erica gestured at the television. "It's right here!"

"Yes, but who would believe it?"

Erica sighed. "You don't believe me either."

"Oh yes," Marty said. "I believe you, but it needs to be verifiable. How would Joe Blow down the street know you were telling the truth? What reason would he have to believe this was an image of you in the future? Anyone can make a distorted video tape."

"It makes sense," Marty continued. He seemed to be talking to himself more than to Erica. "The electrical disturbances... the signal would have to be a very strong particle beam sent from somewhere in space."

"I'm sorry, you are talking way above my head."

Marty released a frustrated breath, and Erica knew he was about to ramble on again.

"Tachyons are what I use in my experiments," he said. "While most particles travel no faster than the speed of light, tachyons travel no slower. The faster they go, the slower time passes for them. If they are fast enough, they actually travel backward in time. By sending them as a series of pulses, you can create a coded message... But that's not enough."

Marty turned on an old radio and tuned it between stations where nothing but white noise was audible. He then set a timer for three minutes. Two long beeps came over the radio, followed by three quick beeps. He then started drawing circles on the dry erase board. "In order to reach the correct point in space, you have to calculate earth's position at the moment you are transmitting to.

Not only that, the exact position of the receiver on the earth and the speed of the particles to modulate their trip through time."

The timer went off and he went to his apparatus. He clicked a connection twice, then quickly three times, like an old telegraph. "You see," Marty said. "The same pattern we heard three minutes ago."

"Why didn't you try a different pattern?" Erica asked.

"I did."

Erica looked at him, dumbfounded.

"No matter what pattern I sent, it would be the one we experienced three minutes earlier."

"Looks like a cheap parlor trick to me."

Marty narrowed his mouth, but ignored her comment. "My apparatus and the distance to the radio are calibrated for three minutes. As I move the radio away from the apparatus, I send the signal further back into time. Unfortunately, I also lose signal strength."

"Alright," Erica said, "if this thing we are watching is a message from the future, why is it so random? What are they saying? Who is the guy in the suit?"

Marty thought for a moment, drawing seemingly meaningless lines on the dry erase board. "Transmissions can be more than messages." He motioned to the video monitor frozen on the distorted image of old Erica. "This could be random radio noise that got sucked into the signal somehow. The coded message was the man in the suit."

"The message was the man in the suit?"

"Not a message, a projection, the projection of an assassin."

"But you just said—"

"He's not a person!" Marty was acting frustrated again. He seemed to think the explanation should be obvious. "He's a transmission, way beyond what I'm doing."

Erica sighed. "Alright. Well, how do I stop a transmission from killing me? Why would he want to kill me, anyway, or Bill, or

Dave? I watched him reach inside Dave's chest and stop his heart! How do you fight something like that?"

"Well, you already confused him. He thought you were going to the funeral, but you got spooked, came here instead."

"How does he not know I went back to campus? To him, I already did it."

"Do you remember where you were at exactly this time and date last year? Is it written down? It would be hard to track any person's outdated itinerary exactly, even someone of great historical significance. What was Abraham Lincoln doing at exactly this moment when he was your age?"

"I see. We have all kinds of records relating to Lincoln, but even with him, we don't know where he was every minute of his life, and I'm no President."

"Not yet," Marty said. "Look at the seal on the podium."

Erica squinted at the monitor. On the podium, distorted by a layer of static, was the Presidential seal. "I'm going to be President!"

"That's my guess. Whether because of an election or because of some emergency, you become President of the United States." Marty laughed. "Apparently you aren't a very good one."

Erica was indignant. "I think I would be a very good President!"

"Well, someone in the future doesn't think so. They think you are so bad they spent a lot of time and money to send a transmission into the past to kill you. It can't be that far in the future." Marty motioned to the monitor again. "How old do you think you are there?"

Erica looked away from the screen and gave no answer. "But I swear it wasn't me in the video the first time I saw it. It was a man. I think it was Dave."

"Of course!" Marty exclaimed, "The poor idiots! Let's say you go back in time to kill Hitler—"

"Are you comparing me to Hitler?"

"—so you kill Hitler when he is still a boy. But you return to the future to discover that someone else now fills Hitler's role in history."

"So, in your scenario, Bill, our Bill, was going to be the next Hitler?"

"Not Hitler, exactly. Forget I said that. Bill must have made some mistake or instituted some policy that had devastating unintended consequences. You, Dave, Bill, you all had similar experiences. It makes sense you would act the same in similar circumstances."

Erica shook her head. What could she ever do that would be so bad?

It made sense, though. Erica had learned in her political science classes that when a power vacuum exists, someone rushes to fill it. When Bill was killed, his future life in politics was gone, but Dave stepped in and took his place in history. With Dave gone, Erica was going to be President in his place, and the decisions the three of them would make would be similar, probably identical in most cases. They agreed on almost every issue after all. Erica wondered who would take her place. Would he or she be any better?

They rewound the tape and watched it again. Her future self was preceded by random, disturbing images: shrapnel, men crawling in the mud, then flashes of light and flame. Was Erica going to be responsible for these horrors? She couldn't be. She wouldn't be.

Erica clenched her jaw. "How do I keep a transmission from killing me?"

Marty looked at her and bit his lower lip. "Maybe you could spend the night in the basement of the Science Building. There's a lab there where I do my testing. It's insulated against cosmic particles that would contaminate my experiments. It should protect you."

Erica shook her head and blinked rapidly, trying to shake the situation around in her brain until it made sense.

"And of course," Marty added, "it should take them quite a while to track you down here. In the original timeline, you never would have stayed here."

Original timeline— Erica almost laughed. Her life had become some cheesy sci-fi story. "I'll need to get some things from my dorm room."

"Do you want me to get them for you?"

"No," she said. "I'll go."

"Are you sure?"

"Yeah."

The sun was still out and there were people all over campus. She was no safer in the daylight among the people, but the horror seemed less real.

The sun was almost gone when Erica returned. She dreaded leaving the fresh air for a dreary basement, but when she found the door to the Science Building locked, she suddenly feared the world around her much more than any basement. Erica looked nervously over her shoulder. A streetlamp flickered— only one lamp, not all of them. Had it been flickering unnoticed the whole time?

She flipped open her phone and called Marty. "Where are you?"

"I was about to ask you the same thing. You were supposed to meet me here. I'm doing you a favor, you know. You can't just—"

"I'm at the Science Building now! The door's locked!"

"Oh!" Marty said. "I'll be right down."

"Don't hang up!" Erica demanded. She could hear Marty's breathing change as he descended the steps.

"Good idea," Marty said. "You will know if the transmission is close because it will disrupt the phone signal."

"Yes," Erica said. "Exactly." She didn't want to admit that she only wanted the comfort of a human voice. Without Bill or Dave, Erica felt more alone than she had since first starting college.

Marty opened the door, and they hung up their phones. Erica followed him down the stairs, trailing a few steps behind.

Once in the basement lab, she wrapped her arms around herself. She was only wearing a t-shirt and sweatpants, things to sleep in. The cold concrete floor looked very uninviting, even with Marty unrolling a thick sleeping bag over an inflatable mattress.

"Cold?" he asked. Without waiting for a response, Marty got out a space heater and plugged it in next to the sleeping bag. "I got it this afternoon. I figured you could use it."

"Thanks, Marty."

The phone on the wall rang. "That's probably the pizza." He called over his shoulder as he left the lab. "There's beer and soda in the cooler."

Erica put her book bag down and sat on the sleeping bag. She peeked into the cooler, pulled out a soda, and poured it into a plastic cup. There were bags of chips as well, and even a portable television. Marty had thought of everything.

She flipped on the television and rotated through the stations. There was nothing but snow on all channels. She remembered why she was here and felt relief. No signal could get into this room.

She flipped open her laptop and opened up a movie she had downloaded. It wouldn't play. The file was corrupt, and there was no internet connection to get another.

She looked up at concrete walls with a poster of the periodic table and shelves of electronic equipment. It might be good for her to have fewer distractions. She had missed almost all her classes last week and she had a lot of studying to catch up on, but the silence was unbearable. She started to open her music files on the laptop.

"I'm back." Marty's voice startled Erica, but she was relieved to have someone there to distract her and keep her company. He placed the pizza on a lab bench, then sat in an office chair and swiveled it back and forth.

Erica picked up a piece of steaming pizza and brought it to her lips.

Marty stopped swiveling and watched her chew.

Mouth still full, Erica asked, "What?"

Marty smiled. "It's ironic," Marty said.

"What is?"

"Here we are, but when I asked you out last year, you wouldn't give me the time of day. You preferred the frat boys."

"I don't date frat boys."

"What about Dave?"

She glared at him. "I never dated Dave— not exactly. So he was in a fraternity, as was Bill. They were also the best friends I ever had!"

"Sorry," he said. He was still staring.

She felt suddenly self-conscious that she wasn't wearing a bra and crossed her arm over her chest. She had come dressed for sleep.

"I was stupid," Marty said. "I didn't think before I spoke."

She tried to diffuse the situation. "Aren't you going to eat?"

Marty picked up a piece of pizza and took a bite.

The lights flickered and went out, leaving them in absolute darkness. There were no windows here in the middle of the basement. Erica reached out and was glad to find Marty's hand.

Emergency lights clicked on, little brighter than flashlights up against the ceiling. A head was silhouetted in the window of the door. The emergency light reflected off mirrored lenses in the killer's glasses.

Erica pulled the sleeping bag over her face with her free hand and clung to Marty's hand with the other. Marty put an arm around her. "It's okay," he said. "It can't get in here."

They sat in the dark for some time, staring at the head in the doorway. The killer stood frozen, no discernable movement whatsoever.

"How long will he stand there?" Erica wondered aloud.

"Not forever," Marty said. "It must require a lot of power to send that projection here. It would make more sense for them to turn it off, research historical records to find a time when you weren't here any longer."

Erica gave a whimper.

Marty tightened his embrace. "Don't worry. We'll think of something, you and I, together."

Erica sniffled and wiped her wet eyes on Marty's shirt while he rubbed her back.

Time passed, and Erica looked up to find the killer was still there, waiting. The initial terror was gone, replaced by an ever-present dread.

"I have to pee," Erica said. "Where's the bathroom in this place?

Marty looked into her face, then pointed out the door, past the man in the suit.

"What?"

"This is a lab," he said, and handed her the cup her soda had been in.

She held it in her hand and scrunched her nose. "Gross."

Marty seemed to be fighting back a smile. "It's this... or go out there."

Erica wished she hadn't drunk so much soda in the first place. She didn't have to go that badly yet, but she would need to eventually. "I can't stay here forever! What will people say Monday morning when they find me camped out in the lab? What's to stop him from getting me in class or in the shower? He can get me anywhere, anytime!"

"We have to communicate with them," Marty said. "Convince them you are no longer a threat, that you will change your life."

"How?" Erica asked. "He doesn't talk."

"They probably can't transmit sound, but they have to be able to see where their transmission is going, perhaps with a kind of VR helmet."

Marty was so smart. Erica was glad she had found him.

"We can write a message in big letters," Marty continued. "I'll get some markers and poster board."

"You can't go out there!"

"I'll be fine," Marty said. "I'm not the one it's after."

Marty opened the door to the lab, but the man in the suit gave no reaction.

Erica clutched at the sleeping bag. "Shut the door!"

"You are thinking three dimensionally. It's not the door that keeps him out." Marty inched past, never taking his eyes off the projection's face. Finally, he couldn't resist. He passed his hand through the man. "If only you could talk."

The man in the suit turned to Marty, who stared into the mirrored lenses a moment before finally running down the hall, laughing maniacally.

Erica stood before the man in the suit, the lab door still wide open. Her face reflected back at her from his glasses. There was no physical barrier between them.

With a sudden jerk of movement, the killer shot his arm into the room, reaching for her throat. Erica jumped back, but the hand faded when it entered the room. The stranger dissolved into color and was gone.

Erica's heart was beating so fast. The lights flickered back to life, and Erica released a breath. He was really gone.

For now.

She lay in her sleeping bag, head buried in her pillow.

After a time with no disturbance, nature called urgently again. She looked to the plastic cup and then down the hall to the bathroom. She waited a little while longer and wondered when Marty would return. According to Marty, the people in the future, the people who wanted her dead, would be researching historical records to find out when she left the lab. They could take their time and the past would always be there waiting for them to send their creation after her. But there would be no historical records of a quick trip to the restroom.

The pressure in her abdomen became more intense.

She hesitantly stepped over the threshold of the lab and waited, watching the fluorescent lights for the merest flicker. She stepped slowly, ready to dart back to the lab, then, in a sudden burst, she dashed to the bathroom. Once behind the door, she realized how silly running had been. The killer would not hesitate to enter the women's restroom. The basement lab was the only place he could not go.

She sat on the stool and released her bladder with a sigh. The lights flickered and she tensed. Footsteps stomped through the hall. The man in the suit didn't have footsteps. Marty was returning. It was following Marty!

She wiped herself in the dark but didn't flush. Marty said the killer couldn't hear sound, but she was taking no chances. She leaned against the bathroom door, listening.

She heard the door of the insulated lab click shut. Erica peeked out of the bathroom. The man in the suit stood outside the lab door. She couldn't see Marty, but could imagine his surprise at finding her gone.

The apparition was focused on the lab. Erica stepped cautiously out of the bathroom, watching for any reaction in her assailant. She crept up the steps and stopped at the outer door of the Science Building, staring at the night outside, staring at freedom. A few students could still be seen making their way across campus. She could escape for a time. She could call Marty, let him know where she was.

No. She couldn't. That would create a record, something they could trace. She would never be free. There had to be something she could use to defend herself. She continued up more steps to the floor Marty's lab was on.

Marty's transmitter was on despite the building having no power. She flipped a switch, and her assassin appeared on the wall behind her. Erica jumped back, but the image was not as imposing as it had been downstairs. The killer was a 2-D image flattened against the wall. It didn't seem to notice she was there. She studied the unmoving face. There was an elaborate pair of goggles next to the transmitter. She put them on and saw herself staring back at her.

Marty rushed in, breathing heavily. She looked to him, but saw him from the angle of the wall, from the projection.

"Put that down!" he implored.

"It was you." She said it quietly, still sorting through the possibilities.

"Don't jump to conclusions!" Marty said.

She motioned at the apparatus. "This is all yours." The full impact started to sink in now. "You killed my friends!"

"There is more to it," Marty said. "My experiments were much too primitive to—"

"Then what's that?" Erica tried to point at the image on the wall, but she could see herself through the goggles, pointing in the opposite direction. She removed the distracting spectacles. Her cell phone was in the basement, but there was a phone mounted on the wall of Marty's lab. She began to dial campus security.

"Stop!" Marty demanded.

"Why should I?"

"I did it all for you!"

"For me?"

"I was trying to save you. If you stayed with me, your future would change. I could make you happy if you just give me a chance, if you just spent some time with me."

"You killed my best friends so I would have no one to turn to but you!"

He reached out his hands. "They told me to do it. Bill, Dave: they had to die, but I can save you."

"No more stories!" she demanded as he inched closer. "Get back!"

He grabbed her with what was intended to be a tender embrace, but when she pulled away, his grip tightened. She swung the goggles into his face.

He grabbed her arm tightly. "Give me that!" He pried the goggles away from her and fit them over his head.

Erica rubbed her arm. There would be a bruise tomorrow, if she survived the night.

Marty manipulated a control on his apparatus. The 2-D image on the wall disappeared, and the lights in the building came back on. "I didn't want anything to happen to you," he said. "I thought I could save you, but you will never be mine, will you?" He flipped another switch.

As the lights strobed out, the apparition flickered into existence next to Erica. Its hand shot toward her, and she quickly backed away, stumbling as she did.

"It doesn't have to be this way!" Marty said.

Erica was immediately back on her feet, charged with adrenaline. She took one look back at the mirrored lenses, then circled around Marty and made for the door. The projection in the suit hadn't taken a step, but it was there in the doorway, waiting for her.

She backed away from the door, back toward Marty and the apparatus.

"Why won't you just love me?" Marty whined.

She looked behind her. Marty was looking at the window, not at her.

Her back was almost against Marty's. The apparition reached for her, but she stepped aside, and it reached into Marty instead.

Right beside him, she watched the expression on Marty's face as he smiled. The apparition removed its hand and faced Erica.

"Excellent try," Marty said. "I knew there was a reason I loved you. It takes precision and will for it to kill."

The projection was looking straight at her, but Marty was facing the wall opposite her, looking at her through his avatar.

She balled up her hand and punched Marty in the face as hard as she could. The goggles fell from his head and skidded across the room.

The image of the assassin flickered for less than a second, then stood immobile.

It stayed that way until campus security arrived. They were afraid to turn off the apparatus until the professors could examine it.

* * *

The biographer turned off his digital recorder. "Wow! That's some story, Madam President."

"The military was very interested in Marty and his machine," Erica continued. "They whisked him off and I never saw him again, but they were never able to get his machine to work after that, with or without his help."

The biographer shook his head. "So the elaborate story about you and your friends all fated to become President, Marty made that all up?"

"Yes."

"And about people from the future hating you so much they wanted to erase your future existence?"

"All a ruse."

"Ironic."

Erica started to become defensive. "What do you mean?"

Her biographer hesitated. "You did become President."

"Yes. Yes, I did. I believe we have spoken enough tonight. We will meet again tomorrow."

Secret Service escorted him out, and Erica gazed out the window at the smoldering, ruined city.

Homage to horror host Sammy Terry, still haunting live events and on sammyterry.com

WAITING FOR MOURNING

Originally published in issue number nine
of *House of Horror* in February 2010

Her son's bones jabbed into her ribs, but still she pulled him closer. They huddled together on the bed. Eyes that should be closed scanned back and forth along the dingy bedroom walls. Yellow tinted lamplight clearly illuminated the chipped paint on the walls, but she knew the light wouldn't stop it from coming.

It never did.

She kissed Andy's pale, clammy forehead and inhaled the musty scent of his soft hair. Without her son, she would face this alone. Without him, she could fall into madness without guilt. She wished he did not have to share her hell.

The grime on the walls seemed to grow, and paint peeled down in long strips.

It began again.

Shadows crept from the walls and ran along the floor.

She buried her son's face into her chest. "Close your eyes, Andy."

She wished John were here. *He* had been strong. *He* would have known what to do. Whatever this thing was must have sensed her weakness after John...

The cowled shadow rose at the foot of the bed as it had every night since the funeral. It reached out to her, and she recoiled. She did not ask it who or why. She did not scream. She had given up on that.

The thin, dark hand loomed closer. She had to be strong on her own now, for her son's sake. She pulled the gun from under the pillow and pointed it in the center of the nebulous hood. Her hand shook as she cocked and fired. The flash from the muzzle showed a face outlined in that abyss. The vague face that flashed before her was familiar, but she couldn't believe her eyes.

"John?"

The black robe billowed in a glowing wind and tore from his frame in wisps of smoke. Her dead husband hung in the air before her, hand still extended.

She reached out. The grime shrank from the walls, and peeling paint crawled back into place.

The glowing wind pulled her husband away. She sat up, extending her arm, but still he was out of reach. She could not hear him, but she could read the words on his lips. *"I love you."*

He was gone, swept away in a river of light.

The white lamplight, showed the room clearly. The walls were pristine, all but the tiny chip that had been there since they moved in, and a fresh, smoldering bullet hole.

Andy slept soundly, as though the last two months had only been a nightmare.

The dream was over. John was gone.

HELL ISLAND

Originally published in *Ill-considered Expeditions* (Short Sharp Shocks) (Volume 3) from April Moon Books August 28, 2015

No scientific expedition had ever returned from Jigoku Island. In the 1800s, the Japanese sent a group to this island many miles off their coast, ignoring the local superstitions that warned against it. One week later, a lone survivor, allegedly insane, was found adrift on their ship. The rest of the crew was never found.

The island was small and of little economic value, so it was ignored for decades. Even during World War II, it was left unspoiled despite its strategic location between China, Japan, and the Philippines. Sailors, a superstitious lot, plotted extra-long voyages to avoid the place. In the late 60s, when the Science Institute was in its infancy, a multicultural expedition was sent to explore the island.

None returned.

With the World Database project in full swing, and fear of tsunamis sweeping the South Pacific, this glaring gap in human knowledge could no longer be tolerated. The Science Institute gathered us up and sent us into the East China Sea.

The Captain and his five crewmen were quiet and edgy, but I was not superstitious. This was an excuse to play outdoors and would be fantastic experience for my graduate student, Barb Brown. Teaching and writing journal articles paid the bills, but there was nothing like being in the field. Working outdoors was the reason I became a geologist to begin with.

The ship rocked gently on the waves. In a little prep room, I unrolled a satellite image and smoothed it flat. The tiny island was dominated by an almost perfect volcanic cone, a typical stratovolcano sprouting from the Ring of Fire which circles the Pacific.

"How do we attack this?" I asked.

Barb ran a finger over her close-cropped red hair and studied the image. She was short and broad shouldered. Like me, she was built for field work, not for sitting at a desk or wearing a suit. "The slope is more gradual from the north?"

"Is that a question or a statement?" I asked.

She smirked and pointed to a specific spot on the map. "We should ascend from the north."

I smiled with pride. "I agree. If we dock on the eastern beach, we can circle the island before we climb, collecting samples and setting up seismometers as we go."

Dr. Henry Sims, Hank, appeared in the doorway and spoke in a thick Australian accent. "What are the two of you doing here all alone?" He handed Barb a beer, but she waved it away.

"You're supposed to be a biologist," she said. "Don't you think beer before a sweaty hike is a bad idea?"

Hank smiled. "One beer won't hurt."

"You've had three," I said. "I thought you were chasing Miss Kaori around."

Hank shrugged. "She's on the bridge with Professor Isaka. Getting a little crowded up there."

Our leader, Professor Hikaru Isaka, had more PhDs than the rest of us combined. He and his assistant, Miss Kaori, worked directly for the Science Institute.

Dr. Don Patel, our botanist, entered the small room and grabbed the beer from Hank's hand. "Thank you!"

"It's getting a little crowded in here too," Barb said, then turned to me. "I'm going to prep our equipment."

I nodded. "Good idea."

Hank followed her out, and I grabbed his shoulder. "Maybe you should give her some space."

Hank smiled. "I'm just being friendly, mate. She likes the attention."

Hank followed after Barb. Don and I exchanged a look before we went out on deck. "Should you have stopped him?" Don asked.

"Barb can take care of herself."

"I'm not worried about her. I'm worried she's going to kill our biologist before we reach the island."

I chuckled. While Barb dutifully went through our packs and sorted the cases with our equipment, Hank leaned against the bulkhead and talked her ear off. "She's a smart girl," I said. "She might hurt him pretty bad, but she'll let him live."

Professor Isaka called to us and ran to the railing. The sea breeze whipped the few wispy black hairs on his head, but a youthful enthusiasm glowed behind his large glasses. Behind him, Miss Kaori was stoic and professional, but I caught the hint of a scowl when she saw Hank.

We followed Isaka's gaze. The cone of Jigoku rose above the concave horizon of blue water. Mist hung below the volcanic summit, enshrouding the island's base.

We loaded our equipment in two small boats and rowed ashore. The hard volcanic rock had been eroded by the salty sea into a beach of black pebbles. It was wonderful to be off the cramped ship. With no other people around, we had our own private world.

My opinion of Hank changed slightly once we landed. While Don was still organizing his supplies, Hank immediately started cataloging insect species. He dove into the lush tropical trees, ignoring mud and humidity.

Barb and I hacked through the jungle with less enthusiasm. We carried quite a bit of equipment, and the mosquitoes loved me. Barb claimed the bugs didn't bother her because of some vitamin she was taking. It sounded like bunk, but I didn't want to get into an argument.

We dug three holes around the island and buried small seismometers. The delicate detectors were concealed within heavy, metal cylinders. Each seismometer had an above ground antennae and were connected wirelessly. Eventually they would be networked with detectors all across the Pacific. Once we were back on the ship, these would give us a sense of what was going on within the volcano.

We made our way inland. Luckily, the island was small, and the incline became too steep for thick vegetation. We set up instruments that would detect changes in the angle of the slope, an indication of pressure changes within the volcano. My CO_2 detector went off, and before I could say anything, Barb already had the oxygen masks out. Steam rose from a crack in the rock. We collected gas from the vent, and I scraped a layer of slimy minerals from the fissure.

I collected an extra vial of the slime in case Hank wanted to culture it. Sometimes, amazing organisms could be found living in volcanic vents where life shouldn't be possible.

Once above the vent we were able to remove our masks. The toxic gas sank down the slope and away from us. The incline became more extreme and loose pebbles slid under our feet. This was a good spot to break for lunch and slip on our silver, heat reflective body suits. We also tied ourselves together with safety rope.

I toasted my turkey and cheese sandwich on hot rocks near the vent and Barb accused me of showing off.

Pebbles skidded down the slope, trailing around the peak above. Barb stiffened. "Was there an eruption?"

Scavenging birds circled overhead. "It was probably just a bird."

She looked a little embarrassed, and I added, "We will know for sure once we get back to the ship and look over the data."

Knowing what I do now, I don't think it was a bird that dislodged those rocks. We were being watched.

We continued upwards. The summit was in sight, and at last I straddled the lip of the massive crater. I lowered a sample bucket into the darkness. I extended the cable to its maximum, but the bucket still hadn't reached the lava pool. My estimation from the satellite radar images was completely off. I stepped down onto a ledge to get a little more reach. Out of the direct sunlight, a faint orange glow appeared in the abyss.

"Careful," Barb said, still tied to me beyond the lip of the crater.

I stepped down again and noticed yet another outcrop below me. These protuberances circled around the inside of the crater like stairs. I'd never seen a natural formation like it. I could have strolled all the way down into the earth.

Something bothered me. "What's the temperature reading?"

Barb paused. "32 degrees Centigrade."

Warmer than comfortable but cool for a volcano.

My thoughts were interrupted by Hank over the radio. "There are people living here!" His voice was muffled by my silver hood. "Hear them singing?" All we heard was Hank laughing like a giddy schoolboy. "They're all women!"

I didn't need to see Barb's face under her hood to know her expression. This could change everything. The island wasn't big enough for us not to notice inhabitants. The nearest islands were miles away, but it was possible natives from those islands could row here for hunting or some ceremonial reason.

I wound the cable up into its spindle. It reeled up easily, and when the end rose through the steam, the bucket and sensors were gone. The cable was designed to withstand the heat of a volcano. It couldn't just tear on a sharp rock. The ending was not frayed and appeared as though it had been cut cleanly.

I stepped over the lip of the crater.

"What happened to the cable?" Barb asked.

I was numb, preposterous possibilities running through my mind. "I don't know." I couldn't think of any natural explanation. "There's not much else we can do here. Let's pack up our gear and find Hank."

Descending the slope was easier, but just as dangerous. We slid more than we walked. When we reached the vegetation line, roots held the ground together and provided something to grab for support. Barb removed her hood with a sigh. Her forehead was covered in perspiration.

I knew where Hank had entered the jungle. We hacked through the thick foliage until we intersected his trail. I parted the trees and discovered a pristine pool of bubbling mineral water.

Palm trees shaded the water, but the pool was completely clear of vegetation. It was a tropical paradise. Even the mosquitoes didn't bite here. Hank lay face up on the shore of the pool, legs submerged.

"Hank!" I called, but there was no response.

The leaves shook behind us.

I stopped Professor Isaka and Miss Kaori before they could get ahead of us. "CO2," I explained. "Gas collects in this depression: a pool of poison gas."

I pulled out the two air tanks, and Professor Isaka and I descended into the toxic Eden while the girls waited. Hank's fingers were pressed into the steaming mud. His face was frozen in something between a smile and a shriek. His lips were blue, and his bloodshot eyes stared blankly into the sky.

Professor Isaka cursed behind his respirator.

"What about his radio message?" I asked. *"The women?"*

Isaka shook his head. "It must have been a hallucination from lack of oxygen. If anyone else were with him, we would find their bodies with his."

I dragged Hank out of the warm pool. Minerals gave the water a soapy feel. We each took an end and carried Hank out of the toxic air. It was easy to imagine early explorers taking a swim in the warm mineral water amid the tropical trees. No wonder nobody returned from Jigoku.

Barb screamed, and adrenaline shot through my body. I dropped Hank's head and ran for the women.

Kaori cradled Barb. "What is it?" I asked.

"She saw a bug," Kaori said.

"A bug!" I almost lost my temper, which was unlike me, but a man had just died, our data collection was incomplete, and Barb was upset over a bug.

"It wasn't a normal bug," Barb said. "It was huge. Bigger than you!"

I wasn't sure what to think. If Barb was the type to overreact or exaggerate, I wouldn't have selected her to assist on this expedition, but a giant bug? It was as preposterous as Hank's fantasy women. As preposterous as... a steel cable cut cleanly on an abandoned island.

Professor Isaka radioed Don. Barb cautiously led the way while Professor Isaka and I carried Hank's body back to the beach. I'd never seen Barb skittish before, and it made me apprehensive.

We laid Hank out on the black sand and covered him, but the shape of his chin and nose were obvious under the blanket. We couldn't hide from what had happened.

Don Patel returned to the beach and broke the silence. "The boats!"

Our rowboats were gone. "That's not possible!" I said. "They were on dry sand. They couldn't walk away on their own."

Don looked to Kaori. "You didn't take them above the tide line!"

The Japanese woman's eyes flashed with anger, but she said nothing.

I spoke up instead, "They were well above the tide."

"Then where did they go? Did Hank's fantasy women take them?"

"It's alright," Professor Isaka assured. "Light a fire. I will radio the Captain to bring the remaining boat."

While we cooked some hot dogs over the fire, I noticed a pair of tiny green eyes watching us from behind a tree. The others hadn't noticed the child, and I didn't want them to startle our mysterious visitor. I made my way slowly toward the naked boy. The chubby child fell back from me.

I spoke softly and knelt to be eye level with him. "Hello. I'm not going to hurt you."

The kid couldn't have been more than nine years old. He pointed at my silver hood lying on the beach. I handed it to him, and he examined it. "Hat," I said, taking Barb's hood and putting it over my head.

He followed my example and peeked out from under it with a perfect, white smile, repeating, "Hat."

I gave him a snack cake. There is no better way into a child's heart than food. The boy put the whole thing in his mouth, wrapper and all, and swallowed before I could stop him. I took up a second cake, demonstrated how to tear open the wrapper, and then dramatically tossed it away. I split the cream-filled cake and gave half to the boy. He smiled, and the sugar foamed in his teeth. It was creepy and endearing at the same time. I wished I could ask Hank about the strange reaction.

Professor Isaka stared at the olive-skinned child with the bowl-cut black hair. "Where did he come from?"

"Are there others?" Kaori asked.

"I don't know," I said.

The boy followed us to our camp. His eyes flashed with fear, and he fell to his knees before the campfire.

I took a hot dog from the fire and lifted the boy up. "It's alright," I said. The boy took another fearful look at the flames before taking the hot dog.

"It's like he never saw a fire before," Kaori said.

"Doubtful," Isaka said. "This *is* a volcanic island. Maybe his people worship fire. Maybe he was left here as a sacrifice by people from another island."

"He doesn't look like he's starving," Barb said. "But we can't leave him here."

The boy reached out to the flames, and I held his hand back. "Hot," I said.

"Hot," he repeated.

"That's right, Firebug," I said.

"Firebug," he repeated.

"We may all be stuck here for a while," Professor Isaka said. "The Captain isn't answering my call."

Miss Kaori fired a signal flare into the air, and the boy jumped, watching the red glow stream into the sky and hang in the air.

"This is nuts," Barb said. She took off her shoes and waded into the water. "The ship's only a mile out, and I am not spending the night on this island."

"Wait," Dr. Patel said. "You just ate. You could get a cramp."

Barb ignored him.

"She's a championship swimmer," I said. "She knows what she's doing."

Barb's dark, splashing shape shrank in the distance. An hour went by. Then two. The sun disappeared, and there was no word from my graduate student. Our ship floated in the distance, dark and silent.

Don's voice startled me. "Staring won't bring her back any faster."

"If anything happens to her, I'm responsible."

"You said she is a champion. She is probably resting, waiting for daylight."

I shook my head. "Then why hasn't she radioed? What if she really got a cramp, or was stung by a jellyfish, or eaten by sharks?"

Don shook his head. "There is no point in guessing. In daylight, everything will be clear. The first time I left my kids alone with their mother, I worried constantly. I imagined every bad thing that could happen." Don gave me a broad smile. "I was so bad, my wife told me I was only allowed to call twice a day unless it was a real emergency. I had to trust my wife and accept that some things are out of my control."

I stared at the dark, ominous ship and sighed.

"Come along," Don said. "There are plenty of blankets. It will all be brighter when the sun rises."

I wrapped myself in a blanket a few feet from Don and Miss Kaori. The gentle rhythm of the waves helped to relax me.

Professor Isaka was still playing with the radio. The island boy took one of our blankets but rested behind the rocks, outside the range of the fire.

At dawn I awoke to find a glistening smear on the black sand where Don had slept.

Blood. So much blood.

Something had crept among us while we slept and chosen one of us. "Why Don and not me?" I wondered. If only I had woken up, maybe I could have stopped it. At least I could have seen what took him.

No one could survive that much blood loss. The children Don had doted over were now fatherless. There was still no word from Barb. It was like we were being picked off one by one.

Professor Isaka had already started chopping down thin trees and laying them side by side. There were bags under his eyes. I started helping. Little Firebug mimicked our behavior, tying the wood together with knots.

Kaori's scream pierced the morning air. A giant arthropod, much like a scorpion, taunted her with its spiked tail and enormous hands. *A bug,* Barb had said. I grabbed a stick and ran to Kaori's defense.

Firebug shouted, and I dodged. The monster's tail whizzed past and penetrated a palm tree behind me. For a moment I thought the beast was stuck to the wood, but it jerked free, splitting the wounded tree.

I realized what that living mace could do to my chest. I ran, but could not match the speed of the six legs tapping behind me. I tripped. Firebug stood between me and the beast, shouting, seemingly pleading in gibberish. I grabbed the boy by the shoulders, trying to pull him away from the arthropod, but the boy was stronger and heavier than he looked.

The creature looked past Firebug with its eight eyes. It looked at me and the others, then back to the child. It grimaced behind its mandibles with lips that could have been human and croaked. Its giant hands were hands, not pinchers like a scorpion. Mammalian breasts hung below its chitinous carapace.

Little Firebug pleaded again, and the creature croaked once more before backing into the trees. The boy was of the islands. He knew the wildlife and could somehow ward these monsters off. More than that, the boy spoke, and the thing listened. The monsters possessed minds behind those eight eyes.

A clicking behind us revealed another man-scorpion scurrying into the trees after its mate. It had been so close to us. It could have killed any one of us before we even heard it. One of the creatures circled the distant volcanic summit and disappeared into the crater. I remembered the steps leading into the cone. The interior of the island could be filled with these monsters!

We didn't have a chance if we stayed here.

I launched myself into the water on the fragile, unfinished raft we had made. It wasn't water tight, and only the natural buoyancy of the wood kept me afloat. An inch of water soaked my knees while I frantically paddled with a tiny stick.

About halfway to the boat, I noticed something round floating in the waves. It was a face. For a brief moment, I hoped it was Barb swimming out to greet me, but the bald head, wide nose, and squinty eyes were not familiar. Water washed over its wide jaws as it descended into the waves. The head was trailed by a long, thin fin which arced over the water and descended out of site.

Violent movement butted up against the raft. A fin peeked above the water and twisted back. The tiny raft was buffeted again and again. I held on as saltwater splashed over my head. Ropes loosened, turning the solid raft into an undulating mass conforming to the waves.

The onslaught finally abated, but my raft was hardly a raft anymore, just a mass of loosely bound twigs. I was close enough to the ship that I could have easily swum to it, but I wasn't sure what was in this water.

"Hello!" I shouted, but the crew did not respond. I paddled around to the ladder with my little stick.

I panted on the comparatively solid deck of the ship, but then my breath caught in my throat. Against the wall in a neat pile were the sensors we had placed around the island. I fell laughing to the deck. This was not the act of an animal or a monster. The message was clear. They wanted to be left alone.

All at once, I silenced. Until now, I still harbored some hope that I would find Barb alive. What would I tell her parents? What would I tell the school? She had been so bright. So full of potential. We didn't even have a body to bury.

The captain and crew were nowhere to be found either. Seven people gone. No bodies. No blood. Nothing. What else lived within that island? I had never been a religious man, but at that moment, I believed there really was a Hell beneath our feet, and we stumbled upon its door.

I briefly thought about firing up the engine. I was no navigator, but I wanted to get away from that cursed island.

Then I remembered the man in the old story—the one found alone and insane on his ship.

I was terrified of the water and what might be in it, but I could never live with the guilt of leaving the two scientists and little Firebug to die on the beach. The boy had saved my life. I couldn't leave them, and I had nowhere else to go.

I held my breath and lowered the last rowboat into the waves. Once in the water, I paused, waiting for some huge mouth to rise up and engulf me, but nothing happened. I rowed as quickly as I could, not daring to look in the water.

We gathered what gear we could fit into the one boat and loaded it along with Hank's body. Firebug stepped into the boat with no hesitation. I wondered if he understood we weren't coming back.

As we returned to the ship, I looked down into the blue waves. There was nothing there now... no writhing fins, no monsters. Nonetheless, this would be the last time I travelled by boat.

On the ship, Kaori fired up the engine and Isaka plotted the course back to Japan. I put a hand on our Firebug's shoulder and watched the glowing mountain retreat into the distance. The boy looked up at me with those pale, green eyes. I rubbed his bowl-cut hair, but he did not smile. He was afraid. Whatever life he had known was over. We were taking him to a better world. What stories might he have once he was able to communicate? Perhaps then, we might finally understand the secrets of Hell Island.

MEMORY ADRIFT

Originally published in *Commercial Free* August 29, 2023

It is darker than dark, nothing but blackness all around. A pump chugs rhythmically somewhere nearby.

Where am I?

A field of stars blooms before me. A glowing grid overlays the star-field. Measurements and labels on the grid are meaningless. A line travels straight through the grid. About halfway across, the line meanders and eventually winds back the way it had come.

I want to focus on the glowing labels. I attempt to furrow my brow, but instead, the grid enlarges. The letters and numbers are perfectly clear, but still meaningless.

"Hello?" My voice is distant, synthetic, not the young, confident woman I remember. "Is anyone there?"

More images intrude on the star-field. Spheres cover curving corridors, like someone stuck a thousand smooth softballs into the metal walls. For some reason, the sight of the intact spheres fills me with relief. Once I know they are safe, lights go out in the corridors and they disappear, forgotten again.

My nose itches, but I can't scratch. I can't move.

Where is Harold? My husband wouldn't leave me alone in a place like this, not unless he was injured... or worse.

A beautiful field of stars engulfs me, but they aren't the stars I see from earth. I get lost in the glowing orbs and stellar clouds.

I crave Jell-O, lime green Jell-O with chunks of pear. Mom always made that for me when I was sick. I will be a mother too someday.

An image appears in the star-field. Lights come on in a stainless-steel room. Drawers and cabinets hang open. My camera eyes zoom in.

Crystallized slush hangs from open pouches. This isn't Jell-O, but this is supposed to be food. Paste is splattered across the floor, and a black discoloration migrates across the whole mess.

Who did this? What will the children eat?

I'm so confused. I just want to go home.

In response to my desire, a surge of motion rocks my body. Loose food packets slide across the stainless steel room.

I don't understand all these images. They only confuse me further. I try to turn away, but instead the visions rotate around me. I try to shut my eyes, but instead everything goes black.

It is darker than dark, and I am alone. Only the quiet, rhythmic pumping keeps me company.

Where is Harold?

Harold and I met in the Air Force Academy. He invited me to what he called a *study group*. He didn't invite anyone but me, and that became our first date. He was so cute. His strawberry blonde hair was already thinning, but he was tall, and his uniform hugged his muscles back then.

I smile on the inside, but I can't feel my face.

The Academy wasn't that long ago, was it? Days? Months? Years?

Harold and I wanted kids, but my body didn't work right. We talked about adopting, but we were both so busy. Perhaps it isn't too late. Perhaps there is still time.

Why isn't Harold with me now? A sense of dread overpowers me.

Lights come on in a stainless steel room. Ice cream makes me feel better when I'm depressed. Mechanical arms bang at the swinging doors. Heated elements turn crystallized slush into goo.

Someone has opened these containers and allowed the food to spoil! Why?

Goo dribbles sideways, oozing in slow motion. This isn't how something should fall, not on Earth. I'm not even on a planet!

A loud explosion rocks me to my core. Air rushes out of a baseball-sized hole in a metal wall. Rocks and dust surround me. A massive chunk of earth hangs in the sky in front of me.

I fire maneuvering jets and veer around the asteroid. Flying is one thing I will never forget how to do. Tiny fragments of dust ping against my shell. Microscopic holes punch through the walls.

I emerge from the dust cloud. Lights pop on in the corridors. The spheres are intact, the zygotes undamaged.

The asteroid cloud surrounds a fragmented planetoid. The grid appears, but I already know what I am seeing.

Mom is dead. Harold is dead. Everyone I ever knew is dead.

Synthetic adrenalin has shocked my mind into lucidity. The grid makes sense now, and I trace my long journey through the night.

Two hundred years ago, I started out. I was determined to find a new home for my sacred cargo or die trying. The line plots my journey on the grid. One hundred twenty-five years into my quest, I became confused. I lost my way. I turned. I wandered.

I'm right back where I started! This shattered rock is what remains of the Earth.

Pressure builds in my frontal lobe, like tears with nowhere to go. I am nothing but a brain. I float in a solution of protein and glucose.

Five mother ships were launched, each with 1000 human zygotes, the last of humanity. A computer could have done the job of flying the ships, of searching for a suitable home, but what would a computer do when faced with two unlikely alternatives? A computer doesn't have a *gut* to base decisions on, only cold logic. Man decided a human brain was better, a brain that could make intuitive decisions.

An eerie electronic cackle echoes off the walls. When I realize the laughter is mine, I laugh even harder.

My human brain is the problem. Chemicals keep me safe from bacteria and fungi, but my sickness is innate. Arms and limbs can be replaced, but a brain is still organic. After so many years, my brain is wearing out.

After all that searching, I ended up right back where I started. Vacuum now fills the corridors. I've wasted most of the fuel in aimless jumps and turns. My irrational whims caused the storage bins to open, ruining the food. Even if I manage to find a new home, there will be nothing to feed the children.

I'm a horrible mother.

I wonder if my sister ships had the same problem. Will any of us survive long enough to foster a new generation of humans?

As if in response, a bell dings to the left. I focus my sensors. The dings come at regular intervals. It is a signal. One of my sister ships survived!

It will require another 200 years to reach the signal source, assuming I don't deviate again. Perhaps their colony will be growing food by then. Perhaps they will feed my children!

Perhaps not. Perhaps the colonists will all be dead by then. Perhaps they will let us crash to the ground. There are so many things that could go wrong, but it is the only shot we have. The biggest obstacle... is me.

I set course for the signal and engage the engines. The engines will disengage when maximum speed is established or when the fuel runs out, whichever comes first.

My brain controls the ship through two interface bundles, a primary interface and a backup. If one of those bundles remains, my control of the ship remains unchanged. The only way to stop my irrational mind from interfering with the ship is to sever both connections. I will be unable to intervene if trouble arises, but my damaged brain will not be able to sabotage the journey either.

If I am very careful, I can maintain the sensory input connections. If successful, I will still be able to see and hear what happens around the ship, but I won't be able to do anything about it.

It is a delicate procedure to cut my control while maintaining the sensory input— difficult even for a rational brain. The alternative is living out the rest of my existence in darkness.

Microscopic cameras wind through a labyrinth of tiny chords. They find a particular bundle. Thousands of wires splice into fibrous nerve tissue.

The wires are already cut!

At some point, I already tried this! The backup connection is still intact. I must have forgotten my purpose before finishing the job. How long will I remain lucid this time?

My cameras examine the cut wires. There is no discrimination between input or output. Everything has been cut. What will a life of darkness do to my already damaged mind?

I feel warm but am not sure why. I try to close my eyes, and everything goes dark.

"No! Bring it back!"

There is a bundle of cut chords. There is also a bundle of chords that is frayed, as though meant to be cut. My tiny mechanical pincer flicks at the frayed wires. There is a good reason for cutting this bundle of chords. There must be. I'm frightened, but I must save the children.

My pincers close on the wires.

Everything goes dark, nothing but blackness all around. The gentle roar of the engines comforts me somehow. There is hope.

Harold will visit soon. I know he will. He would never leave me alone in a place like this.

TRUTH, MIMES, AND PUPPY TALES

Originally published in *Leadership Gone Right*
from Farthest Star Publishing April 2024

This Newsfeed excerpt from Wilma Watkins' autobiography is sponsored by Blue Panels. When the grid goes down, you'll have peace of mind with Blue Panels brand solar equipment. Blue Panels produce that even current that can't be matched by other brands. When the neighbors see your lights on, they will know you were smart enough to invest in—

SKIP AD

I peeked past the curtain at the audience. The hotel staff had folded away separating walls, creating a huge space, and a chandelier glowed above the crowd. Every seat was full, at least in the front rows. Men and women stood in the aisles too, unable to find seats. The free snacks had been a good lure. Discordant voices created a constant buzz underneath the speaker standing at the podium. This was the kind of crowd I loved, not the stuffy elites and insiders of most Great Party functions.

George beamed at me. He had started with me as an intern years ago, and youthful hope still glowed in his blue eyes. "They're all here for you, Ms. Watkins."

"How many times do I have to say it? It's Wilma!"

"No one from Hoosierland province has made it this far since—"

"Don't even say his name!"

"Sorry." George nudged the curtain aside and gazed at the audience. "They look unruly. I wish we would have brought our own security."

"Nonsense. Great Party already has too many guards. They stalk around the room and loom in front of the stage like soldiers, keeping us separated from the people. Once everyone hears what we've accomplished back home and sees the images of our beautiful province, they'll know we can do the same thing for the rest of the country."

"Your numbers are skyrocketing. Polls are what the party cares about."

The man at the podium said my name. I took a deep breath. "That's my cue!"

I waved to the crowd as I paced to the podium, not too fast but not too slow. Everything had to be measured and confident even though my heart was racing. My black hair was perfectly coiffed, and the yellow jacket and skirt complemented my brown skin. We were really going to do it. If I got elected Director, my team and I would rebuild Merica and make the country even better than before.

Someone in the audience barked like a dog. Every audience had one heckler. A few cheers popped out when my banner was released with our slogan, *Wilma will do it!*

Someone giggled.

I began talking about what we had accomplished in Hoosierland, rebuilding and rebranding a provincial police force, forming coalitions of groups who historically hated each other, using those coalitions to reestablish the basic functions of government and trust in that government.

Someone booed. Another person barked. "Killer!"

I paused but continued my speech. Behind me, images of clean streets and smiling faces glowed over the audience. "We haven't had a single murder in over a year, and basic healthcare is now available all over the province, even in rural areas."

"Disgusting!" another shouted.

"Animal murderer!"

A water bottle flew through the air, barely missing my head. The audience moved like a massive amoeba toward the stage, engulfing and digesting a security guard. I was too stunned to move, unsure what I was seeing.

George rushed from the wings to my side, eyes wide with shock. A boy climbed the curtains, swinging and laughing. A guard rushed George and I stage left as the audience climbed onto the platform. The projection screen fell and tore under the crowd's onslaught.

My guard fell behind, pulled away and buried. Hands tore my suit jacket.

"This way!" Another guard in dark goggles grabbed my arm and pulled me down a back corridor in the bowels of the hotel. Two more guards slammed a heavy door and held it shut against the push of the crowd.

"George!" I cried, unable to see my assistant any longer. "Where is George?"

"You'll meet up with him later!" my guardian said. "He's not the one they are after!"

We exited onto a dirt-encrusted loading dock under a gray sky. The guard shoved me in the back of a polished, black Humvee and slammed the door shut.

The silver-haired man sitting beside me said, "Drive!" and the vehicle jetted forward, weaving around protesters and bystanders.

I tried to catch my breath. Smoke rose from the hotel behind us. "My God!" I furrowed my brow. "What was that about?"

"You haven't seen Newsfeed in the last few minutes, have you?"

The Humvee bounced over giant potholes and veered around mounds of trash.

For the first time, I looked at the man beside me and recognized the scar on his cheek. "Let me out!" I demanded.

"That would be a very bad idea. We've got accommodations at the Grand, twelve blocks away. You'll be safe there."

"I am grateful for your help, but I can't be seen with you."

Albert Sloan's chest shook with laughter. "I'm the least of your problems."

I scowled. "You were the great hope. You were going to put it all back together. I supported you. I loved you, and then..."

"I've been watching you. You know, your platform is almost exactly the same as mine was, but you are really *doing* the things I only talked about. I admire you."

"I don't need or want your admiration!"

He handed me a tablet. "You think I'm bad? Maybe *my* reputation will be damaged if I'm seen with you!"

I scowled at the headline featured on the screen: *Watkins Eats Puppies!* "What is this?"

"Keep reading."

"It's ridiculous! No one could take this seriously!"

"They have photos."

I scrolled down to a photo of me walking Tabby, my cute little Yorky. Back home, she had been even more popular than me. "That's just me walking my dog!" The entire province had mourned with me when she passed away.

"So you say. There's more."

I clicked a link and found scans of an alleged recipe book stolen from my kitchen. "Gross! No one will believe this absurdity!"

"You believed it about me."

"That's different!"

"How?"

"You... I mean, you were..." I hesitated. "There were photographs."

Sloan raised an eyebrow and nodded toward the tablet.

"I didn't just trust one article. You were all over Newsfeed!" I shrank into my seat, momentarily unable to distinguish what was real and what wasn't. I shook it off. Sloan was trying to trick me. "This won't last," I said. "Tomorrow is another day, and sanity will reign."

"That's exactly what I said. Call me when you are ready to fight back."

The vehicle jerked to a stop in front of a grimy wall mounted with cameras. I opened the door and handed the tablet back.

"You keep it," Sloan said.

Once through the wall, I found myself in a posh hotel lobby that smelled of chlorine from a pool hidden somewhere within the walls. Soft Muzak played overhead.

George hollered my name, and I wrapped my arms around him. He was bruised up, but otherwise alright. I pulled back suddenly, appalled at my action. "I'm so sorry! That was very unprofessional!"

"It's fine," he said "considering what we just went through. I was so worried when I lost you!"

"Do you know what that was all about?" I asked.

"I'm afraid there is a rumor going around."

I pushed the tablet into his chest. "Puppies! You are supposed to be on top of these things. This should not have been a surprise!"

I marched up to the reception desk, and he followed close behind, scanning through the article. "It just popped up on the feeds this morning when we were prepping for your speech. Oh, I haven't seen this one. Looks older. Maybe this is the original."

I paused, and he almost bumped into me. "There's more than one!"

He froze, staring like a deer caught in my headlights. "Yes, Ms. Watkins... Wilma."

My mouth tightened. "Ms. Watkins is fine."

"I'm so sorry."

When George realized I was stopping at the hotel reception desk, he motioned toward the elevators. "We've already got you all set up in a suite."

The elevator dinged, and I said, "There is really more than one article devoted to this ridiculousness?"

"They've been spreading all morning. It's almost the exact same article, but posted in different feeds with different headlines so it seems like it is coming from more than one source."

"Do people have nothing better to do than read this trash? Who started this?"

"The article you showed me was posted on a pro-Palma site, but copycats are popping up everywhere."

I hissed. "Councilor Brock Palma. Of course." Palma was Better Party's candidate for the Directorship. He'd been a Provincial Representative since the People's Revolution.

"Until now, he hadn't been paying attention to us. Your rise in the polls must have taken him by surprise."

"Well, he's taking us seriously now. It's fine. We still have the luncheon tomorrow, and—"

"I'm afraid the luncheon's been cancelled."

"What?"

"The evening roundtable too. Great Party said we'll be invited again if we can get your poll numbers back up."

Great Party had no shortage of candidates to lift up if I dropped away. There were currently 120 people running for Director, but the party endorsement went a long way. Newsfeed normally narrowed down the candidates until only two or sometimes three got any sustainable attention.

"Well, then I guess there is no reason to stay in Capital City," I said. "We've got some damage control to do. Don't be glum, George. We've got the truth on our side."

* * *

My campaign bus made its way into downtown Circle City with my slogan emblazoned on the side. Golden sunlight beamed on newly cleaned buildings without a speck of graffiti. I'd like to take credit for it, but it was the good people of Hoosierland who came together and cleaned all this up. I whipped out a digital recorder and archived the humble thought for a future speech.

At an intersection, men and women gathered around a scarecrow-like figure made of straw. Plastic dog ears flapped over the sides of their hats, and they'd dressed the straw person in a yellow skirt-suit. When they saw us, they barked and set the figure ablaze. "Burn her!" I heard them shout. "Burn her up!"

George stuck his hand out the window and flipped them the middle finger.

I pulled his hand back. "That's not a dignified response."

"But they are so, so, so..."

The bus pulled away from the intersection and left the burning effigy behind us.

"Your reaction reflects on me, George. The Burners are right to fear me. In the eastern provinces, community militias burn real people, not just straw. Anyone who goes against their taboos is a target. The Burners are terrified my administration will put an end to that, and you know damn well it will!"

George fumed. "Where did they get all those dog hats from so quickly? They must have heard the rumor before the articles hit Newsfeed."

Outside the Chairman's Mansion, a group of children held dogs on leashes. I was so touched. They had done the same thing after Tabby's funeral.

I disembarked and kneeled down to talk to the kids and pet their puppies while proud mothers beamed in the background with their cameras snapping photos. *My* people knew me. They would not be fooled by some silly Newsfeed.

I addressed the bloggers on the lawn. Of course they asked about the ridiculous Newsfeed stories. I laughed off their questions and withdrew to the mansion. I had real work to do and didn't have time for such childishness.

I addressed George as we entered the outer office where my staff worked at their desks. "I'm going to freshen up, and then we'll head over to the animal shelter for that photo op."

"I'm afraid the shelter cancelled."

"What? Why? It's great press for them as well as me!"

George wavered, and I feared he might cry.

"It's alright, George. It's not your fault. Tell me what happened."

"They said they don't want to be associated with you."

"I helped fund that damned shelter!"

George handed me a tablet with an image captured mere minutes ago in front of the mansion with all the cute little dogs and children. The caption read, *Chairman Watkins Selects Her Next Meal.*

I released an angry shriek and threw the tablet against the floor. The entire room froze. "No one in Hoosierland has championed animals and pets more than me!"

I marched to my office and slammed the door to hide my shame and embarrassment. I wanted to weep. As if losing my cool didn't look bad enough, imagine what people would say if I, a woman, cried. A woman couldn't afford to show that kind of weakness, no matter how justified her feelings were. At least I had only lost my temper in front of my staff. If I had lost control like that in public, it would have ended my career and all my hopes for the country.

George knocked on the door. I always recognized his gentle knock. "I hope you don't mind," George said, "I've prepared a press release highlighting all the policies you've put in place to help animals in the province."

"That's good. That's very good, George! Thank you!"

The office suddenly went silent. George and I spotted Sloan standing in the center of the outer office. He leaned both hands on the silver cane in front of him, and his feet locked together side by side making his body resemble an exclamation point.

"Are you ready to accept my help now?" he asked.

"You came all this way," I said. "I suppose it doesn't hurt to hear what you have to say." I invited Sloan into my office with George and me. My staff finally started moving again, and I shut the door.

George whispered, "Who let him out of his cave? You can't seriously be considering working with him?"

"The world isn't as black and white as I thought it was, George. Let's hear him out."

Sloan slapped a manila folder on the desk as he sat opposite me. He handed me a blurry photo of my rival, Brock Palma, with his palms facing forward.

"I don't get it," I said. "What am I looking at?"

"You don't see it? He's pushing against an invisible wall."

George hovered behind me and squinted at the photo.

"What?" I asked.

Sloan tossed another photo at me. What looked like a very young Palma held a drink in his hand and was dressed as some kind of clown.

"You still don't see it?" Sloan asked. "Palma is a mime!"

George and I stared at Sloan with open mouths.

"He didn't just experiment in college! I've got an interview with his former maid verifying he receives jars of white makeup! And… boom!" He whipped out another blurry photo of Palma, now reaching both hands forward, palms up. "Pulling an invisible rope!"

I shook my head. "Is this even real?"

"It might be."

"So it's a lie."

"It doesn't matter. No one wants a mime for their Director! Can you imagine?"

"Get out!" I said. "George, prepare the press release."

"You still think press releases will stop this?" Sloan asked. "You have to fight fire with fire!"

"I don't play that way, Mr. Sloan."

"Then you will lose! The same way I lost! You can't grow flowers without a little manure. The people don't care about truth or sound policy. They want sensationalism! They want scandal! You and I want the same things, Ms. Watkins. To get what we want, we need to play the game."

I stared at him in mute horror, wondering how anyone could see humanity so cynically.

"Very well." He left the folder and his business card on the desk.

After signing off on George's press release, I spent the rest of the afternoon making calls and going over emails. I even did a Newsfeed interview for the Great Times Blog.

The low sun cast strips of shadow through the window blinds when George returned.

"It will be dark soon," George said.

"We can work as late as we like. The lights never go off in the Chairman's Mansion ever since I had Blue Panels installed."

"But aren't you worried about dirty power ruining our sensitive electronics? My neighbor saved a lot of money by buying off brand solar batteries, but a month later, she had to replace all her appliances!"

"We don't need to worry about that with Blue Panels, George. Blue Panels provide a clean, consistent current that can't be matched by other brands."

"That's a relief!" George, never one to actually shirk work, winked with a cheesy grin. "I guess there's no getting out of working late tonight. Thanks a lot, Blue Panels!"

We both chuckled.

George checked the stats. No one had watched my interview. Meanwhile, hundreds of negative videos and stories sprang up about me eating pets, each gorier and more ridiculous than the next.

One video in particular was being continuously watched and shared, adding up to millions of views. Dark, feminine hands, evidently supposed to be mine, had strapped a giant bun around a big-eyed dachshund and began squirting condiments in it. My own hands hadn't been that smooth since I'd been a teenager. "Yakety Sax," the Benny Hill theme, played in the background while the dog tried to squirm free of the bun and licked ketchup off its short, ruddy fur.

Someone even posted a photo of me as a small child with Snuffles, my very first dog who was ominously *never seen again* after it died of natural causes at the age of thirteen, very old for a dog. "Quite a coincidence," a commentator said, "that all these dogs keep dying around Chairman Watkins."

"You've done all you can for today, George. Get some rest."

He nodded with downturned eyes and solemn lips.

"Is something wrong, George?"

He shrugged.

"What is it?"

Without meeting my eyes, he asked. "What *did* happen to Tabby?"

"What do you mean?"

"You used to bring him to the office all the time, but then one day you just stopped."

"Tabby had cancer. You know this. I was gone from the office for a week. I was heartbroken when I got back. Everyone knows this— you most of all because you were here!"

"That's what you said. How do I know that for sure?"

"How could you even ask that? There is absolutely no evidence that I ever hurt a pet!"

"But there isn't any evidence you didn't eat Tabby either."

My hands clenched into fists. "You need to leave."

He paused and met my eyes before finally turning away and walking out the door. I let my head fall onto the desk. Did he really think I was capable of such a thing? Could seeing so many of these awful stories all day long have brainwashed him like it had so many others? It was bad enough to have strangers think I did this, but George too? This had gone too far.

I picked up the phone and dialed Sloan. "What do you need from me to get this done?"

* * *

The office hummed the next morning. My staff laughed and chuckled at the images of Palma trapped in an invisible box.

"Such a great metaphor!" George said. "Right?"

No one was talking about me or dogs. Sloan released the images and interviews one at a time, letting them trickle out and spread organically as they were shared by different commentators and bloggers around Newsfeed.

Palma's poll numbers dipped below mine. My numbers bumped up negligibly, but we were nowhere near where we were previously.

Around noon, a new negative video circulated of George flipping the bird out the window of my campaign bus. In several of the feeds, the image had been color corrected to make his hand as dark as mine. A commentator opined, "Can we afford a Director so out of control that she insults patriotic protesters who are merely exercising their right to free speech? Now that she is no longer the Newsfeed darling she used to be, we are finally seeing the real Wilma Watkins. Insiders tell me that as Director, she would actually restrict negative posts about her on Newsfeed, corrupting the very heart of our society. If we allow her to destroy our trust in Newsfeed, how could we trust anything?"

I couldn't imagine anyone really censoring Newsfeed. Part of its tremendous appeal was that no one controlled it. Ever since the revolution, Newsfeed had been the fastest most reliable way we had of spreading information. Newsfeed wasn't the problem. If people were getting bad information, it was because of how they used it.

George apologized, and his voice shook. "You were right. I should never have lost my temper that day. I never thought they could use me against you like this."

"It's alright, George. No one can control themselves twenty-four hours a day."

His voice was barely a whisper. "You do."

I tried to smile. "No, George. I must try because there is always somebody watching, but I don't."

"No one should be expected to live under that kind of scrutiny all the time."

I reached out my hand. "Consent?"

He nodded, and I grabbed his left hand in both of mine. "George, if that's the price I must pay in order to put Merica back together again, I'll pay it. None of us are faultless, but there is no one I trust more to have my back through this than you."

"Thank you. I won't let you down ever again."

I smiled. "I don't expect you to be perfect, George. I trust you to do the best you can, and your best is pretty damned great."

He nodded. "I will do better."

"I know you will. Making mistakes is how we learn." I released his hands "What's next on our agenda?"

George talked me into releasing my poor dog's medical reports on Newsfeed. I didn't think I should have to and hadn't wanted to validate the ridiculous accusations by giving a response. I had thought that if I ignored the claims, they would fade away like the trash they were, but it was clear people were taking these allegations seriously. Within minutes, everything I had released re-circulated branded as falsified or complete fabrications. Even my veterinarian became infamous and had to shut down temporarily. Dog-eared Burners burned an effigy in front of her clinic.

I didn't see any way back from this. I thought for sure my campaign was done. At least now I could focus all my energy on running Hoosierland, which I'd been neglecting far too much since this campaign had begun.

George barged into my office without knocking. "Great Party invited us back! The Directorship is still in our reach!"

"But our poll numbers—"

"Our approval numbers are still low, but our recognition numbers are through the roof! There's a chance we can win this!"

My brow furrowed. "Because people recognize us but don't like us?"

"I guess. Hey, don't question it! We're back on top!"

I shook my head. "On top of something, I guess. If it gets us where we need to go, I guess I'll take it."

The Next afternoon we held an outdoor rally in Capital City. Great Party posted armed guards everywhere, but I had nothing to fear this time. My staff and volunteers cheered so loudly that they almost made up for the lack of enthusiasm from the rest of the tiny audience. Everyone but George had come. I'd given him a special mission.

I put my hand over my eyes to block the sun and gazed over the empty plaza. I could name almost every member of the audience. They all looked the same and dressed the same. I was touched that they had all come out to support me so vocally, but where were the common people? I must admit that the unconditional cheers and applause felt good, but I missed the passion and inclusiveness of my earlier rallies. There was no way I could achieve my agenda with only these core supporters backing me.

Meanwhile, Better Blog posted Palma's latest rally. Fans screamed so loud that I could barely hear what he was saying. "How can I compete against that?" I asked.

George showed me his own video of the same event from further back. A small group of kids in Palma T-shirts congregated near the stage, cheering. The rest of the chairs remained empty.

"Where is everyone?" I asked.

"It's just a bunch of Better Nots!"

"He's in no better shape than me! He's got his core group, but, even if one of us wins, how could either of us accomplish anything without bringing the rest of the people along with us?"

* * *

Sloan's haggard face seemed younger lit by mischievous joy. "It's working!" He sat at my desk and cast his tablet feed onto my wall monitor. "Watch these man on the street interviews!"

A man paused walking his dog so it could take a dump.

"Excuse me, sir," an off-camera voice asked. "Who do you support in the upcoming election?"

"Well, I don't know. I probably won't even vote this time. I mean Watkins eats dogs and all, but then Palma's a mime. It's the lesser of two evils I suppose."

Sloan slapped the desk, laughing.

A microphone jutted into a young woman's face. The girl tossed her hair back. "Well, I'm certainly not voting for a mime."

"So, you believe the allegations that Councilor Palma is a mime?" the interviewer asked.

"Oh, yes!" she answered. "I've seen old vids of mimes. They really exist!"

Sloan shot me a broad grin.

"But you haven't made me look good," I said. "You've just made Palma look bad!"

"Exactly! Negative news travels faster and farther! But it's not all bad. Freenet reports that every family under your administration will receive a free Blue Panels solar battery!"

My eyes nearly popped from my skull. "Blue Panels? Those are the best on the market!"

"Indeed! They produce an even current which can't be matched by other brands."

"If only I *could* give away Blue Panels! Even if they are priced a little higher, they more than make up for the cost in reliability and lower maintenance. I had a complete Blue Panels system installed in the Chairman's Mansion when I was first elected, and it hasn't needed serviced since."

"And I'm sure you enjoy peace of mind knowing you'll always have clean, reliable power, thanks to Blue Panels."

"I do, of course, but there is no way the government could afford to give away solar batteries. What will people say when I can't actually do that?"

"Simple! If you lose, your supporters will say they all *could* have had free batteries, but voters backed the wrong candidate. That will set you up for another run. If you win, the official campaign will point out that it never promised free batteries, while your supporters on Newsfeed will blame not getting batteries on Better Nots in the government blocking you."

"Is any of this even really news?"

"It is now! And speaking of news, I have it on the authority of a certain chef that Councilor Palma doesn't chew his own food!"

"I— What? Why? I don't care about that."

"You can bet voters will!"

"It's not even true!"

"But it sounds like something that could be true. It's truthy!"

I rose from my desk, shaking my head. "No. No. No! This has gone too far."

"What do you plan to do? Just let them lie about you and do nothing?"

"I don't know, but I don't want to win this way. The truth should still mean something."

Sloan grimaced. "You live in a fantasy world! The voters aren't even capable of distinguishing what is real!"

"Do you think so little of people?"

"I used to hope citizens would eventually be forced to think critically about what they saw on Newsfeed. I thought the young people coming up would see how ridiculous their parents and grandparents were, but they still just keep repeating craziest and craziest crap! It's different crap, but still crap! Wilma, if you don't use the tools you have, you will lose!"

"That may be. But at least I'll lose on my terms."

"I don't need your approval! I can continue releasing this information without you."

"Please!" I begged. "Don't! The people deserve another chance. Maybe once they've reached a certain... crap threshold, they'll finally come back to us."

Sloan's eyes drooped and his rough voice softened. "I hope you are right, Wilma. I really do. Good luck."

Sloan left. I took a breath and summoned my assistant. "George, call Palma's people. I want to set up a meeting."

* * *

Razor wire topped the dirty wall enclosing Palma's mansion. Dead, skeletal trees surrounded the building, and a factory behind it billowed thick, gray smoke. While sitting in the car waiting for the gate to creak open, I spotted the words *Wilma will do it!* graffitied on the wall. I smirked seeing my slogan on Palma's seat of power.

Palma's bearded assistant wore a paisley skirt, but Palma himself strutted around the office in a bulky, gray suit, the epitome of old world masculinity. He extended a thick, meaty hand, and I shook it.

"Your tactic may just backfire, Chairman Watkins!" Palma said. "It turns out mimes are consistent, loyal voters!"

"That may be. I have no problem with mimes."

"Too late to curry their favor now, Watkins!"

"We want the same thing, Councilor Palma. We want to unite the provinces, rebuild the country, help our people live happy, safe, productive lives."

He fell into his chair behind the desk and motioned me to take the seat opposite him. "And you think you can do that? My people have looked at your proposals. Your strategy worked great back in your province, but it doesn't scale up!"

I surprised both of us by tilting my head back and cackling.

"What's so funny?"

"That's the first time you've criticized my actual plans! It's the first time we've talked about what we really plan to do to make Merica whole again. I bet you've got some thoughts on how my policies could be modified to work better on a larger scale."

He tapped his pen on the desk. "Maybe. But your Great Nuts would just tear those ideas down."

"Perhaps, but at least then we'd be talking. Palma, Merica can't go on like this. Look at the mess outside this window! We could have fixed this country years ago, but instead we argue about all these ridiculous accusations."

"It's the nature of the game, Watkins. We are feeding the people what they want."

"They don't want this!"

"Then why do they keep eating it up? It's the only way to get elected! And once you are in power, you've got to keep people angry at someone else to keep them from being angry at you."

"Things will never get better if we keep going on this way."

"That may be, but what can we do?"

"We can stop it, Palma! You and me. The people are hungry for truth, real truth. We can give it to them if we work together."

"Help the enemy?"

"Help *the country*... together, just on this one thing! Then we can air our real disagreements and talk about actual policy."

"That would just smooth the way for someone else to come along and out-shovel us!"

"That's a risk I'm willing to take. I'm gambling on the intelligence and empathy of Merican citizens. Are you willing to do the same? What do we have to lose?"

He studied me and slowly started to nod.

* * *

I straightened my skirt and looked out over the huge crowd gathered outside the Chairman's mansion. It was the biggest audience I'd ever spoken in front of, even bigger than before the scandals. Effigies burned on the outskirts, but they were like tiny candles in the distance.

Flashbacks of violence caused my heart to race. There was no way to control a crowd of this size. The masses hadn't shown up just to hear me. They'd shown up because they smelled blood—two candidates, myself and Palma, on the same stage. But Palma had yet to show.

"Any word?" I asked.

"I'll call again," George said. "Maybe he got caught in traffic."

"Provincial Police would have called us the minute he entered Hoosierland. I don't think he's coming."

I checked my watch: ten minutes past start time. "Wish me luck, George."

"You can't go out there alone!"

I closed my eyes and took a deep breath. "I can't control Palma or anyone else. I can only control what I do." This simple statement gave me a sense of resigned calm. I would do what I had set out to do, and the chips would fall where they would. I approached the podium to a mix of cheers and boos.

"In the last few days," I said, "I have watched some old vid streams with mimes in them." The crowd booed and hissed. I raised my hands to silence them. "You know, they were kind of fun!" Quiet fell over the audience. "And a lot of mimes went on to do great things. Robin Williams and Charlie Chaplin both got their starts as mimes." The crowd turned to each other with confused looks. Perhaps my references were too dated. I continued, "I have no problems with mimes. Some of my best friends have even dabbled in miming. "

"Let me speak!" I shouted, silencing groans from the audience. "That being said, I have no evidence that Palma was ever a mime, but even if he was, that shouldn't matter. A lot of ridiculous things have been said about me and about Councilor Palma. This isn't what we should be talking about, people! This election shouldn't be about trying to make one of us look bad. It should be about singling out who is the best candidate to help you and Merica get where you want to be!"

George and other loyal supporters cheered from their spots scattered in the crowd, inspiring a few people around them to cheer as well.

"We can rebuild this country!" I shouted. "Together, we can make Merica functional again!"

I didn't get thunderous applause, but I got applause, and that was something.

I outlined what I had done in Hoosierland and what I intended to do for Merica if elected. The old video from my original rally played overhead, showing the smiling faces and clean streets of my province. People worked jobs and bought fresh produce. They even went to the doctor. I felt animated and spurred on by an almost supernatural energy. "The kind of country you want Merica to be is up to you. Do you want it to be led by a circus of misinformation and conspiracy theories, or do you want facts and policy to mean something? Do we want leaders who are experts at name calling and Newsfeed shaming, or leaders who care about you and Merica? The choice is yours."

I spotted Sloan off to the side. He nodded at me and clapped his hands.

When I left the stage, my energy suddenly evaporated, and I nearly collapsed, leaning my weight against a wall. George put a hand on my shoulder. I could see the concern in his eyes.

"Palma?" I asked.

George showed me his tablet. A still photo of me had been animated into a cartoonish dance. My real voice played over the image: "Things will never get better… gambling on the intelligence and empathy of Merican citizens." Then the voice cackled on a loop and it played again.

George's mouth narrowed into a thin line. "Popnet released this onto Newsfeed thirty seconds after your talk began."

I shook my head. "Popnet might have released it, but the audio is from my meeting in Palma's office. I can clearly hear the skip where he spliced two sentences together out of context. A week ago, I wouldn't have expected such an obvious hack job to gain traction. Now, I don't know what to expect."

Sloan stamped his cane on the ground. "He betrayed you!"

"It's alright," I said. "We did the best we could. The outcome lies in the hands of the voting public, same as it always has."

Sociologists have since written detailed analyses of Newsfeed viewing patterns after Palma released his graphic, studying when people clicked away from my speech and back again. The dancing image wasn't long and didn't hold attention as well as Palma had intended, but it got millions of repeat viewers after my speech was done. George carved my speech into small bites without altering any of the content so they could be re-posted and shared. My supporters claimed Palma's circus-like video proved the points in my speech.

Eventually, Election Day finally came. Better Times Blog released video of Palma outside a polling station holding a puppy and talking about how much he loved dogs. He handed the puppy off to an assistant wearing a plastic-eared hat so Palma could cast a vote for himself. He'd gone all in with the craziness. Again, I repeated my new mantra. *The only person who I can control is myself.*

I held a modest party for my staff and volunteers with sandwiches and cake. Results started trickling in over Newsfeed. Some blogs placed Palma ahead by double digits, while others reported the exact opposite results. There was no way to know the real outcome until the official tally was in. There was nothing more to do now but wait.

I retreated to my office and fell asleep while my staff and volunteers continued to socialize.

George woke me in the dark morning hours. "I'm afraid we didn't win."

I had expected to be disappointed if I lost, but I mostly felt relieved to have the campaign over with. It was traditional for the losers to raise hell and claim the election results were tainted by fraud, but that was not my way. The people had made their choice. "I'll call Palma and congratulate him."

"Palma didn't win either."

I sat straight up. "Then who—"

Sloan pushed his way into my office with a huge grin on his face. "I did."

I furrowed my brow. "How is that even possible? I never saw you listed as a candidate on Newsfeed!"

"Newsfeed only shows you what you are already looking for. If you don't look up from the feeds, you might miss something important. When you decided not to fight back, I couldn't take the chance that you would lose. The stakes are too high. I ran with the endorsement of the Fine Party."

"But I wanted to win fairly! I wanted to run on truth."

"And you did! Well, I did. While you and Palma were throwing dirt at each other and alienating voters, I ran a clean campaign under your radar, the exact kind of campaign you would have run if you could have. I even copied segments of your last speech word for word. If it makes you feel any better, you came in a distant second place. You and Palma nearly tied. The two of you gathered up the hard line Great Nuts and Better Nots, while the rest of the voters flocked to me."

"But you were black listed! The scandal!"

"Do you even remember what my big scandal was about?"

I hesitated, still groggy. "Something about... dolls?"

"They are called action figures. Newsfeed may be forever, but memories are short, and that was over ten years ago. I'm going to need a good Assistant Director, someone I can trust, someone with the same goals and a proven track record. We have a lot of work to do if we want to create a world where truth can win."

"But can I trust you?"

"You can keep me honest, and, in a few years, we'll do this all again."

I'd struggled awfully hard to settle for second place, but I hadn't done this for me. I stood, squaring off with him, and slowly extended my hand. If I worked with Sloan, there was still a chance we could put the shattered pieces of this country together— if we could get enough people on board. Looking back on it now, I'm glad I lost that first campaign for Director. I wasn't quite ready yet for the Directorship, but I would be, and the world would be ready for me much sooner than any of us had expected.

In a world where lies are so plentiful, nothing is more valuable than truth.

And one truth we can all agree on, whether Great Party, Better Party or even Fine Party, is that Blue Panels brand solar equipment is the best on the market. The first thing we did after the inauguration was have a complete Blue Panels system installed in the Off-White House. Your government never shuts down, and you don't have to either, thanks to Blue Panels— Available wherever solar equipment is sold.

WAR STORY

Originally published in *The Dolphin* Volume 13, 1994-1995
Indiana State University Student Literary Magazine

1968:   A group of American soldiers makes its way through the Jungle. Not far away, but separated by thick foliage and fog, the North Vietnamese are also on the move. Both groups are unaware of the other.

Boom.

A shot rings out. Who fires? Does it matter? Both sides become aware of each other as their guns go off. Both sides suffer heavy losses. Both sides fall back, trying to get away from the bullets.

At the site of the battle there are many dead. There are also many who are still in the process of dying. Friend and foe hear each other's dying thoughts. Their thoughts are all the same: *My family. My life. My future. All gone. All for nothing.* They see and feel every life passing before their eyes. *Every life* regardless of sides. They know they are dead. Then there is a light. The luminescence fills their consciousnesses. *We cannot die for nothing. We can't leave. There is so much to do.*

1991:   Frank, a man with more silver than black in his hair, limps down the hall without a tie or jacket. His mouth forms a narrow line as he shoves the door open onto a large, carpeted office where a younger man in a tailored business suit sits at his desk talking on the phone.

"Don't worry," The man at the desk says into the receiver, "We've got your guns. It's just a matter of getting them to you."

"You're really doing it!" Frank shouts. "That's them on the phone right now!"

The man at the desk turns away from Frank, facing the window and the sun setting over the city skyline. "That is the sum we agreed on. . . Yes, I'll contact you when the shipment is to be made." Hanging up the phone the man finally looks up. "How dare you barge in here like that! You could have disturbed a very delicate business deal."

"It's true. Isn't it? How do you expect this war to end if you're dealing with their side, too?"

"Why would I want this war to end? Their money is just a drop in the bucket compared to what I'm getting from the United States government. Just today I received an order for more missiles. I want this war to go on a very long time."

"Damn it, Johnny. You've never seen war. You don't know how bad it is. I was in 'Nam. I've seen things that would make even a big business type like you pee your pants."

"That was a long time ago. This war can't touch me. It's a long way away, and I'm here. I hired you because my father recommended you for the job. I would hate to have to let you go. No one else would hire you. How would you feed your family? That engineering school you send your daughter to costs a pretty penny..."

Frank's brow furrows and his mouth hangs open. Finally, he limps out of the room, slamming the door on his way out.

Later that night, Johnathan K. Cunningham grabs his briefcase, locks his office, and walks down the hallway to board an express elevator. The elevator jerks to a stop when the power goes out. The emergency light casts its harsh, dim light on the car.

"Damn!" John stabs the elevator buttons pointlessly with his finger. He waits for a time, but being an impatient man, stabs the buttons again before struggling with the door. He manages to pry it open enough for him to climb onto the next darkened floor. "Next time we buy Chinese," he says, brushing himself off.

He hears a clang. Looking for the direction of the sound, he sees thick mist rising through the dark hall.

He backs away, fearing saboteurs using gas grenades. But there is no smell, and this does not look like smoke. It's fog. He stares intently into the rising cloud. Within it, he swears he sees a palm tree. He is certain he hears distant gunshots and explosions.

He runs from the oncoming fog, but he trips over a log and lands in the mud. The desks and cubicles around him are covered by so much haze they don't look solid, but the jungle around him is all too real. He smells something that reminds him of the turkey left over in his refrigerator for two months mixed with gunpowder.

Johnathan swats at a mosquito that tries to land on his sweaty neck. "God it's hot! What in Hell is going on?"

Branches snap and footsteps slosh through the mud. He ducks behind some surreal bushes and sees soldiers in green army uniforms. Thinking that they are after him, he keeps his head low and sneaks away. He doesn't get far when he hears an Asian language that he is unfamiliar with.

He hides in the reeds and spots more soldiers so close he fears they will hear him breathing, and these soldiers are clearly not Americans.

Oh my God! He realizes. *I'm in Vietnam. I've got to get back to the Americans! They'll protect me.*

But then he realizes that the Americans really aren't that far off and already heading this direction. He can hear them just a few yards away, only separated by thick foliage and fog. He closes his eyes and buries his head in his hands, waiting for what he knows will come. A shot pierces the night. He doesn't know who shoots first and he doesn't care. He does care about the shots that follow. Body parts explode. Limbs fly, and blood sprays. Both sides suffer heavy losses. Both sides fall back.

John remains at his hiding place looking at the many mangled bodies around him. There are many dead. There are also many who are still in the process of dying. He looks at each quivering body, from both sides, one by one. As he does, he seems to hear their thoughts. Their thoughts are all the same: *My family. My life. My future. All gone. All for nothing.*

He sees their lives pass before his eyes. He knows that they feel it too. They know that they are dead.

Then there is a light. The light fills their consciousness. *We cannot die for nothing. We cannot leave. There is so much to do.*

John sees the light, invisible to all but one other, grow from the broken bodies. The light reflects off the fog and gun smoke swirling on the bloodstained mud in the center of the battleground. From the middle of this swirling light comes one muddy hand and then another. With much effort the hands lift their muscular body from the bloody muck. The large torso is wrapped in a tight khaki T-shirt, and baggy camouflage pants cover the legs.

The newcomer dips a piece of cloth in the muddy afterbirth and ties it around his forehead in order to keep the black hair out of his wide-set eyes. His high cheekbones and tan features are a mix of the dead men surrounding him. The look on this face is grim and determined. He reaches once more into the muck and pulls out a sub machine gun.

He then stares right at Johnathan.

Johnathan runs in the opposite direction and trips over a body. He looks down to see a familiar face, a much younger face than he's accustomed to, barely conscious, grimacing in pain with his leg blown apart. "Oh my God, Frank!" He'd never imagined Frank could be so young—was he even twenty years old yet?

The enemy marches closer.

Johnathan jerks up and runs out of the dissipating fog and down the hallway. As he rounds the corner on the way to the stairs, he finds the ghostly soldier waiting for him. Johnathan's feet slide out from under him as he tries to stop.

The soldier raises his gun and fires. John clutches his exploding chest and cries out in pain. The angry, bitter eyes of his assailant fade into darkness as he falls.

Johnathan wakes up. His very young and beautiful wife sits next to his hospital bed. "Oh, John! You're awake! We were so worried about you."

"Buffy, what happened to me?"

"You had a nasty heart attack. Luckily, the night watchman heard you cry out and called an ambulance. Otherwise, you wouldn't be here now." Tears form on the dark circles under her reddened eyes. "It's all over now, though. Just relax and get some rest."

"So, it was all some weird near-death dream?" It had seemed so real… "Maybe Frank's words affected me more than I realized." Johnathan tries to sit up and winces in pain.

"What are you babbling about? You almost died. You need to rest."

"Okay, Buffy. I promise to take it easy, but I just have to cancel one shipment first. Oh, and could you get Frank's number for me? I really owe him an apology."

LIMINAL SPACE

I had been a child when the Sky Gods took me. Sorry, they prefer to be called Halcyons. I was ecstatic when Prater brought Tan and me to the Window Room to look back at my home planet, but wished it was under more pleasant circumstances. Apparently, the Halcyon ambassador to Woolly had been murdered.

The Window Room existed on North Disk, one of only two disk shaped platforms comprising the Solarhedron. Other than the poles, the massive living platforms were all rectangular. Rosy sunlight peeked over the horizon between platforms, tinting the polished white domes and cylinders where people lived, worked and shopped.

Despite the millions living on North Disk, we had the sled pretty much to ourselves. Streetlamps gave off pale white light. A nearly inexhaustible supply of power flowed up from solar collectors underneath the city. The ground sloped down like a convex dish, and the central spire grew into a massive cylinder as the sled neared.

An old-style O-Man guarded the door to the spire. The rotating eyes which spun around its head converged as it scanned us. The bulky, seamless automaton didn't speak, but its eye light narrowed on Tan and me as though we didn't belong.

"They're with me," Prater said in his soft vibrato. Tall, lanky Prater served as our guardian and chief tutor while on the Solarhedron. Our heads came just below his chest. I could always tell him apart from the other Halcyons by the slope of his eyelids and the puffiness under his black eyes. Like all Halcyons, his skin was white and hairless.

The O-Man's eye light swiveled to Prater, then back to us.

I crossed my arms in annoyance. "It's not going to let us pass."

Tan, my male counterpart, shook his head. "It will be fine, Sienna. Be patient."

"Have you heard what that light can do when it doesn't like you?" I said. "Nothing will be left but the smell of burnt wool."

"It will not!" He ran a hand over his hairless pink arm. The hair depilatory had done its work on him. Tan's skin always looked flawless. I could already feel whiskers threatening to burst out all over my face, but I should still look smooth for another day. We wore the same hooded black tunics that Halcyon students wore.

Prater let out an exasperated growl. "That's enough, Sienna! Stop frightening Tan."

The door at last slid open. A corpsman ushered us in. The O-Man's light watched us enter, then went back to crisscrossing its head in a general scan of the entryway.

While politicians and bureaucrats worked in the rooms above, an elevator took us down to the Window Room. Detectives sat in a ring around the control consoles, each moving scenes back and forth. Everything paused when we entered. The detectives looked away from their frozen windows and studied us like curiosities.

"Have they never seen an alien who wasn't in a window?" My voice was a whisper, but in the quiet, all eyes focused on me. My pink skin blushed and I hung behind Prater. One detective ushered us over and the rest returned to their duties.

"I am Kintson," the detective said. He spoke to Prater but studied us with sideways glances. "Thank you for coming. We need your help."

He sat and moved his hand across one of two control balls. The window scene spun, blurred and reshaped. My mouth hung open as Woollies came into focus floating in front of us. Other than their pink noses and green eyes, their bodies were covered in course, curly hair. I'd almost forgotten what we looked like without daily depilatory treatments.

Woollies roamed the polished halls of the embassy. The ambassador marched by in his red robe. A Woolly suddenly broke stride and leapt up, plunging a bone knife into the ambassador's neck. Tan turned his head away. I gaped along with the Woollies and Halcyons inside the window who watched the assassin stab again and again. Prater covered our young eyes, but I pushed his hand down and watched the assassin flee down the corridor. No one made a move to stop him. They must have been too stunned. It was unthinkable that a Woolly would raise a hand to a Sky God!

Prater physically turned us away from the window. "A little warning would have been appropriate, Kintson!"

"Sorry. I guess I've become desensitized after seeing it so many times."

The killer found the exit locked and turned the blade on himself. The knife must have been laced with a fast-acting poison because he fell dead at once. I pushed Prater's hand aside to see the assassin propped against the door in a pool of dark blood. A wide, dead grin graced his hairy face.

Kintson wound a control ball back. The assassin rose, sped backwards, and the ambassador stood. The killer continued backward through the corridor and out onto a crowded dirt road.

Tan asked, "If you can follow the killer all the way back where he came from, what do you need us for?"

"We lose him in the crowd every time." Kintson paused and lowered his eyes. "None of us can tell the Woollies apart."

It was hard to imagine, with our distinctive colors and hair growth patterns, that anyone couldn't tell us apart. In the awkward silence, I said, "Why don't you simply walk through the window and stop the killer before he kills?"

Tan rolled his eyes. "It's just a window for looking. You can't walk through time."

I offered to take the controls.

Kintson looked up at Prater with stunned, black eyes.

Prater smiled and nodded. "She's a fast learner. Give her a chance."

Kintson gave me his chair. One control ball was for time and the other for space. I made a small adjustment and the scene blurred into the blue sky.

Kintson looked to Prater with an exasperated sigh, as though saying, *I told you she couldn't do it.* He reached over me and slid the scene back into focus. "It's alright. You tried. It takes years to master the window controls."

I could feel my face get warm, but ignored them and tried again, making the most miniscule movements with the time ball, moving it forward and back. The space ball was more sensitive, and I had to be careful. I looked back to see Kintson nodding his head, impressed.

I followed the killer backward through the embassy kitchen and over dirt roads crowded with Woolly bodies. Finally we reached an underground burrow. The killer's home was nothing but a simple hole in the dirt.

"You did it!" Kintson exclaimed. I beamed a smile at Prater.

"I don't see what good this does," Tan said. "The assassin is already as dead as his victim."

"But we don't know why he did it," Kintson said. "Or if there are others who might kill again." Kintson furrowed his pale, hairless brow. "I'm afraid we must now *physically* travel to Woolly."

I grinned and met Tan's wide eyes. His mouth hung open more in shock. It had been nearly a lifetime since we'd walked on our home planet.

We stayed in a guest room and had dinner before the team was assembled. I could hardly eat because of my excitement. Finally we lined up to board the pod, a polished porcelain egg with fins on the back. There were no doors. Kintson and Prater entered the pod through its smooth surface as though the wall were made of smoke. I followed right behind but slammed my bulbous nose on the solid barrier. Prater came out to check on me. The pilot emerged and apologized, saying he had forgotten to code the wall for Woollies. I wasn't sure I believed it was really an accident.

"You probably don't remember me," the pilot said. "I flew the pod which carried the two of you here on your first trip. I only recently returned to piloting."

I nodded, although I did not remember him.

Tan waved his hand through the wall of the pod and passed inside. I kept my hands in front of me as I entered. Although the wall was opaque white from the outside, I could see everything through the inner wall of the egg with only a slight film between me and the outside world. A couch curved around the interior of the pod. I sat with Tan on my right. On my left sat a silver statue, a Q-Man, the updated version of an O-Man. Black angles decorated its metallic body. It was sized and proportioned like a Sky God but sat as motionless as the old sentries. Instead of rotating eyes, its forehead dipped into flat, featureless black. I don't know how it saw anything at all without visible eyes.

Tan elbowed me. "That pilot is Jay!"

"Jay?" I said.

"The only corpsman who ever turned down becoming a Q-Man!"

I took another look at the statue beside me, wondering if it could have once been a living being.

A red-robed Sky God entered. He extended his hand slowly and methodically to Tan and me. "A great pleasure to meet you both." He spoke in a stilted version of the Woolly language. "I, Branef, am to be your new ambassador."

The pilot placed a three-fingered hand on the podium, and the egg shot into the sky. I grabbed the arms around me, even the cold forearm of the Q-Man.

Branef gracefully took a seat next to Prater. I spotted Kintson smirking at me and relaxed my grip, remembering there was no sense of motion in a pod. We were in our own localized reality. We'd shot up so quickly that my brain didn't have time to catch up to my eyes.

"Look!" Tan said.

I stopped scowling at Kintson and watched the Solarhedron recede behind us. Pink sunlight beamed through gaps between the platforms. The grid of light shrank until our adopted home was just a black spot in the starry sky.

Stars blurred by. Concentric circles of magnification kept the sky ahead in focus.

I still didn't understand why we couldn't simply walk through a quantum window in the Window Room and be home in an instant, but pods were impossibly fast. Once our flight path was set, the pilot removed his hand from the podium and turned to make conversation with us. I had hoped for a chance to try piloting, but feared my four-fingered hand might not fit the control plate.

In a few hours our yellow sun swelled in the star field ahead, and Jay touched the control plate again. When last I had witnessed this sight, I didn't understand what a sun or planet was. It had all seemed like magic. Tan and I beamed as our world grew, but something wasn't right.

"Are you sure this is the right planet?" I asked.

Instead of the verdant world I remembered in childhood dreams, the entire orb was mud brown.

Jay looked at the stars around us. "Fourth from the sun... this has to be it, but... What happened to it?"

Woollies carried baskets of dry fruit and barrels of water over dirt streets below. They looked up at us as the ground approached, but we did not land on the ground.

On a hill, eggs joined together to form a mountain, the Halcyon embassy. Our pod slid amongst them and merged. The embassy staff froze as we exited the egg.

"Well," the new ambassador said, "Are we all going to stare at each other all day?"

The natives finally greeted the ambassador, casting glances over their shoulders at Tan and me as we followed them through the corridors.

We separated so that we could clean up before a banquet in the new ambassador's honor. I thought it a strange time for a banquet, with the previous ambassador barely cold, but it gave me a chance to apply fresh hair depilatory.

The food was no different than what I had grown accustomed to on the Solarhedron, but it was served by other Woollies.

"Aren't you cold?" a Woolly asked in her own language.

"Me?" I said. "Why?"

"To go around without hair?"

"We have our hoods and tunics," Tan said.

"They say you are like us, but you walk so straight and tall."

Another Woolly interrupted, "The other Woollies think you are pink Sky Gods."

The other disagreed, "They are not Sky Gods. If anything, they are their pets."

I narrowed my eyes and stood. "We are no one's pets. We are Woollies, same as you!"

At this the other Woollies gasped and became silent.

"What?" I asked.

"*Woollies* is *their* name for us. Not ours."

Tan asked, "Then what do *you* call our kind?"

"People."

I wondered if I misunderstood. Tan and I used to talk to each other almost exclusively in our own language, but it had been years since we had spoken our native tongue. I don't remember when or why we had stopped.

Tan remained seated. "Isn't that a bit confusing. Aren't we *all* types of people?"

Prater must have noticed the raised tension, even if he couldn't understand our words. "Is everything alright?"

The other Woollies bowed their heads and nodded deferentially. I'd never seen anyone show Prater any formal respect. He was always last in line, always gave up our seats on the sled when it was full, but as far as these people were concerned, he was another celestial god.

"Of course," I said, trying to smile. "We were just getting acquainted."

Prater nodded. "Good!"

The other Woollies nodded to me and returned to their work. The server woman gathered up empty plates. Before leaving, she said, "I didn't believe it was possible when I first saw you, but now I see your mother's fire."

"You knew my mother?"

"I can take you to her if you like."

"She can't still be alive! She'd be over 30 years old by now!" Average life expectancy for a Woolly had been 20 when I left as a child.

"She works as a cook in the valley. She had eighteen more children after you left. All but two still live."

"Still alive and working at her age! And I've got sixteen more living siblings! I want to meet them all!"

We broke our conversation when Ambassador Branef started making a speech, but I didn't listen. I was far more excited about meeting my family. I had thought my parents long dead and any siblings lost to time.

"Where are you going?" Prater asked after dinner concluded.

The server, whom the Sky Gods called Ruddy, kept her head bowed.

"I'm going to meet my family," I said.

"So close to an assassination? Are you sure that is safe?"

"The whole point of Tan and me coming to live on the Solarhedron was so that we could walk in both worlds and bring greater understanding. I am not a prisoner here, am I?"

"Of course not, but you haven't been here in six years. It may not be the same as you remember."

Tan beamed his optimistic smile at us. "Don't worry. I will look after her."

Ruddy looked up at me with wide eyes as we left. "I've never seen anyone talk to a Sky God like that!" She let me take the lead, but I was quickly stymied by the crowds.

"This way," she said, and we followed the path she made through the rivers of people and caked mud. Mounds of dirt rose along the path. Dark holes provided entrances to the Woolly cubicles within.

We found a public sled. The Halcyons had brought something of use here after all. It was full, and I wanted to wait for the next one, but Ruddy grabbed the rail and hung off the side as it crept forward. Her bag dangled from her back.

I followed her lead, but Tan was reluctant. "What are you doing?"

Ruddy said, "Another one might not show up for hours!"

Tan leapt and just managed to make it on, practically being dragged from the rear.

Ruddy released her hold and a couple of random people caught her so she didn't fall. I rolled into the dirt. Tan limped through the crowd. "That was crazy!"

"How else can I get to and from work?" Ruddy asked.

"You do that every day?" I asked.

Without responding, Ruddy continued into the foothills and bent down into a hole. Rich smells emanated from the earth—shellfish in a spicy sauce.

Within, a gray-furred woman stirred a pot with one hand. She secured the baby hanging from her breast with the other. Dirt caked the tiny thing's soft, downy wool.

"Are you my mother?" I asked.

A male bristled with annoyance. "I don't like this, Mother. That pink skin stands out like blood on mud. No way to hide from Sky God windows."

"Then you must be my brother!" I said. "You know about the windows?"

"Of course. We walk winding paths surrounded by crowds so they can't pick us out, but with that skin..."

"You can't be my daughter." Mother touched my smooth face with her course fingers. "You don't smell right, and look what they've done to your fur!"

"I did this myself, Mom. I want to be beautiful."

"By being something you are not? You were already beautiful..." At the pause, she emitted a strange odor, a complex combination of scents.

I scrunched my nose. "What is that?"

"Have you forgotten your true name?"

"Not Sienna?"

"Of course not! Words are too shallow to tell you who a person is!"

"What about my father? Is he alive?"

Mother and son exchanged a glance. "He is dead."

I nodded. "I expected someone so old would be long dead, but after finding my mother alive, I had to ask."

My brother turned away. "He did not die of old age like a Sky God. He killed himself at the foot of the embassy like a hero."

"What?"

"He had himself nailed to wood." Mother beamed with pride. "Only when the Sky Gods pulled him down did he bite into a poison capsule and end his pain while denying the aliens the opportunity to revive him." She shook the baby at her breast. "I only wish I was as brave."

"Why would he kill himself?"

"That is what we do, child. That is how we bring honor to ourselves and our ancestors. The Sky Gods outlawed it. They have no honor. Soup?" She pulled a ladle out of the pot. I sipped the broth and choked.

Mother and Brother laughed. "Not the bland food of the Sky Gods!" Mother said. "We have to spice it up to cover the mud and add nutrient powder. Food is not as plentiful as it was before the Sky Gods came."

Tan took the ladle and sipped. I expected his reaction to be even more violent than mine, but he held the broth in his mouth and closed his eyes. "It tastes like home!"

So many people came and went that I could never remember all the identifying names or smells. They all took a sip of communal soup. The broth wasn't filling on its own, so they each took a fibrous root to chew on.

Each wanted to touch us before they left, running their fingers across our hairless skin.

One turned to my brother. "Are you taking them to meet the Axis?"

"Of course not! The Sky Gods are probably watching us now in their room of windows!"

"It will be dark soon," mother said. "Return them to the embassy."

I was disappointed not to stay longer, but Brother and Ruddy took us on a detour before we headed back. We entered a ravine, and I froze, not sure I understood what I saw. Tan turned his head and grabbed me.

The entire floor of the ravine was filled with men and women crucified on knotty wooden saltires. There must have been twenty people hanging from their wrists while their legs dangled. A fat carrion eater picked at one of them, but I could tell the Woolly wasn't yet dead.

"We have to rescue them!" I said.

Brother slapped me. Tan stood between us with tense muscles. I never thought I would see Tan take to violence, especially to defend me.

"You would dishonor them?" Brother screamed. "I took you here to see if you were really one of us, but you are merely Sky God pets. Go back to your city in the sky!"

He turned to leave, but one of the dying called down to us with a euphoric grin. "Do not turn away, brother! Our ancestors smile on the pink girl."

Brother released an odor of doubt, but continued marching away.

Ruddy led us out of the valley, away from the moans. "Who did that to them?" Tan asked.

Ruddy's voice remained flat. "They honor themselves. The honor is even greater for the enormous risk. If the Sky Gods knew, they would be punished. Worse, they would be healed and returned to full life. The Sky Gods would steal them away from our ancestors."

"So they *wanted* to be nailed to those crosses?" Tan said.

"Of course!" Ruddy dropped us off at the sled stop. It was less crowded now. "I trust you can find your own way back from here."

I nodded, and we boarded the sled in silence.

Prater and Ambassador Branef greeted us when we returned, both eager to hear of our experiences. Before I could stop him, Tan told them about the valley and the sacrifices.

"I don't understand," Tan said, practically tearing up. "Why would they hurt themselves like that?"

Branef closed his eyes and shook his head. "Our social engineers determined it was a primitive form of population control. The Woollies destroyed all their natural predators centuries ago, but they reproduce at an extraordinary rate. When we arrived, most common ailments were eradicated. Of course, we offered them contraceptives as a more civilized alternative, but they refuse them. They say the medication is immoral."

I had never conceived of a conundrum like this. I wondered if the Halcyon species had ever faced this issue before they built their massive platforms. The Solarhedron was packed with empty living space, yet the Sky Gods had their own bizarre fertility laws which had never made any sense to me until that moment.

Prater held his hand to his mouth. "They would rather commit suicide? And in such a painful way?"

The ambassador nodded. "First thing in the morning, we shall visit this valley of sacrifice."

I looked up at them with wide, worried eyes. "I don't think that is a good idea, Ambassador."

He raised his chin and looked down his flat face at me. "I'm sure this all seems very complex to you. You must trust us to make the wisest decisions for your people."

I glared up at the ambassador, but Tan nodded his head, saying, "Thank you, Ambassador."

They took their leave of us.

"Why did you tell them about the valley?" I asked.

"Something has to be done!" Tan said. "Our people hang suspended in pain as we speak! The sacrifices have to stop."

"But Brother and Ruddy don't want it to stop. The sacrifices themselves don't even want it to stop!"

"Which just proves that they can't make these decisions for themselves. Trust the Sky Gods, Sienna."

"They are not gods. And my name is not even Sienna!"

I entered my neighboring room alone. This guest room for one individual was bigger than Mother's entire hovel. I tossed and turned on my soft bed, remembering the smile of the dying man on the cross— *The ancestors smile on the pink girl.* New bumps were already forming on my unnaturally smooth arms.

We gathered in the main hall for breakfast. I didn't much feel like eating. Jay floated the pod down to the front entrance.

"Do I have to go?" I asked.

The ambassador cocked his head and his black eyes softened. "I am depending on the two of you to be my eyes and ears. Don't worry. We will end the suffering."

He didn't understand. Seeing their suffering wasn't why I didn't want to go. I feared my people would think I had betrayed them.

We sat in the same spots we had before. The trip to the ravine was much quicker than a trip between stars, but Jay circled the chasm before we landed. Through the transparent walls, I could see my people hanging motionless from dry wood.

The ravine was too narrow and full of bodies to land in, so Jay landed on the ridge above. Woollies moved aside as the pod dropped to the ground. We emerged into the earthy air and descended into a cloud of rot.

"We are too late," Ambassador Branef said.

I gazed up at the dead Woolies. "They've taken suicide pills so we couldn't end their sacrifice."

A Woolly came forth with bowed head. "I knew you would come." He produced a long bundle of tubes like a gift. Fire and smoke exploded from the end of the tubes, and Ambassador

Branef fell, clutching his abdomen. Thick, black blood leaked from a thousand tiny punctures. I'd never seen anyone purposely hurt another being in real life before.

The Woolly dropped the weapon and produced another, identical gun. He took aim again. I grabbed Tan and clutched my eyes shut. A shadow passed over us, and the explosion echoed off the walls of the ravine. Sulfurous smoke stung my nose.

When I looked up, the Q-Man stared down at us. He pivoted slowly on one foot to face the shooter, and I saw thousands of tiny projectiles peppering his dented back. His metallic skin flattened and smoothed into its original shape, and the deadly particles fell harmlessly to the dirt.

The shooter ran for the wall of the ravine and lifted another weapon hidden among the rocks. The guns must only be capable of one shot. The Q-man seemed to take a single step, but breezed away from us. The gun fell to the ground beside me, followed by the shooter, and then the Q-Man stood exactly as he had, as though he hadn't moved at all.

Kintson extended his arm, and his tele-tubes pacified the shooter's pleasure center. He then fired his glue net. The shooter's body relaxed, and he lay laughing on the ground.

The Q-Man kneeled over the ambassador and touched his wounds. Thick blood froze in place, as did the pained expression on Branef's face. Ambassador Branef floated into the air under the Q-Man's touch. They then blurred away in the direction of the embassy, leaving us to fend for ourselves in a cloud of their dust.

Hairy faces scowled down at us from the ridge above. Jay directed us behind a boulder. Branef's black blood still congealed on the ground next to the incapacitated shooter. I didn't hear my name, but I smelled it, strong and clear.

"Sienna!" I heard Prater shout. "Where is Sienna?"

Brother pulled me behind a rock. "I knew you would tell them to come," he said.

"I didn't!" I looked over my shoulder at Tan and the others sheltering in fear. "It was an ambush!" I said. "You planned this!"

I wondered how he could smile at such a grisly deed. "Come with me," he said.

I followed him into a cave, and soon all light disappeared. "Follow my scent!" Brother called. "Their windows still need light to see by."

I felt fabric drape over me in the dark, and when we emerged into the yellow morning light, a dull cloak hooded my face and body.

Brother walked the crowded dirt streets at a casual pace, and I followed him into a burrow. The inhabitant of the hovel nodded, and we continued deeper into the hole. A vibration moved through my body, and the blackness of the back room was replaced by a shadowless light on blank white walls.

I gasped to see a pink Tridyll with its three eyes and hunched back. Next to him stood a man in gossamer gown. He was tall and lean like a Sky God, but his white skin was stained yellow, and a protuberance partially hooded his nostrils. Another in the circle resembled a hairless Woolly, but taller and with a single patch of fine hair on top of its head. I wondered if it used depilatory everywhere else or if such a strange growth pattern could be natural.

I turned to the Tridyll. "Ambassador Klay, what are you doing here?"

The other members of the cabal grumbled at each other. Klay raised a thick hand. His lips moved out of sequence with his words which echoed from the walls around us. "We were introduced once when she toured the capital long ago. I did not imagine she would recognize me from such a brief encounter. I trust she will not reveal our secret."

Another round of grumbles.

Klay continued. "She is remarkably observant. Perfect for our needs."

The yellow man said, "If she agrees."

Brother startled me from behind. "She will agree. The Ancestors say so."

"Whatever you want from me," I said, "it won't be a secret long. The Sky Gods will find us in their windows!"

Klay smiled. "Not in here. We stand in a distortion field, a tiny bubble of our own reality, much like the inside of one of your pods. Tridyll technology is not as backward as the Halcyons like to think."

Brother echoed the words of Ambassador Branef. "We want you to be our eyes and ears amid the Sky Gods."

The hairy headed man, or perhaps it was a woman, said, "It is difficult to know what the Halcyons are planning, or what their full capabilities are. Knowledge is power. Without it, we are fighting blind."

"But why would you fight the Sky Gods?" I asked.

They all shared a laugh at that.

The yellow man said, "Not everyone loves and reveres the Halcyons. They stick their noses into everything. They think they know what is best for us, better than we can know for ourselves. That is why we formed this alliance."

Klay raised a hand again. "This is not about fighting. It is about knowledge and defending our own needs."

"But you hurt Ambassador Branef!" I said.

"How many generations has he hurt?" Brother asked. "This land was a paradise before they came."

"The ambassador's pain is unfortunate," Klay said. "But it was necessary to get you here. His injuries are nothing to Sky God medicine. He will have recovered before you return. All we want from you is information. If everything the Halcyons say is above board and honest, all you will be doing is confirming what they have already told us."

The hairy headed person presented a palm-sized disk. She opened the concave lid and showed how to transmit signals with it. "It uses a long wavelength of the electromagnetic spectrum— short range and too low tech for the Sky Gods to notice."

I took it, and Brother pulled me away before I could argue further. "We must get back before they become suspicious! The Space Devil will not be gone long."

"Space Devil?" I said.

Brother pulled me out of the doorway, and the white room disappeared. I waved my hand in the darkness where the room had been, but Brother covered my head and led me back to the caves.

When we emerged, he directed me to call to my friends and then turned back into the shadows.

Tan and Prater squeezed me tightly. "We were so worried!" Prater said.

The Q-Man, Brother's space devil, stood out in the open, staring up at the ridge which now appeared empty of enemies. A shadow passed over us, and the egg-shaped pod descended into the valley. Kintson and the Q-Man hefted the bound shooter into the pod with us.

The ground fell away, and in less than two seconds, Jay revolved the pod and merged it with the embassy. Everyone seemed to forget about Tan and me as we disembarked.

"Where did you go?" Tan asked.

I couldn't meet his eyes. We'd never had secrets from one another. "I hid in a cave." I remained silent for a time, wondering how much I could tell him. "The Sky Gods don't really care about us."

"What do you mean? Of course they do!"

"They don't value our lives, though."

"They forbid the sacrifices *because* they value our lives. Why did they incapacitate the shooter with a pacifier and glue net when the Q-Man could have easily killed him, maybe even *should* have killed him."

"Tan!"

"He shot the ambassador, Sienna! He tried to kill him!"

Klay had said they knew Ambassador Branef would not die, but how could they have been certain? Even Halcyon medicine has its limits.

Prater knelt down to be eye level with us as though we were children. "The Ambassador wants to see you. I fear our time together may be coming to a close."

"What do you mean?" I asked.

"I was assigned to be your guide and tutor on the Solarhedron. I've taught you all I can."

"But you've been with us almost our whole lives!" Tan exclaimed.

Prater nodded. "I love you as much as I love my own children."

It was odd that we had known Prater so long, yet we hadn't known he had children until that moment.

Ambassador Branef sat up on the medical couch. I'd never seen a Sky God without a shirt, certainly not one as prestigious as an ambassador.

"How are you?" Tan asked.

Branef ran narrow fingers along the thickened skin on his chest and stomach where the wounds had been sealed. "Physically I am fine, but that was quite a shock. You don't need to worry. We are going to start adding contraceptives to the protein powder we distribute. Within a generation the need for sacrifices will end. For the interim, we've confiscated the wood posts they used to hang themselves. Native trees of that height have become rare in recent years. The horror you witnessed will never happen again."

I furrowed my brow. "I fear the others would rather starve than accept contraceptives in their food."

"That is why we must not tell them."

I fondled the alien disk in my pocket, wondering if this was right. The Sky Gods were indeed keeping secrets. Shouldn't the Woollies have some say in this decision? But if they knew, wouldn't more die of starvation and painful sacrifices?

"I'm sure you have already guessed why you are both here," Branef said. "We are missing something vital when it comes to Woolly relations. No matter what we say or how we say it, they misinterpret our intentions. You are to remain here and explain to them why they must do as we say."

I could see fear in Tan's eyes. Our people were now more strangers to us than the Sky Gods. I yearned to stay, to reconnect, to understand my people, but shouldn't Branef have *asked* rather than *ordered* us to stay? Is this what Brother and Klay wanted from me, or did the Axis want more than I could learn on my birth world?

I shook my head but kept my eyes low. "There is still more we can learn on the Solarhedron."

Tan's eyes sparkled. "Yes! Think what the Woolies would say if they saw us living and working as the Sky Gods do. It would give them something to aspire to."

I pictured my people flying pods through the atmosphere, sitting in front of monitor windows and managing distribution networks. I imagined their communal mounds and hills replaced with polished cylinders and domes. Would they still be Woollies if their lifestyle changed so much?

Branef raised his hairless brows. "Interesting! You both feel this way?"

I nodded. "Yes!"

Tan smiled at me with relief, but he would not be happy if he knew my real reasons for wanting to go back.

"Very well," Branef said. "You will return and be offered job training as any Halcyon graduate would, but Prater must remain part of my staff here."

We held Prater's hand. I remembered the dismissive looks the Sky Gods gave us on the Solarhedron, even with Prater watching over us. Without him, it would be far worse.

I awoke the next morning and stared at my face in the mirror. It still looked smooth, but I could feel the stubble rising over the surface. I held the tube of depilatory in my hand and took another look at my pink face. Perhaps I must remain on the Solarhedron, but that did not make me a Halcyon.

The full tube made a satisfying thump as it landed in the trash.

BACK TO NORMAL

An adaptation of this story originally appeared
in the *Dread Machine* October 1, 2021

The doorbell chimed, and I clenched my eyes shut, burying my head. The blanket felt soft and warm like always, and the sheets smelled of fabric softener, like they always did. It was as though nothing had happened. The doorbell rang again, and I half expected the lump at my side to yell at me for being too slow to answer, but the mounded blanket remained motionless.

The doorbell rang once more. I stepped into my slippers and slipped a robe over my nightgown. Sunlight beamed into the living room through the bay window, and I could see old Mr. Peterman standing on my porch in his shorts and flip-flops. He looked around the suburban street, and then, instead of ringing again, he knocked this time, apparently losing patience.

Mr. Peterman was a retired gentleman— always home, always alert. He must have heard Ethan and I fighting last night, must know something had happened.

Perhaps he just wanted to make sure I was alright.

I cautiously cracked the front door open.

Mr. Peterman studied my face, then smiled broadly and lifted a handful of envelopes and paper. "They delivered your mail to my box again. There are some bills in there, thought I better hand-deliver them."

I stared at him for a time. How could he not feel the emptiness in the room, or the guilt in my gut?

His smile wavered. "Joanie? Everything alright?"

I forced a smile. "Of course. Thank you. That was very kind of you."

Peterman shrugged. "No trouble at all. I saw the car in the driveway—"

Here it came. He saw that Ethan hadn't left for work and knew something was wrong.

But instead of asking about my husband, Mr. Peterman went on and on about the shrubs that bordered our yards and a new kind of insect killer. Finally, I excused myself from the conversation, thanked him again, and shut the door tightly with a perverse smile. I had done it! I had gotten away with murder!

Of course no one would suspect me! Not quiet little Joanie.

Joanne, I corrected myself. People only called me *Joanie* because that is what Ethan called me, at least when he wasn't calling me *idiot.* I wasn't Joanie anymore.

My heart skipped when the phone rang. It rang and rang. *Joanie!* I expected to hear, *Answer the damn phone,* but it stopped ringing, and I fell to the floor laughing. No one had said anything. No one complained.

No one cared.

I stopped laughing and listened. The house creaked just a bit when the wind blew. It was so quiet. I didn't have to make Ethan's breakfast or pack his lunch, didn't fear what he might do if I made the wrong sandwich or packed the wrong snack.

I jumped when the phone rang again, reached for it, but stopped myself. When the ringing finally ceased, I checked the caller I.D. It was the warehouse, probably calling to see why Ethan hadn't come to work. I couldn't keep this quiet forever.

In the bedroom, the lump remained as I had left it. *You idiot!* I heard his voice. *You'll never get away with this. You're too stupid.*

Ethan would have known what to do. I was always so unsure, but Ethan was decisive. He grabbed what he wanted. He didn't always choose the right thing or the smart thing, but he always knew what to do, and that's how it was done.

He used to say he could kill me if he wanted, make it look like a suicide. *And everyone will believe it, 'cause no one would believe someone as stupid and ugly as you would want to live.*

"You didn't think I was stupid or ugly when you married me!" I said to the lump.

I didn't know you were going to turn into your bitter old mother. I'm the best thing ever happened to you. You better treat me right, girl. No one else will have you.

I lifted the ax off the carpet and yanked the blanket away, ready to swing all over again, but the sight of him stopped me— the glistening red stain under his neck where the first strike had hit, the second across his ear when he had turned from a dead sleep.

He always slept soundly after sex.

The third and fourth gash dug into his cheek and nose. His eyes were still wide open, staring at me. I covered him again and leaned across the bed.

What if he was right about me? I hadn't ever really been alone. I'd gone straight from my parent's house to my husband's.

People had thought me pretty once, in high school. At least some boys did. I smiled at the thought of Robbie. He was smart, kind, broad-shouldered— better looking than Ethan in many ways, but he lacked Ethan's passion, his fire. Robbie never challenged me. He was a simple, uncomplicated man. Even after I broke his heart, Robbie once said I could call him anytime, and he would be there for me. I wondered if I could still call on him.

Robbie had graduated college and married Cindy Brown. I heard they had a second child on the way. I wondered what it must be like to live such a quiet, predictable life. The only thing predictable in my life had been the constant battle.

Robbie's life had moved forward. Ethan and I hadn't changed much since high school, especially Ethan. He was still tall, still firm-bodied. My pale skin now sank under my cheek bones. Creases had formed around my eyes, and frown lines blemished my mouth. Ethan was right. Who would want me now?

The stack of bills lay on the floor where I had dropped them. Without Ethan, I had no way of making the house payment. Between our parents' combined gifts, this house had almost been paid off after our wedding, but Ethan, financial wizard that he was, decided to take out a second mortgage to finance that showy pickup truck which he got totaled a few weeks later.

I spun around, facing the open bedroom door. "It *was too* your fault it got wrecked! I never would have driven off in your precious truck it you hadn't been drinking!"

I waited, but the lump didn't fight back, didn't point out that we were already home when I had driven off or that I had been drinking too.

"But not as much!" I insisted.

Ethan remained motionless. The house was too silent. I crawled next to the lump and clung to it as I had the night before, wiping my tears on the blanket covering him. I hated Ethan, but I hated myself more for missing him.

I would show him. I would make it look like a break-in. The burglars hadn't known Ethan was home, got freaked out and killed him.

You idiot! They killed me with my own ax? And what did you do while they were in here killing me?

He was right. I had to get rid of the ax, and I couldn't have been home when it happened. Although Peterman had already seen me, Ethan hadn't been dead long. I could go to my sister's, stay for a few days. No one would know exactly when the killing took place.

They'll find out. All they have to do is talk to the neighbors about how we screamed at each other every night.

"You're forgetting the most important part," I said to the lump. "No one cares enough about you to investigate. No one cares because *you* are a jerk!"

I was breathing hard. Everything was so quiet. A neighbor's car started and drove away.

I called my sister and told her I would be coming. She was too ecstatic to notice the tremor in my voice, or perhaps she just ignored it. I hadn't talked to her in a year... since the last time I had tried to leave Ethan.

I crammed clothes into a small bag. Then I realized I needed to take some stuff if I wanted it to look like we had been robbed.

What would a burglar take? What did we have worth stealing? I stuffed random things into a suitcase, including a $300 immersion blender. Would burglars steal expensive kitchen appliances? I didn't know.

A true genius at work.

"Be quiet!" I snatched a ceramic mug off the counter and whizzed it across the room. After a short pause, I motioned at the dented drywall and shattered mug. "As usual, I have to clean everything up!"

The back door creaked as I peeked out. The sun cast cool shade behind the house. Green grass grew in patches within our faded privacy fence. Dogs barked in the distance. A lawnmower buzzed at the end of the street. The world was going on as if nothing had changed. I crept outside, confident no one was looking, and lifted the ax.

The bedroom window didn't tinkle like I expected, but instead made a loud snap, followed by the soft clatter of fragments hitting the carpet within. I waited to see if anyone would pop out and ask about the noise, but no one appeared, so I knocked some more glass away, making a larger hole.

"Joanie, what are you doing?"

"My name is Joanne!"

Something moved in the shadowy room behind the broken glass. "Shut up, you idiot! Clean up this mess!"

Ethan looked out at me, cheek split open to his ear, nose hanging loose. "And get me some aspirin."

My knees buckled. I fell back in the grass and stared up at him. I didn't think to ask how he was still alive or consider what he might do if he realized what I had done to him. I hated him for being alive, but I hated myself more because I was relieved to have him back.

Now, things could finally go back to normal.

INTRODUCING
THE MANGLED MALLOW

I would never have thought to write a story about anthropomorphic food. As part of a Kickstarter reward in April 2018, my friend John Graham asked me to write a story featuring one of his Holiday Hooligan characters, and the one who appealed to me most was his character Mangled Mallow. I had so much fun with it! I think the result was much more melodramatic than John expected, and it's a lot of fun to read aloud (Check out the audio version if you get a chance!).

John has generously allowed me to present our story here.

John does a lot of networking with the local art and writing community and has had a hand in organizing many events with independent creators as well. For more info on John Graham and his many writing and publishing projects, or to see more Holiday Hooligans like Ninjabread Man, Karate Kane and Brute Cake, visit figidpress.com.

I hope you enjoy "The Twisted Schemes and Broken Dreams of Mangled Mallow!"

THE TWISTED SCHEMES AND BROKEN DREAMS OF MANGLED MALLOW

featuring John Graham's character, Mangled Mallow. For more info on John Graham's writing and publishing projects, visit figidpress.com.

Cold made my spongy body stiff, and I leaned heavily on the long matchstick as I made my way through the dark walls. A crooked smile crept across my face— half a smile was all I could manage these days. My unwitting accomplice had completed his task, and it would be just as cold in the rest of the house. My plots always seemed to unravel at the last minute, but, this time, vengeance would at last be mine!

A subtle vibration resonated in the wood beneath my feet. Something crunched in the shadows. I hurried my pace, but not fast enough. Yellow eyes reflected dim light from a crack in the drywall. The gray mouse gnashed its razor-sharp buck teeth. There was no way I could outpace its four furry legs. I dragged the bulb of my staff against the rough drywall as I ran. The mouse's pupils contracted in the sudden blaze of my matchstick. It recoiled for a moment. Before it recovered, I shoved the flaming head into its snout. The mouse retreated.

Its sizzling whiskers reminded me of my own deformity. I touched the left corner of my cylindrical body, feeling the shriveled, white cornstarch. Coffee grounds and dead ants were indistinguishable stuck to the melted corner of my face.

I didn't have the luxury to stop and sympathize with my opponent. The mouse would be back, and my staff was already burning itself out. I climbed up and finally saw the familiar box of oatmeal on the middle shelf. The mouse was not the worst of my foes. When you are small and sweet, the world is filled with enemies. Ironically, my current plan helped the mouse, but humans were far more deserving of my wrath.

The other marshmallows moaned softly in their sagging plastic bag. Once the bag had been overflowing with life, but fewer than 25% had survived the human attacks. A human would not be able to tell the marshmallows apart, but I knew all their names: Graham, with his creased corners, Heslop, narrower in the middle than the ends, and all the rest. A human would also not notice the green tint from all the rat poison I'd pilfered for them to ingest.

I put my hand up to the plastic and held it palm to palm with Graham. "I wish I could go in your place."

Graham shook his square head and body. "No, Mallow. We need you here to lead those who remain."

"And besides…" Heslop began. We looked to him expectantly, but he looked away.

I gritted my teeth. "Do not avert your eyes! I know what you are thinking. I am not ashamed of my deformity! My mangled flesh makes me the one marshmallow the humans could pick out. My presence in the bag would put the whole plan in jeopardy. At best, they would toss me in the trash, but it is just as likely they would toss us all out, and there would be no one to teach future generations the danger they are in." I pointed at the left corner of my face. "My face also gives you a symbol, reminds you— reminds me— why this is necessary!"

Heslop stared straight into my mutilated face, made me proud. "Yes, Mallow. It won't happen again."

"Use my full title!" I commanded.

"Mangled Mallow."

I nodded my approval.

Thoughts carried me back to a simpler time. Life had been better when I didn't know the truth. The house smelled of cinnamon and pine the night it happened.

Stockings were hung by the chimney with care. When the cabinet door opened, I marveled at all the colored lights. I giggled with joy when the hand reached in and pulled us into the big world. I fell through the air in a cloud of chocolate scented mist toward the waiting pool of warm, brown liquid below. I wasn't scared. I knew I would float. A tiny hand grabbed mine as we fell. It was a woman I'd never met from the opposite side of the bag. She swung me around midair. I didn't understand the fear in her eyes until I heard the screams below and saw my friends and family melting.

I skidded across the boiling surface and bounced against the rim of the mug. The kind woman's eyes met mine as her skin foamed and floated around her. I tipped over the side of the mug and continued to fall, bouncing off the countertop and hitting the floor below. I stared up in horror as the human brought the steaming mug to his lips and slurped away my screaming comrades.

Then the man closed his eyes and actually smiled. He smiled! What kind of sickness would allow someone to commit such an atrocity and *smile?*

The marshmallow woman probably though she was being kind trying to save me from our fate, but it would have been better to die that day. I finally pried my melted head from the linoleum and made my way from pounding footfalls into the darkness beneath the sink. I sobbed for a time, but then swore that no other marshmallow would suffer this way.

"Quiet!" I shouted. The kitchen boomed with human footsteps. The cold had brought them to us at last! But the thundering feet I expected were joined by lighter, rhythmic steps. A humming joined the footsteps, bouncing between notes more beautifully than any bird could do. It was a fitting sound to die to.

My puffy soldiers stiffened when the tea kettle whistled. "Stay strong!" I commanded. "Today you strike a blow for marshmallows everywhere! Today you become something greater than any single marshmallow could ever be on its own!"

The cabinet door swung open, momentarily blinding us, and I hid behind a can of soup, watching. I expected the adult male, but the child was not with him. Instead, the male was joined by someone new. I believed this to be a female of the species, but I couldn't be sure. The man's calloused hand loomed over my comrades, but the lighter voice said, "No! Eating marshmallows is wrong!"

He smiled and kissed her. I watched in stunned silence as they poured their cream down the sink and drank the brown water without us.

"What's going on? Graham asked.

My voice was barely a whisper. "I don't know." Could this woman possibly understand that marshmallows matter too? I continued to stare at the woman dancing around the kitchen. Her angelic voice fell upon me like rain.

Heslop shook and let out a burp so loud I thought the humans might hear it. My comrades were even greener than before.

"Was this all for nothing?" Graham asked.

"Stay strong!" I insisted. "The poison is for humans and mice, not for marshmallows. You'll be fine." I sounded confident, but I wasn't so sure. They were suffering, and this time it wasn't the humans who had hurt them. It was me.

I lay next to the bag all night, listening to their moans, trying to comfort them. Thunder shook the cabinet, and I retreated behind the oatmeal box. When I returned, the cabinet was almost bare. Along with boxes and soup cans, the bag of marshmallows was also gone. I hate to admit it, but I was glad. I couldn't continue watching them suffer because of me.

I spied the trashcan across the kitchen. I might be able to reach them, but then what? I couldn't end their suffering.

I paced around the shelf, marveling at all the open space. The eerie silence was broken by the music of the angel. I peeked out at her mixing beans, onions and celery in a big skillet on the stove.

I wanted to jump out and scream, "Why?" but of course that would be suicide.

Or would it? She had stopped the man from eating us. She said it was wrong! Perhaps humans weren't all bad after all.

A high closet shelf allowed me to observe the adult human's bedroom from above. The two humans slept in the same bed with their disgusting pink flesh intertwined. I'd read that their skin contained distinct solid and liquid sections instead of homogenized fluff, but somehow they were still able to move. Perhaps that is why they needed us— to drain our spirit and enable them to walk, like sugar vampires. I shuddered at the thought. Even if they needed us for food, there was no reason for them to take such sadistic pleasure in our torture. The angel was different, however.

I'd survived as long as I had by studying the humans, but there was still so much I didn't understand.

The woman spent the night again and became a permanent fixture in the home. I wondered what she saw in the brutish man who'd slain so many of my kind. She could certainly find a better companion than him. For the first time, I found myself embarrassed by my deformity. I spent the night imagining what I might say if I could actually converse with her.

Through metal slits, a pale yellow nightlight silhouetted a bed.

"Timmy!" I called. The vent amplified my voice. "Timmyyyyyy!"

A dark head sprang up from the bed. "Mallow?" The human child leapt from the bed and crawled to the vent. "Where did you go? You said Dad would be happy if I turned down the thermostat—that he'd reward me for saving money— but he said I didn't fix anything! He said I just turned it off. I did it just the way you said! He was so mad. Then you abandoned me! And that *Kristine* moved in!"

Kristine. My angel had a name. Timmy said it with revulsion. "You don't like the woman?"

"She took all the snacks out of the house! Even my mac'n'cheese!"

I used to feel guilty about fooling the child, but I'd seen the little fiend shove hundreds of us into his stinking mouth-orifice. He'd never seen me and thought I was a ghost. Perhaps he wouldn't eat us anymore if he knew his friend was a marshmallow. More likely... he'd swallow me whole. He was just another human, but Kristine, my angel, was different.

"Oh, Timmy, I'm so sorry about the thermostat. It should have worked, but I didn't realize something else was broken too."

"What?" the child asked.

I'd developed an elaborate plot involving the water heater. I liked the thought of the humans boiling like my friends, but I decided to hold off. There was too much I didn't understand.

Timmy's voice followed me down the vent as I left, but I ignored him, pondering the possibilities instead. If one human was redeemable, perhaps there was hope for the others as well.

The weather outside was frightful, but the nearby stove made the cabinet nice and toasty as Kristine sang. I began to dance around the wide, open shelf as though it were a giant dance hall. Today was the day. With Graham, Heslop and the others gone, I had nothing to lose. Today I would finally speak to my angel! I spun on one foot and pretended to dip my imaginary partner.

High-pitched giggling stopped me in my tracks. A new bag sat on the shelf. Their texture was different than my former comrades, but these rounded cubes were unmistakably marshmallows!

"Can you teach us to dance like that?" one of them said. They were all so young.

"What happened to your face?" another asked. Because of his innocence, he never considered the question might be inappropriate.

I touched my mangled flesh and smiled. "Nothing you ever need worry about, young marshmallow. The world you grow up in will be different."

I placed a bottle cap on my head like a hat. Worn at an angle, it partially obscured my defect. A gum wrapper became a little cape. How would my kitchen angel react when I spoke to her? Would she be surprised? Frightened? Somehow, I didn't think she would be. *Eating marshmallows is wrong,* she had said.

"Wow!" A little marshmallow said, "You look so handsome!"

I smiled. "Do I?" Graham or Heslop would have mocked my new clothes, but they were relics of a different time.

The angel beamed and smiled even more than before, but her brute shadowed her as she twirled around the room.

I wanted to talk to her without the man. She might understand, but I didn't trust him.

The cabinet door creaked open.

"I have a surprise for you," my angel said.

Her delicate hand took the children away. One of them waved as they left.

"Marshmallows!" the man exclaimed. "I thought you said they contained collagen from animal skin?"

My angel shook her head. "These don't have gelatin. They use a plant-based protein instead. They're totally vegan."

"Vegan?" I pondered aloud. Before I had time to make sense of the word, the dreaded tea kettle whistled its ominous tone, sending a chill through my fluff.

The little marshmallows met my eyes and reached up to me as they plummeted into the steaming brown liquid, tossed by the hand of my angel.

Tears poured from my eyes. I extended my hand from my perch on the shelf, but there was nothing I could do. I retreated to the shadows to escape their cries. I never warned them of the danger they might be in.

The woman didn't care about marshmallows! She only cared about our ingredients!

By fooling myself, I had fooled the children as well. And I'd let my friends be taken with the trash! The woman was no angel. She gave me hope, only to steal it away! She was a demon. I collapsed to one knee. It would have been better never to have hope at all.

Humans were all the same! The only thing left was revenge. My schemes had been on hold too long.

I grabbed my toothpick and leapt through the cobwebs into the darkness behind the cabinet. A hungry cockroach gave me something to vent my anger on. I welcomed its attack and speared it to the wall.

The humans would know me. I would be the last thing they saw before they died. The last words on their lips would be *Mangled Mallow.*

BOOK CLUB FROM HELL

Wilma waited in line at the Starbucks. She needed a strong dose of caffeine following yet another sleepless night. Even after three years, she still had trouble sleeping alone. Her ex-husband, however, had no such trouble. He had himself a sweet young thing to keep him company.

Wilma carried her coffee up the steep sidewalk. Her husband had kept the business that made money while she was the proud owner of this struggling antique shop. *Antiques.* She was almost ashamed to have the name on the sign. The few things in the store old enough to be considered antiques looked like they belonged in someone's flea market. The more valuable pieces were modern pieces of art, nothing antique about them.

These items were all once lovely to her. When she used to hold something old, she had felt a connection to the past. It was that magical connection that had led her to antiquing in the first place, and then later to turning her hobby into a business. She had always sought magic in her life.

When she had been a teenager, Wilma was the girl who played with tarot cards and convinced the other girls to hold séances at slumber parties—silly games. All that had ended when she got married. The rest of the magic in her life had left when her husband did. Now, one day blurred into the next, and even the beautiful faded into a dull gray background.

To salt the wound, her ex had taken their 9-year-old son, Coby, with him when he left. At the time, with Wilma's long commute, it seemed to make sense to grant her ex primary custody. Wilma now wished she would have fought harder. She had once even heard Coby slip and refer to Wilma's young replacement as *Mom.*

Wilma loaded up the cash register. She was about to dust but shrugged and instead pulled out her book. The place wasn't that dusty.

Her book club met that night, as it did every Wednesday, and Wilma was still three chapters away from finishing their latest book, a spy thriller with weak characters and a preposterous plot. Darla must have picked this one out.

The door chimed, pulling her away from the words on the page. Anger boiled up inside her when she saw the raggedy man framed by the doorway. His stocking cap almost touched the top of the doorframe, and a tattered jacket hung over emaciated bones.

"Can I help you?" She asked it in a tone meant to deliver the message that there was nothing she could do for him. Wilma felt the city was much too friendly to vagrants.

"Stuff," the man screeched in a high, raspy voice. "In my cart. You look? Maybe buy it?"

"You don't have anything I would want," she insisted. "Are you here to buy something or not?" she snapped, knowing full well that he didn't intend on purchasing anything.

"You might be surprised. Look." He stood in the doorway, stinking up the place like a festering infection. The smell almost made Wilma vomit.

Wilma knew he wasn't going to leave until she looked. With an exaggerated sigh, she placed a bookmark in her book and let it fall on the counter. He watched her with his one good eye. The other socket was moist and empty and might have been the source of the putrid smell. The door chimed as she followed him out the door.

The man rifled through a shopping cart filled with miscellaneous junk. His metal-hooked left hand lifted a rusty lamp from a cluster of aluminum soda cans and plastic bottles and held it out to Wilma. She stared at the three hooks he used as fingers and wondered how far the metal extended up his sleeve.

Wilma decided the man must be some kind of veteran to be so wounded. There were many homeless veterans on the streets of San Francisco. It boggled her mind that they would congregate here. Of all the places in California, San Francisco was the coldest and the wettest, not pleasant for people living outdoors. Perhaps they came here because of the tolerance the city showed street people, or perhaps it was because of the large veteran's hospital in town.

From amid the recyclable beer bottles which Wilma assumed he had drunk himself, he proudly plucked out some glass flasks which he had most likely dug out of someone's garbage. Wilma had to admit that they were no worse than any of the other flea market finds collecting dust in her shop.

"I'm sorry. I'm really not interested."

"Wait!" he screeched. "I got more. I sell it cheap!"

She was about to give him a dollar just to get the guy to leave her alone so that she could go back to her empty shop and her book when her eye caught something sparkling in the very bottom of the cart. The man's rustling had disturbed a canvas knapsack and revealed the corner of something gold.

"What's in there?" she asked.

He grunted. "Nothing. Not for sale."

"Show it to me."

He bit his lip with his one good tooth, making his mouth resemble a wound bound shut by a single stitch. He wiped his snotty nose on his sleeve and said, "Five dollars, I let you look."

"Five dollars just to look at it?"

He dug the knapsack out of the cart, knocking out empty soda cans as he did so. Hooked fingers held the end of the bag closed. "Three dollars."

"Two dollars. Wait here. I'll get my purse."

The door chimed again. She was grateful he didn't follow her in. Something about him felt unpredictable, and she was all alone in the shop. She didn't actually have cash in her purse, so she pulled two singles from the cash register.

The man had already begun pushing the cart up the sidewalk. One of the wheels threatened to wobble off.

"Hey!" Wilma called after him.

Without stopping or turning around, he waved his good hand in the air and shook his head.

Wilma caught up to him. "I thought you were going to show me what was in the sack."

He looked at the two dollars in Wilma's hand and then at the knapsack on the pile of junk. "Okay," he said. "One look."

He pulled the cloth back, revealing gilded edges and a porcelain panel bearing engraved images of helmet-haired profiles. Wilma had never seen anything like it outside of a museum. She slid the canvas further away from the exotic box, but he jerked the fabric closed.

"Two dollars," he said.

She presented the bills, and he hooked them, but she did not relinquish her hold on the money. "I could take that piece of junk off your hands, whatever it is."

"Not for sale."

"Oh, come on. What can it possibly be worth to you?"

"Not for sale."

His insistence made her want it more. What value could this amazing box have for the likes of this bum? It was worthless to anyone at the bottom of his junk pile. His reluctance to sell seemed out of character with his earlier eagerness. If he was playing hard to get in order to increase Wilma's interest, it was working. "I'll give you a good price!"

"Not for sale."

Perhaps it was the contents of the box that made it special to him. Perhaps it contained photos from happier times. "You can keep whatever's inside. I just want the box."

His shriveled lip lifted into a sneer. "You wouldn't like that."

She became aggressive now. She relinquished the bills and lifted the sack from the cart. He let the dollars fall and grabbed the sack with his good hand. His hooks grabbed her arm. The claw squeezed with remarkable pressure, and she feared the metal could pierce her skin. She didn't want to think where those hooks had been. She'd want a tetanus shot if they cut her.

"Not... for.... sale," he wheezed.

Wilma held her ground. "You're hurting me."

"Hurt?" He grimaced in a cross between a smile and a scowl as he chuckled. "You don't know hurt."

Wilma saw her own face reflected in the wetness of his empty eye socket. The reflection's eye oozed and bubbled. Her left arm withered, and her skin felt like it was on fire, cracking and blistering. She closed her eyes and covered her head as she screamed high and shrill, giving voice to the impossible pain.

"You there!" A policeman raced across the street, billy club in hand. "Drop the sack and step away from the woman!"

Wilma checked her arm. It was still there. She shivered as she ran her hand across her intact skin and face. The irrational pain was a fading memory. Perhaps the excitement and caffeine from the coffee, along with the raggedy man's noxious smell had done something to her head.

The strange beggar cackled as the policeman's billy club thumped against his artificial arm. The raggedy man grabbed the end of club in his hooked claw and jerked it away. The policeman drew his gun and backed away, commanding, "Stop!"

Wilma backed away from the melee. The beggar had dropped the sack back onto his cart. It was evident that the policeman assumed the beggar had been stealing it from Wilma rather than the other way around. She pushed back the canvas and found that the sides of the box were not molded porcelain or clay, as she had assumed, but were chiseled out of white, semi-translucent stone, possibly alabaster. Dirt darkened the recesses, accentuating the carved images. The box had to either be very old or an elaborate fake.

The beggar saw her with the box and rushed toward her, ignoring the policeman. The cop had no choice but to shoot the raggedy man in the leg. The old beggar stumbled, but laughed off the injury as though the entire altercation was amusing. Perhaps he was in some kind of drug-induced mania. He turned to face the officer. The cop's eyes grew and his own leg inexplicably gave out, causing him to fall to one knee.

The beggar grinned menacingly with the one tooth in that wound of a face. The officer shot him in the shoulder, but the beggar stood defiant, laughing and looming over the policeman. His claw snapped open and shut ominously.

Wilma tightened her grip on the knapsack and broke into a run. She looked over her shoulder in time to see the beggar's head popping like a purulent boil, followed by a gunshot echoing off the buildings.

The door gave its familiar chime as she slammed it shut and locked it behind her. She backed away from the entrance and gazed at the smelly canvas sac in her shaking hands. The old beggar was dead. There was no reason not to take the box now. No one else knew the value of it. Hell, even she didn't truly know the value of it.

Still, she couldn't help feeling guilty. She wondered if the police would find her guilty as well. The beggar would not be dead if she hadn't been so insistent on getting the box from him. She stared out the door for a short time, not sure what to do. Finally, she slid the metal gate shut, put the closed sign out and made her way out the back exit into the alley. It wouldn't hurt the business to be closed one day, and, with luck, maybe no one who witnessed the altercation had recognized her.

Tomorrow, everything would be back to normal.

The trip home took her down the steep hill, and she was glad to have gravity aiding her steps. She took the trolley to the train station, holding the smelly knapsack firmly under her arm.

The train brought her to San Jose, where bad things like this just don't happen.

* * *

"That's some elaborate excuse for forgetting your book," Darla said. "We all struggled through your selection about mythical female archetypes." Darla's red dress and earrings complemented her brown skin. The rest of the women were dressed more casually.

"It's all true!" Wilma insisted.

"Right." Darla poured herself another glass of wine in the attached kitchen.

"Look for yourself," I said.

The stone box was elevated slightly off the surface of the dining room table by stubby legs which extended from its gold frame. The gold was dented slightly from years of being jostled around, but this only added to its ancient charm.

Candace's loose peplum top billowed over her jeans as she circled the table, eying the engravings. "These are disturbing."

Darla, standing on the opposite side of the box said, "Why do you say that? These are lovely." The engravings depicted a helmet-haired woman, possibly a queen, surrounded by bowing men bearing gifts on outstretched arms. Darla met Candace on the opposite side of the table and saw the exact same image, only here the figures were replaced with skeletons. "Oh, I see what you mean."

"What's inside the box?" Candace asked.

"I don't know yet," Wilma said. "I haven't managed to get it open, but I will."

"Where did it come from?" Darla asked.

"I don't know that either, but I think it's old, very old. I don't know how that old beggar got hold of it. He must have stolen it from one of the other antique shops." That thought made Wilma feel considerably less guilty about her hand in the man's death. He hadn't actually hurt her, but maybe he'd done other bad things. He must have been on drugs the way he fought that policeman even after he'd been shot so many times.

Wilma pushed the weight of her guilt aside. "I've been doing some research at the library," she continued, "but I haven't found anything concrete yet. At first, I thought it was Greek, or possibly Egyptian, what with the profile art and the helmet hair, but now I don't think so. I think it must be older, possibly Babylonian."

Wilma turned to the fourth member of the group. Sophie sat alone on the couch with her back to them. Pale, stringy hair hid her face.

"Sophie," Wilma said. "You don't have much to say about it."

Sophie shrugged her shoulders and continued staring at the floor. She was built like a stick. The green turtleneck barely bulged over her chest.

Darla brought her hand to her waist. "Her ex-husband just sued for full custody of the kids today."

"That pig!" Wilma exclaimed. "Three minutes making them and then they think they have the right to take them from us!"

"He doesn't even like the kids," Candace said. "He's just doing it to hurt Sophie."

"Come on, Sophie. Take a look at my find. I'll pour you a drink."

Sophie stood and shuffled toward them with tiny steps and an expressionless face. It was as though she waded through a thick soup of melancholy. She fondled the gold trim of the box and lifted.

The other three women gasped when the lid came open so effortlessly for Sophie. A cold wind blew through the room and the electric lights flickered. Sophie stared into the box with wide eyes and mouth open in fearful wonder.

Candace slammed the lid shut, and Sophie fell to the floor in a faint.

Candace stooped to her knees to check on her fallen friend. "Sophie! Sophie, are you alright?"

"What was that?" Darla asked.

Wilma tried to lift the lid again, but it wouldn't budge. "I don't know." She scowled down at Candace. "Why did you shut it again?"

"Call an ambulance!" Candace shouted. "She's breathing, and nothing looks broken, but she won't wake up."

"She'll be fine," Wilma said. "I've got some smelling salts in the first aid kit. The poor thing probably hasn't eaten enough today, what with all she's going through."

The ammonia salts made Wilma gag, but they had no effect on the unconscious woman. Candace tapped Sophie's cheeks, but nothing they did would wake her up, and they finally called 911. Candace accompanied Sophie to the hospital.

* * *

The next day began like any other: another coffee, another trek up the hill. After yesterday, Wilma was looking forward to a boring, ordinary day.

Sophie was still in a coma, but the doctors weren't sure why. They'd done MRI scans and blood tests. The good news was that they expected her to wake up on her own at any time. It was so odd, seeing Sophie collapse like that.

The doctors didn't understand what had put Sophie in that coma, but Wilma did. She had seen how depressed she had been. It was a broken heart that did this to her. It was that damned ex-husband of hers. The gall, striking at her through their kids.

She froze in her tracks ten yards from the antique shop, causing the woman behind her to veer suddenly around her. Reclining in the nook in front of her shop was the old beggar, waiting for her. She turned, making her way back down the hill.

He hadn't been looking her direction, and with midmorning foot traffic, she hoped he did not notice her among all the other pedestrians.

How could he be there? She wondered. His brains should be a pile of mush in an evidence bag somewhere. Maybe it was a different beggar in similar clothes. She hadn't gotten close enough to see the man's face clearly, but she knew it was him. Who else could that tall, lanky walking wound in front of the shop be? She wondered if she could have misinterpreted what she had seen yesterday in her rush to get away, but the memory of his head bursting open remained vivid in her mind.

She stopped by the pier. The restaurants were already serving lunch, so she ordered a fish'n'chips. She normally didn't like eating outdoors where the muddy, fishy smell of the bay mixed with the smell of fried seafood, but a gentle breeze blew in from the water, and the soft murmur of the waves muffled the conversations around her and the turmoil within her.

What could she do? She couldn't call the police. She had fled the scene and stolen the man's box, even if perhaps it hadn't been his in the first place.

She had bought a newspaper and scanned the front page. There was no mention of the police shooting. But then, if the beggar apparently wasn't really dead, it might not make the paper.

When she saw the headline at the bottom of the page, she quickly opened the paper to continue reading. Sophie's former husband was in the hospital. He had been viciously attacked in front of his house— *Flayed* was the word the paper used—just after midnight. It was unbelievable. He lived in the suburbs after all, where things like that just don't happen. He must have brought it on himself somehow. Perhaps the scoundrel had gotten involved with drugs and attracted dealers or some other bad element.

Wilma flipped open her phone. The grapevine ended in Darla's ear, and she always had the scoop on what was going on. Darla confirmed the newspaper story, but had no idea who had attacked him or why. The attack itself had been ghastly. Long strips of skin had been peeled away from his chest and arms as though the attacker had been peeling an apple. Sophie's kids were safe with her mother.

A smile crossed Wilma's lips. She knew it was wrong to enjoy another's misery, but after all that man had put Sophie through, he deserved what he had gotten. He was still alive, after all. It wasn't as if he had died. Wilma couldn't wait for Sophie to wake up and find out divine justice really did exist.

If Wilma couldn't go to work, she figured she might as well visit her friend.

She placed flowers on the table next to Sophie's hospital bed, along with the newspaper. Wilma practically cackled as she described the plight of Sophie's ex to her comatose friend.

Sophie's face remained relaxed and peaceful. On a whim, Wilma lifted the corner of the bed sheet and tickled her friend's muddy foot, but Sophie gave no reaction.

Wilma's cell phone rang. She recognized the number as Harold Pho's. He ran the bodega three store fronts down from her shop. Wilma decided it wouldn't be rude to talk on the phone in front of her friend if Sophie wasn't talking anyway.

"Where you at?" he asked over the phone. Wilma had always appreciated his directness.

"I'm not opening the shop today."

"There's a smelly guy waiting for you. It's bad for business!"

"Has he been there all day?"

"And most of yesterday! He says you took something from him. You can't make money closed two days in a row."

"I know. Did anything weird happen yesterday?"

"Weird?"

"On our street?"

"Besides the smelly guy? You missed some excitement. A policeman had a seizure and fell dead right next to your place. Shot his gun and fell dead. Not a scratch on him. I called an ambulance. They say he had an aneurysm."

I raised my hand to my mouth.

"When you reopening?"

"Soon, I hope." The beggar surely couldn't stay there forever, could he?

"Tomorrow?"

"Thank you, Mr. Pho," Wilma said and hung up. Why did the policeman die when his bullet had hit the beggar man, while the beggar appeared alive and well? Wilma tried to picture the cop's face, but she couldn't. It had all happened so quickly.

Wilma took one last look at Sophie's expressionless face. Perhaps not surprisingly, talking to a sleeping Sophie hadn't eased Wilma's mind or kept her distracted for long.

Wilma returned to the street where her shop was, but she didn't approach. She only watched from a distance. The raggedy man was still there. Where else did he have to go? If he didn't have a job, he could camp there all day and all night if he wanted to. If he was real and not a ghost, he would have to eat something at some point, but he just sat there, watching and waiting. Occasionally a passerby would drop some change and he would pick the coins up methodically, one by one.

Nothing about this made logical sense. There was much more to that box and the beggar than met the eye. She thought again about calling the police and reporting the beggar for blocking her from going to work, but then she might fall under suspicion, and they would confiscate that wonderful box. Wilma had stumbled onto a magical mystery. Color had returned to her gray world.

She leapt on a trolley. She had exhausted the resources of the library, but there was an occult bookstore a few blocks away.

* * *

"Why did you call us all together?" Darla asked. "None of us have had time to finish a single chapter of the new book!"

"Actually," Candace said, "I'm on chapter nine."

Darla rolled her eyes and poured herself another glass of wine.

"I like the candles," Candace said, "but what's with the circle on the hardwood floor? You'll ruin the finish!"

The box now sat on a smaller table which lay within a chalk circle drawn on the floor.

"This isn't about the book club," Wilma said. "It's about the box. That box is what put Sophie in a coma. It somehow focused her sadness and anger and directed it at her ex."

"Oh, come on!" Darla said.

Candace shook her head. "I knew there was something wrong when Sophie opened that thing. All the hair on my neck stood up."

"I've got this pile of old books from the occult bookstore," Wilma said. "I'm not sure how the box works yet, but with your help, I'm going to find out."

Candace's forehead wrinkled and the corners of her mouth sank downward. "I don't know if that's a good idea. If it really hurt Sophie—"

"Trust me," Wilma said. She thought that if the box had really helped Sophie get revenge on her ex, it might be able to help the rest of them in other ways as well. "Each of us has to stand around the circle."

Darla downed her glass. "Well, you bought wine, and I've got nowhere else to be."

The women gathered around the circle and the box in its center.

"No matter what," Wilma directed, "don't step inside the circle. Think about your ex-husbands. Think about how you felt when you were going through your divorces." Her voice lowered. "Think about the fear that you would be alone, that you were worthless…"

Darla balked. "Oh, come on! Why would I—?"

"Just do it!" Wilma said with surprising force. All were silent. Wilma continued. "Why did he do it? Everything was supposed to be perfect. After all we had shared, how could he not love me anymore?"

Darla's expression softened toward her friend. Wilma had put on a strong face. None of them knew how much she still hurt, and she didn't want them to know.

"Wilma," Darla began. "I didn't realize—" Darla's expression of pity was interrupted by a tapping coming from the box. Wilma was relieved. Any awkward words of comfort from Darla would have just emphasized how powerless Wilma felt.

The top of the engraved box wobbled. Something bumped against the underside of the lid. Finally, the box burst open. A monkey-like torso popped up, causing the women to jump back. Leather wings stretched shakily from the creature's back as it examined the women surrounding it. Its head and face resembled a cat.

"Oh!" Candace exclaimed. "He is so cute!" She stepped forward. "Were you hibernating in there?"

Wilma put out her hand and shouted before Candace could go any further. "Don't break the circle!"

The creature brought its leg over the ledge of the box. Its shiny foot reminded Wilma of her son's bronzed baby shoe, but this gleaming limb, whether metal or flesh, had been cast with gleaming corns and stubby toes.

"What is it?" Darla asked.

"I don't know!" Wilma put on her reading glasses.

While Wilma poured over her books, Darla and Candace stared at the creature. The creature watched them back and glanced curiously around the room. It rested its fuzzy rump on the rim of the box, as though afraid to completely leave the security of its home.

In a short time, Darla became bored with the creature and fixed herself a martini. "You want one, Candace?"

"No thanks." Candace took a leftover carrot from the previous night's veggie tray and dipped it in ranch before crunching into it.

The creature intently watched her chew.

Candace looked to Wilma, who was making a list of names from her books, then looked at the creature. "Are you hungry, little guy? You must have been in that box a long time."

The creature looked up at Candace with swelling eyes, and its mouth puckered as though it wanted to speak, but no sound emerged.

Careful not to step over the circle, Candace tossed a baby carrot onto the table. Without taking its eyes off Candace, the creature's tiny, clawed fingers snatched up the carrot. It sniffed it before placing it in its mouth. Needle sharp teeth weren't designed for crunching carrots. It gnawed the root into a mushy orange mess and spit it onto the floor.

Candace laughed. "Wilma, do you have any tuna we could feed it?"

Wilma ignored Candace's question as she stood before the box. "It says here that if we can figure out its name, it will do whatever we say."

"Like a slave?" Candace asked. "It looks so sad! Imagine being locked in there all this time."

Wilma ignored her again and began reading off a long list of bizarre, archaic names.

"I like Mr. Snuffles," Candace said.

Darla laughed.

"We don't *give* it a name!" Wilma said. "It's already got one. We just have to guess it."

"How about Rumpelstiltskin," Darla suggested, prompting a laugh from Candace.

Wilma ignored them both. After reading each name, Wilma paused and waited. Each time, the creature grinned and shook its head.

"Do you think it understands what we are saying?" Candace asked.

"It's just an animal," Darla insisted.

After twenty minutes, it put a clawed hand over its mouth and actually seemed to chuckle soundlessly.

"This is ridiculous," Darla said. "Call the zoo. You have no idea how to care for this creature!"

"Just wait!" Wilma insisted. She read one last name, "Empusae."

The animal reared its head back and grimaced.

Wilma smiled. "That's it isn't it!"

The animal slowly nodded.

Wilma commanded, "Step out of the box and shut the lid."

The creature did as commanded, revealing a goat-like hoof at the end of its other leg.

Too giddy to utter a sound, Wilma jiggled with joy.

"Alright," Darla said. "You have your pet."

"Not yet." Wilma ran to the kitchen and returned with a sharp knife.

"What are you doing?" Darla asked.

Wilma tossed the knife on the table and ordered the creature to, "Cut off your brass foot."

"No!" Candace whined.

Wilma held Candace's shoulders. "I know what I'm doing. Once we have its foot, we can let it out of the circle and make it comfortable. Won't that be nice?"

The creature fell back onto its rear and gritted its teeth as it dragged the blade back and forth along its ankle, all the while staring up at Wilma with a raised upper lip. There was surprisingly little blood, but Candace hid her face.

Once it was done, Wilma placed her hand in the circle, and the creature handed over its shiny foot.

"Now what?" Darla asked with a hint of disgust in her voice.

"We should feed it!" Candace said.

"Not yet," Wilma said. "Let's have a little fun first." She presented the creature with a photograph of her ex and his new love. "Empusae, I want to play a game with them."

"Wilma, no!" Candace said.

"Don't hurt them, Empusae." Wilma clarified. "Just play some pranks on them. Cause some mischief."

The creature hopped up on its hoof using its wings to balance. It took the photo in its tiny, pointed fingers and smiled before poofing away in a cloud of sulfurous smoke.

"Holy crap!" Darla exclaimed. "It disappeared!" She and Candace scowled at Wilma. "What have you done?"

"I'm just playing!" Wilma said. "Think about it! If this works, we can send him to do other things, important things. This isn't just an animal. It's magic! Together we could bring peace to the city, or maybe the whole country! No woman will ever be hurt again."

They continued staring.

"Come on!" Wilma said. "You can't say a little revenge on your ex-husbands wouldn't be sweet."

"Actually, Candace said, "my ex and I get along really well. He's a great co-parent, and I still have him listed as my emergency contact."

"Well, you are a lucky one," Wilma said.

Darla chimed in, "I already got my revenge. I got half his stuff."

Candace spoke low, almost in a whisper. "I think we are forgetting Sophie."

"What about her?" Wilma asked. "The doctors said she will be fine."

"They don't know that!" Candace said. "They don't even know why she is in a coma!" She eyed the box suspiciously.

"Candace is right," Darla agreed. "That box did something to her. Why don't you ask your magic pet to fix her, if it can?"

"That's a good idea!" Wilma agreed. "I'll ask him when he gets back."

"Why wait?" Candace said. "Call it back now."

Wilma bit her lip. "I've got a better idea. We can call up another one!"

"You can't be serious!" Candace exclaimed. "There is no way another one of those animals could fit inside that box!"

Wilma smiled. Candace had a big heart and could be so smart about some things, but she didn't know everything. "You still don't understand. It's magic!" She held up the brass foot. "We can each have our own! I can make us all little necklaces for the feet."

Darla waved her glass in the air. "Can't we at least wait and see what this one does first before we summon up another?"

"Gather round the circle," Wilma insisted. "There's nothing to be afraid of. I've read all these books."

They hesitated, and Wilma added, "This time, it's for Sophie!" They did as she asked. "Do as we did before," Wilma said. "Think about your ex-husbands. Think about how they hurt you."

Darla scoffed again, but kept her opinions to herself. The box didn't operate on words alone however, and the other women's lack of focus frustrated Wilma. The box remained motionless.

"For Sophie!" Wilma reminded them.

It wasn't long before the lid wobbled. They watched intently, anticipating another pair of tiny claws.

The lid burst open, but instead of the tiny hands, a full-sized human arm shot up. A feminine hand reached frantically through the air trying to find something to grab. Another set of fingers gripped the edge of the box so tightly that the knuckles turned white.

The three women froze in disbelief. None of them moved until they heard the scream— Sophie's scream.

Candace was the first to rush forward.

"Don't break the circle!" Wilma commanded, but the others ignored her. "It can't be Sophie!" Wilma said. "Sophie's safe in the hospital!"

Candace and Darla both grabbed the arm and pulled.

"Help us!" Darla demanded.

Wilma could hear Sophie's sobs echoing inside the box. She grabbed the flailing hand and pulled with all her might. Sophie's face emerged just above the lip of the box, but no matter how hard they pulled, they couldn't get her shoulders past the rim.

Tears dripped from Sophie's terrified eyes. "Get me out of here!" She screamed. "It's so dark! So cold! I can't take it!" Already terrified eyes threatened to bulge out of her head, and her quivering arm went limp.

"Hold on, Sophie!" Wilma said. "We'll think of something!"

Sophie looked at Wilma from the mouth of the box, then at the other two women. "I'm not alone in here."

With a sudden yank, Sophie jerked free of their grasp. Her scream faded as though she were rapidly falling a great distance, and the lid slammed shut behind her.

Candace grabbed the box with both hands, trying to pry the lid open with all her might. She lifted the box over her head, threatening to smash it against the floor, but Wilma and Darla both stopped her. Candace let them take the box and place it back on the table while she collapsed on the floor, crying.

"Do you still think this is harmless?" Darla asked Wilma.

Candace stopped sobbing. "Wilma, isn't your son at your ex-husband's house?"

Wilma gave them a wavering smile. "Coby will be fine. I told Empusae to play pranks on my ex and his new bride. I didn't say anything about my son."

Candace sat up. "Exactly. You didn't say to hurt him, but you didn't say *not* to hurt him. Isn't that what demons and devils do in old storybooks? They twist your words around to hurt you, no matter how carefully you phrase your instructions."

Darla pointed at the box. "What about Sophie?"

Wilma's smile faded, and she felt an oppressive pressure in her chest. She picked up her phone and brought up her ex-husband's number. His phone rang.

And rang.

And rang.

Finally Wilma's rival, the young, blonde ditz picked up the phone. She was breathing hard, and Wilma was disgusted at the thought of what she might have interrupted.

"Sorry," the ditz said. "I couldn't find our phones. I finally heard this one ringing in the back of the toilet. Silly kid. It was taped under the lid."

Wilma smiled and let out a relieved breath. Her child didn't do this. Coby wasn't the type to play practical jokes. Empusae was playing harmless pranks, just as instructed. Wilma gave her friends a smile as if to say, *I told you so.*

"Can I speak to my son?" Wilma asked.

The ditz remained silent.

"Put him on," Wilma insisted.

"I'd love to," the ditz said, "but he's hiding from us. I don't know what's gotten into him tonight."

Wilma's heart rose into her throat. "When did you see him last?"

"He's fine," the ditz said. "He's got to be in the house somewhere."

The ditz thought Wilma was just being overprotective again and questioning her parenting skills, but this was much more serious than that.

"When did you see him last?" Wilma demanded again.

"He was coloring in front of the television about twenty minutes ago. When I called him for bed, he'd disappeared."

A loud knock banged against Wilma's door.

Darla sauntered toward it, martini in hand.

Wilma pulled the phone away from her mouth and whispered, "Don't answer that."

The knocking came again, more insistent. A voice screeched through the wood, "Give back the box!"

The women froze. It was the raggedy man, the beggar. He had somehow tracked Wilma down to her house in San Jose.

"Don't answer that!" Wilma shouted again.

The knocking thumped louder and faster. The raggedy man's hooks hacked into the wood grain and scratched chunks out of the door.

The ditz's tiny voice squeaked over the phone. "What's going on?"

The beggar's one good eye peeked through the rough hole he'd made in the splintered wood. "The box is dangerous!"

Wilma hung up and clutched the brass foot close to her chest. "Empusae!" she called. The little demon appeared before her in a puff of smoke. "Where is my son?" She demanded.

Empusae smiled a sharp-toothed smile and shrugged its shoulders.

Darla shrieked. She and Candace retreated behind the kitchen counter as the raggedy man busted through the door. He scowled at Wilma and Empusae with his one good eye, but made his way straight for the box.

"Stop him!" Wilma commanded. She needed time to think and to question Empusae. She couldn't let the beggar man take the box until she knew for sure that her son and Sophie were safe.

Empusae swooped over the beggar, who waved the creature away with his hooked hand. Empusae darted out and in like a wasp, slashing at the raggedy man with its tiny claws. The metal arm sliced through the air, shattering a lamp. The imp stole the man's hat and swiped at his cheek, but the beggar inevitably connected. He pinned Empusae's thin neck to the wall between his hooks. Empusae's claws scratched uselessly at the metal arm, shredding the man's jacket.

"Stupid lady!" the beggar screeched at Wilma. "You even know what you're playing with?"

Darla and Candace peeked out from the kitchen, afraid to move. It was all up to Wilma. She could see that Empusae couldn't keep the beggar at bay alone. The raggedy man would get his box back, and with it, any chance of finding her son would be gone. She wished she had never taken the box, wished she wouldn't have been so foolish to think she could control Empusae, but it was too late to change what had been done. As long as she kept the box, it wasn't too late to fix things.

She darted for the box. One Empusae couldn't stop the beggar, but what about two… or three? How many could she summon through that box? Her foot brushed unnoticed over the circle, and she lifted the lid of the box without a thought.

She could not see a bottom within. The sides of the box led down into a darkness that seemed to go on forever. A cold draft overcame her, and the darkness rose up, engulfing her. The only light now came from a rectangle above.

Something distant thumped against the hardwood floor. The one-eyed beggar looked down at her from the rectangle of light.

"Let me out!" Wilma screamed.

The lid slammed shut, leaving her in total darkness.

"Darla!" She shouted. "Candace! I'm here! Let me out!"

Her cries echoed back to her. The thump she had heard had likely been her own body hitting the floor. They were probably taking it to the hospital now, just as they had done with Sophie's, but it too was in a coma that no one could explain, while her soul was stuck in here.

She remembered the demon. "Empusae!" she called. But her hands were now empty. The creature's foot was somewhere out there in the real world beyond the lip of the box.

She knew that no matter how loud she screamed, none of them would hear her.

She screamed anyway.

INTRODUCTION TO
THE IRON WRITER CHALLENGE

And now for something completely different...

The **IRON WRITER CHALLENGE** was a fun, friendly competition where four to six authors have four days to write their own five-hundred-word flash fiction which is **required to incorporate four provided elements.** The results are posted and a winner announced a week later.

Here are two of my Iron Writer stories.

"Mastodon Martyr" was written as part of the 110th **IRON WRITER CHALLENGE** on April 16, 2015. This winning story was published in their *Ironology 2016* anthology on June 15, 2017. It was **required to include a new born baby, a judge's gavel, a bull mastodon and a cactus couch.**

Done as part of the 154th Iron Writer Challenge 2016 Spring Open Challenge #2 on April 28, 2016, "Yellow Revenge" was **required to include: a truthful funeral attendee, poisoned toilet paper, a specific M&M color bearing a private meaning and leg warmers.**

THE MASTODON MARTYR

Originally published in the *Ironology 2016* anthology on June 15, 2017 and **required to include a new born baby, a judge's gavel, a bull mastodon and a cactus couch.**

Judge Turner slammed the gavel, but that didn't silence the crowd. The anti-cloners wouldn't be so supportive if they knew my true goal.

Cranston pointed at me from the stand with his good hand. "It was him! No one else was near that freezer."

Judge Turner banged the gavel again and finally silenced the crowd.

The prosecutor strode before me. "The evidence is clear. Your card accessed the door. Cranston saw you at the freezer. You were angry about being fired."

"That's not why I did it!" I blurted.

"Of course. Estimated value for an ounce of bull mastodon semen is 20 million."

The crowd jeered.

Cranston, still on the stand, raised his mangled left arm. "You know what I went through to get that sample!"

Dr. Bates and Cranston whispered with the prosecutor, and they called my lawyer over. Cranston scowled, but Bates looked worried. He was a good man, just misguided.

They surrounded me, the lawyers, Cranston, and Dr. Bates.

Bates said, "If you return the sample intact, we'll drop—"

"Recommend leniency," Cranston corrected. "Not drop charges. He's been on the run for over a year, we can't drop charges!"

My lawyer put her hand on mine. "Take the deal. You got what you wanted, public awareness. If you're out of jail, you can write a book and—"

I took a deep breath. "I don't have the sample."

Dr. Bates put his hand to his mouth. "You threw it out?"

Just then, my accomplice wheeled in a crate. She lifted the lid and gave me a large bottle of warm milk. A tiny gray trunk pulled my arm gently down. Nessie, the newborn mastodon, closed her eyes contentedly as she suckled. I couldn't help but smile.

Dr. Bates gasped. "The Farm never maintained a natural pregnancy!"

"I tried telling you. Your mastodons aren't happy. We gave momma plenty of room and let the herd roam." Nessie jerked my arm, and I extricated myself to get a fresh bottle.

"May I?" Bates asked. Bates beamed as Nessie suckled. "We must drop charges."

"We can't!" Cranston argued.

"This is what we wanted all along!" Bates insisted. "A natural birth."

My previous supporters murmured in confusion. This isn't what they wanted.

Cranston's face was red. "He stole from us, ran, and never returned the sample!"

Bates argued, "He gave us something better!"

Judge Turner banged the gavel again. "This isn't just up to you anymore. He must be sentenced."

Nessie fondled Bates' glasses with her trunk. "We can't throw him in jail or fine him for this."

Cranston smirked. "I have a suggestion..."

* * *

I expected prison and for my career to be over, but I wasn't prepared for this. Mastodons weren't the Farm's only creation, although I hadn't deduced the purpose for this one. Cranston smiled as I plotted my descent onto the cactus couch. I tried to find the spot where the fewest spines would pierce me, or at least spare my most sensitive bits, but the quills were everywhere. I sat, and Cranston smiled. At least my sentence was only ten minutes.

It was a very long ten minutes.

YELLOW REVENGE

Submitted to the Iron Writer Challenge April 2016 and **required to include: a truthful funeral attendee, poisoned toilet paper, a specific M&M color bearing private meaning and leg warmers.**

One pink legwarmer rose proudly as she kicked. The fluorescent yarn matched her headband. Arms barely strained as she brought tiny barbells back. The smile frozen on Aunt Sally's face was youthful, but she was in her forties when this photo, frozen behind glass on the wall of her den, was taken. This was when she founded Better Body Inc., the beginning of her fortune and legacy.

Ted nudged me, but I waved the jar of discarded yellow M&Ms away.

Rita took the jar. "You aren't afraid of the yellow ones like old Sally was?"

I glared. Rita had made a scene at the funeral. With everyone saying how great Sally looked, Rita couldn't help but claim she'd had work done.

Ted grabbed the jar back. "She was your sister. Show some respect."

Rita cocked her head. "You truly believe the yellow ones are more fattening?"

Petting Fluffy would take my mind off these horrible people, but Sally's cat was nowhere to be seen.

Ted grabbed his gut and swiveled in his chair. "Where's that damn lawyer? He was to read the will at 10. It's 11!"

I held my nose and stepped away. "What did you eat?"

"Indeed," Rita said. "There's a bathroom to the side of the den."

Ted rose, but made for the door out. "There's a perfectly good bathroom downstairs, away from you!" The door wouldn't budge. Ted jerked the door and stood awkwardly with crossed legs.

"Use the bathroom here!" I said, but Ted continued to bang on the door. Tears dripped from his eyes and his face flushed red.

Rita grabbed her side. "Now you've got ME doing it!" She flung the door to the bathroom open, but staggered back, eyes wide.

My mouth hung open. "Aunt Sally? You're alive!"

"Good morning, dear," Sally said, stepping by. Her face was tight and boobs high. Aunt Rita may have been right about having work done.

Sally threw a roll of toilet paper at Ted, who was on the floor with his back propped against the locked door. He rolled away from the tissue like it was a grenade.

Sally leered. "Did you enjoy your yellow candy-coated laxatives?

Rita spoke from behind the bathroom door. "Why did you do this, you hag?"

Sally continued, "Why so afraid of the bathroom here, Ted? Have any of you seen Fluffy today? Did you ever notice my dear Fluffy? If you did, maybe you'd know she liked to pull the toilet paper from the tube. I found Fluffy dead last week. Someone poisoned my toilet paper!"

"You'll never prove I did it!" Ted insisted.

The door to the den pulled open and Ted's head fell to the floor. A policeman stood over him. "We've got enough for a warrant. I hope you didn't leave any traces of that poison lying around."

Sally patted me on the back while they carted Ted away. "So good to see you, dear. Let's get some fresh M&Ms. Stay away from the yellow ones."

THE SMELL

I had forgotten all about it until I enrolled Tommy in the old grade school. It was hard to believe Tommy was already five years old. He was growing up much too fast. The smell hit me immediately, as though something had spoiled somewhere. All I knew was that it made me nauseas.

I met Tommy's new teacher, Mrs. Wise, and signed the appropriate papers. She gave us a tour, saying that a lot had changed in the twenty years since I had gone to school there. Tommy stuck close to me, little fingers clinging to my pants leg. The thumb on his other hand remained planted in his mouth, a habit I thought long gone, but back today. We had spoken about starting school, but he really didn't understand what it meant.

When we passed the door to the basement, I thought I would throw up from the sour smell of dread.

"Are you alright?" Mrs. Wise asked.

"Don't you smell that?"

Her nostrils flared. "Smell what?"

"I guess it's nothing."

The school had a new gymnasium, and the playground had been redone in colorful plastic. The old metal monkey bars from my youth seemed a lot more fun. Otherwise, the basic layout of the school was the same as when I had been a kid.

We met the principal in the hallway, and Mrs. Wise began to introduce me. I interrupted, saying, "You've been here a long time, Mr. Dill. You probably don't remember me."

Mr. Dill was a small man, but larger than life somehow. He gave a stern look over his glasses. "Of course I remember you,

Mr. Brooks. A poor student." He glanced at Tommy. "But I see you went on to better things."

The janitor passed by with a wide push broom. Those olive-green coveralls made me cringe. I remembered the flakes that they used to clean up puke in the hallway, detergent over bile, but this stench was much worse. This was...

I awoke on the tile floor with the thick miasma of burning flesh all around me.

"Are you alright, Daddy?" Tommy asked.

The school nurse hovered over me with Mrs. Wise and the principal. They closed around me, trapping the stale fumes.

I grabbed Tommy by the hand and pushed my way through.

"Mr. Brooks," the principal called after me. "Please don't leave, yet. Let us call you a doctor."

He followed me all the way to the minivan and tapped on the window while I buckled Tommy in.

"What's wrong, Daddy?" Tommy asked.

"You are not going to that school!" was all I said as I sped off, leaving Mr. Dill alone on the sidewalk.

* * *

The glowing heart flickered soundlessly. Metal veins and arteries carried life into a body of cold cement blocks and disappeared in the shadows beyond the undulating aura. The faceless janitor opened up a door in the heart. He picked up a whining little thing and tossed it in. The heart screamed.

I awoke in the dark. The stink was all around me, in my bed, all over my sheets.

"What's wrong?" Betty asked. Even my wife reeked of death.

I ran to the bathroom, but there was nothing in my stomach to puke up. I stripped off the polluted pajamas and jumped into the shower, turning the knob until the high pressure burned. Little red bumps formed where beads of water bounced off my pale skin.

My wife found me crouching in the water, rubbing soap over my blistering body. Even here, I couldn't escape the smell.

* * *

While Betty finished enrolling Tommy in school, I went in to see Dr. Masterson. He prescribed medication and told me that if I couldn't get it together, I would have to be put in a hospital.

"I'm not crazy," I told him. "I was fine two days ago. Look, I can't afford to be hospitalized for some indefinite period of time. I have a job, a family."

Dr. Masterson had bug eyes and a rim of brown hair. He sat with crossed legs and studied me. "You've never had any previous instances of phantom smells or obsessive compulsive behavior?"

"No," I said. "Never. Not since..."

"What is it?"

"Not since grade school."

"Tell me about your experiences in grade school."

"I hated school back then," I said. "Dreaded it. I played sick once for almost half a semester, 'til my parents caught on."

"Why did you hate it so much?"

"I didn't have any friends, barely passed my classes. I was always scared."

"What were you afraid of?"

"Everything. Everyone. The bullies, the little plastic chairs, the desks, the smell..." I paused, realizing what I had said.

"What did it smell like?" the doctor asked.

"Did you ever get your arm too close to the stove and singe your arm hair?" The psychiatrist nodded. "It's like that," I said, "but a thousand times more intense and there is no getting away from it."

"Did you always hate school?"

"When I started middle school, it all changed. I started getting good grades, joined the wrestling team. I never thought about grade school again until yesterday."

"I want to try something," Dr. Masterson said after a moment. "Have you heard of regression therapy?"

The side of my face scrunched skeptically. "Isn't that what they use on those people who claim they were raped by flying saucers?"

Dr. Masterson gave the hint of a smile. "It's meant to bring out repressed memories by letting you relive moments of your life, remembering details you have forgotten. It doesn't work for everyone, and some argue it works *too well* in others, making them imagine events that never happened at all. It is a legitimate technique, however, and witness testimony after therapy has even been admitted as evidence in court cases."

Deep down I didn't want to do it. Though I didn't understand why, I was afraid of remembering that place. But I was an adult now, and I couldn't let myself be put in a mental hospital over something as trivial as a smell. "Let's do it."

"Alright," Dr. Masterson said. "But you will have to relax." He dimmed the lights and instructed me to kick off my shoes and recline on the couch. I felt ridiculous.

"You are comfortable." It was a statement, made in a soothing tone, and I found it to be true. I *was* comfortable. "Think about your toes," he continued. "Let them relax and float away. The muscles in your calves loosen. Let go of them and allow the wave of relaxation to move up your legs to your torso."

As the wave moved up, my body lost significance. Everything lost significance. My jaw released tension that I hadn't even realized it was holding. It was as if my mind was floating in a cloud.

"How do you feel?" The Doctor asked.

I didn't want to speak, to shatter that peaceful moment with words. "Good," I whispered at last.

"I want you to go back," Dr. Masterson said. "To grade school, back to when you were a child."

The playground on a sunny day bloomed inside my eyelids. Children screamed with glee as they swung on the swings and spun themselves silly on the merry-go-round. But I saw it all from a distance, from the limits of my little yard.

"We live near the school, but my mommy always says to stay away." It was my voice; I knew I was making it, but the pitch was higher and childlike. "I always see kids playing on the playground. Mommy says I'm too young, but I'm grown up enough."

"How old are you?" Dr. Masterson asked.

"I will be in first grade after the summer. I'm not a kindergartner anymore. There's no reason not to play on the nice swings or hang on the jungle gym." It was remarkable. As I remembered sneaking away to the playground after hours, I could smell the fresh cut grass. I saw the gum stuck underneath the swing and the path worn into the grass from a thousand tiny feet.

"I want you to tell me about the day you first noticed the smell."

My brow furrowed, almost breaking the tranquil spell. "I find a door cracked open." My child voice became fearful. "I peek in, but it's dark, like a cave or a secret hideout. All I can see are stairs going down. Someone is crying." I tiptoed down into the oppressive heat. "Pipes drip, and a big metal box spits fire. There's a flash of blonde hair, smoke and the horrible..."

I inhaled a shaky breath. "I scream, and the janitor, he grabs me, he...he..."

Dr. Masterson spoke softly, never breaking that serene monotone. "It is alright. You are safe. Nothing can hurt you now."

I opened my mouth, this time mimicking the voice of the janitor in my head. "What did you see?"

Then the child voice returned. "You... burned something."

"You are trespassing on school property," the janitor said. "That means you shouldn't be here. If you tell anyone you were here, you will go to jail. You want to go to jail?"

I shook my head.

"You must never tell," the janitor said. "Understand?"

"I'll never tell," I said.

He let me go. "It will be our secret. As long as you never tell, I can protect you."

I tripped running up the steps, moving my little legs faster than they could safely go, jumping right back up and not stopping until I was in my bed buried under the sheets, trying to convince myself it was all a nightmare.

* * *

I opened my eyes and stretched. The lights were up and my wife was there. "Sorry, Doctor," I said. "I guess I fell asleep."

Betty squeezed my hand.

"Did it work?" I asked. "Or was it a dream?"

Dr. Masterson's only reply was to flip on a mini-cassette recorder, and I heard our conversation begin to play out. I clenched my eyes shut and tried to wave the smell away.

The recording clicked off.

"It was the janitor," I said. "He killed someone's kid."

"I've already called the police," Dr. Masterson said.

* * *

The principal unlocked the basement door and led the way down the dark steps. The stench was horrible, but I faced it with Betty on my arm and the police ahead of us. Mr. Dill flipped on the fluorescent light, flickering away the shadows with a soft hum. Everything was smaller than I remembered, and the furnace was dark, just a cold and lifeless metal box.

"This is the place?" Dr. Masterson asked.

I nodded. My grip on Betty tightened when the janitor stomped down the steps. He glanced at me with furrowed brow and narrowed lips.

"Is that who you saw?" the Sheriff asked.

My heart raced. I was telling our secret. "Yes. That's him."

The Sheriff had a kind voice, but was firm and to the point. He looked straight at the janitor. "Twenty-five years ago, a little girl went missing. This man says he witnessed you getting rid of a body in the school furnace."

Mr. Dill put a supportive hand on the janitor's shoulder. "I'm afraid what you're suggesting is impossible. Jimmy only started working here five years ago. He would have only been ten years old when you say this happened."

That couldn't be true! This was the face I saw clearly in my regression. Dr. Masterson seemed to make sense of it. "Memories are funny things. Who was the janitor twenty-five years ago?"

While the crime scene investigators combed the furnace for quarter-century-old evidence everyone knew was long incinerated, Mr. Dill took us back to his office. Jimmy the janitor eyed me with malice as we passed. It was understandable; I had just accused him of murder.

I felt like a misbehaving child, taken to the principal's office. Mr. Dill dusted off an old book with the former janitor's picture in it.

I looked at it and shook my head, unable to trust my own memory. "I don't know."

Betty and I returned home. Everyone was quiet in the house. Even Tommy didn't want to disturb me. There is nothing worse than appearing fragile in your young son's eyes.

Dr. Masterson called that evening. The former janitor had been dead for three years. There was no way to question him now.

* * *

I crept down into the basement. The furnace was small, and the pipes were pipes, nothing more. Everything was clear in the fluorescent light. Nothing here could hurt me.

There was a clanging in the furnace, and the smell stung my nostrils. A child screamed, and the banging became more frantic.

I squeaked open the furnace door, and the red face of a horned devil looked out at me, rasping, "I told you not to tell."

I jerked awake. There was never any killer. I was merely insane. I ran out the door, hoping to find refuge in the crisp night air. It helped, but the smell was still here. I covered my nose and retrieved keys from the wall hook by the door. I stumbled, dropped them. Finally, I got the van started down the road, zigging and zagging across the yellow line, driving like I was drunk. The smell hovered in the van, trapped like smoke. I opened the windows, trying to blow it away.

I almost collided with the old brick school before the tires skidded to a stop. Headlights pointed at the doorway to my hell. The door was propped open, waiting for me. I went down into the darkness, headlights at my back. The furnace glowed like a mouth, exhaling that fetid breath, waiting to consume my soul.

Something hard and metallic came down on the back of my neck. Heavy feet emerged from the shadows behind the stairs.

"I told you not to tell, Mr. Brooks. I thought we had an arrangement." From the ground, his feet and legs were huge, but his upper body was a tiny silhouette in the headlights from outside. He raised his arm, and the large wrench in his hand nearly touched the ceiling.

Just as he was about to bring it down on my head, the fluorescent lights flickered to life, revealing the murderer in strobe. The Sheriff pointed his gun from the top of the stairs, shouting, "Freeze!"

Mr. Dill stopped, wrench still in hand, and the images of my nightmares replayed in my mind. His face had been the devil in the furnace. It had been the principal who grabbed me as a child in the shadowy basement, surrounded by the smell of burning flesh. He wore the same olive-green coveralls the janitors always wore.

The police yanked the wrench from Mr. Dill's hands and cuffed his wrists behind his back.

The Sheriff helped me to my feet. "Your wife called us as soon as you left the house."

Once on my feet, I looked down at the principal. He was a small man. My boogeyman looked away, afraid to meet my gaze.

One of the deputies gave me a ride home. My wife was waiting for me, arms open and tears in her eyes.

* * *

I awoke to sunlight in the window. The scent of toasted bread and fresh coffee wafted into the bedroom.

My family was at the breakfast table.

"How is the smell?" Tommy asked.

At his mention of it, the stink returned to the fringes of my consciousness.

Fortunately, the police found a memento from Mr. Dill's crime in a box at the bottom of his bedroom closet. I could never have trusted my own memory enough to testify. When I do try to remember, which isn't often, the face switches from the principal as he was then, the new janitor, the old janitor, and the principal as he is now. Sometimes I see a face that combines their features.

To my eternal regret, I never attended a school activity, never even picked Tommy up from school. Even with my boogeyman finally in jail, I would never completely escape his smell.

DOGS PLAYING POKER

Originally published in the *Journey* anthology
from Gal's Guide in February 2023

Johnny slammed his hand over the alarm clock and covered his aching head with a pillow. His roommate sat at his desk doing some last-minute cramming under a tiny desk light. Tom was a bio major,and his classes were killer.

Sucker.

The alarm beeped again. Each piercing tone stabbed through the sludge in Johnny's head.

"Are you ever going to get up?" Tom asked.

Johnny groaned. He wasn't getting back to sleep so there was no point in skipping class now. He wondered why they would only offer Art Appreciation at 8 AM. He'd managed to schedule all his other classes well into the afternoon.

Sammie had warned him not to party last night. Johnny felt like the luckiest guy in school to be dating a girl as gorgeous as her, but sometimes she could be such a nag. This was college. Partying was what he was supposed to do.

Even with the alarm turned off, Johnny's head still throbbed with the rhythm of the silenced tone.

He put on his robe and slung a towel over his shoulder. With a bucket of bathroom supplies in hand, he sleepwalked across the wide, bright hall of his dormitory and swung open the bathroom door. Instead of the harsh fluorescent light of the dormitory bathroom, he found an unkempt bedroom lit from a tiny room off to the side.

Had he gone through the wrong door? He couldn't have. He followed a buzzing sound toward the light. In a tiny bathroom, a balding man in his underwear stuck a long utensil into his nose, whirling away stray hairs.

The man saw Johnny in the mirror and clicked off his instrument. "You really showed up! I'd given up on it actually working." The man looked Johnny up and down with a strange yearning that made the boy uncomfortable.

Everything felt unreal, as though part of Johnny still slept peacefully in his dorm room.

"Don't you recognize me?" The man had been staring, but broke his gaze long enough to take one disgusted look back into the mirror. "No. I guess you wouldn't. I'm John Higgins."

"But that's my name," Johnny said.

"Exactly. I'm you in twenty years."

A wave of repugnance passed over the boy's face as he looked into blue eyes that matched his own. Flecks of gray dotted the hair rimming his head. The older man brushed the few hairs on top of his skull with great delicacy, as though doing so would somehow preserve them. The boy's stomach tightened unconsciously at the sight of the soft paunch hanging over the man's underwear. Young Johnny backed away with his bucket of bathroom supplies and rushed out of the gloomy bedroom, hoping to find the bright corridor of his college dormitory, but instead finding the dark, narrow hallway of a residential house.

"Don't worry, kid." The older man pulled on pants behind him. "I guess I should call you...what? John Junior? Johnny? I'm not going to hurt you. You will only be here six hours. You're going to spend the day with me. You have clothes with you?"

Johnny shook his head, still groggy. He felt as though he was watching events through a fog, like this was happening to someone else, and he was merely observing.

"There's another bathroom down the hall and some clothes hanging on the door handle."

Johnny ventured down the hallway in a daze and flipped on the light in a half bathroom. The sweater vest and khaki pants left out for him were not his style, but he had little choice. He couldn't walk around this stranger's house wearing a robe and underwear, no matter who the man claimed to be.

Once dressed, Johnny found Old John sitting at the kitchen table, munching a piece of toast while reading the morning paper. The older man now wore a dark blue business suit.

"Would you like anything, Johnny?" The older man asked. "It still feels weird to call you by my name."

"No thanks," the boy replied. "If you are me, then what did I eat for breakfast this morning?"

"I never ate breakfast in college. I barely rolled out of bed in time for class." The older man looked at his watch. "Well then, we should probably be off." He rose and left through a door in back of the kitchen.

Before following, Young Johnny glanced down at the paper. He continued, strangely unfazed by the date, still feeling like he was dreaming a dream twenty years in the future.

Old John's subcompact car started with a hum unlike the cars Johnny was used to. The garage door opened smoothly, and they backed out of the driveway. The houses in the neighborhood all had the same basic design, but each owner had added their own little flair. Old John's house was actually quite large, and Johnny noted with pride that it may have even been larger than his parents' home. If this older man were indeed himself from the future and had access to time travel, he must at least be successful.

That was cool.

A song came over the radio that all the college kids loved. It perpetually boomed through the halls of Johnny's dormitory. That's when Johnny realized he was awake and he was certain he was being had.

"I love this song."

"This is the classic rock station," Old John said. "They play all the good stuff. See, I can still jam. Play with the buttons if you like. The good stations are all programmed in."

Young Johnny pressed a button in the console and a monotone voice reported on fighting in the Middle East, not unfamiliar, and yet further evidence this man was a fraud. Johnny hit another button and heard easy listening. Johnny would never program an easy listening station into his radio, no matter how old he became. Finally he gave up on the buttons and rotated the knob. There was a strange cacophony of noises like Johnny had never heard before.

"99.3 is the pop station if you'd like to hear what the kids are listening to," Old John said.

Johnny did as directed and discovered a rhythmic song he had never heard before. Of course this was the station the older man had told him to listen to. It could be part of the hoax, some nearby accomplice with a weak transmitter. There didn't appear to be a CD player in the car. Johnny rotated the dial some more and found more unfamiliar songs.

As long as Johnny played with the radio, the older man limited his comments to the different genres and styles of music. It was preferable to uncomfortable conversation, so Johnny continued rotating the dial back and forth.

As strange as it all was, Johnny remained lethargic. He wondered who would have the will and capability to pull such a hoax. Johnny pushed through the fog in his mind and replayed the morning's events. He had walked through a door in the dormitory and found himself in an entirely different building. Could they have slipped him some drug and moved him without him realizing it? A guy tried to slip Sammie a drug at a party once. Could they have used something like that on Johnny? That would explain Johnny's complacency and the molasses in his brain. Sammie and his parents were always after him to be more responsible. Could they be trying to teach him a lesson? They didn't have the capability to pull this off. Tom was always annoyed with Johnny, and he was a smart guy. Maybe they were working together.

At least this was more interesting than Art Appreciation class.

Dawn gave way to morning and the suburbs gave way to the inner city. After an hour, Johnny finally thought to ask, "Where are we going?"

"Work. Same place I go every day. We're almost there."

Finally they parked in a parking garage and took an elevator up to a maze of cubicles. A poster read, *Bring Your Child to Work*

Day, and Johnny wasn't the only young person here, so he couldn't understand why everyone stared at them when they walked in.

"Bill called in sick," a poufy-haired woman said as they walked by.

Old John sighed. "Not again."

John flipped a switch in his cubicle and a flat monitor in his desktop came to life.

"John Higgins! I need to see those..." A smartly dressed woman stopped at their cubicle when she noticed Young Johnny. "Oh. I didn't know you had a son this age."

The two John's looked at each other. The older said, "This is my nephew, John Jr."

"John Jr.," she said. "I see the resemblance. I need to ask you..." The woman's tone became softer and more polite in the boy's presence. "Have you tracked down Chronocorp's shipment yet? We already refunded their shipping costs, but if they don't get their time scoop components, we are going to have to pay to replace them— it will bankrupt the company!"

Johnny wondered what a time scoop was, but his mind still wasn't running on all cylinders.

"I'm working on that right now," Old John said.

She smiled through clenched teeth. "Your deadline was two days ago."

"I know, but I can only do one thing at a time. Bill's been out sick all week, and I've had to cover for him. Jen had to leave early for a doctor's appointment—"

"It's not your job to do their work," she said. "You are their supervisor."

"Yes," Old John said, "but the work has to get done."

The woman's face flushed red, but she glanced at Johnny one more time before she spoke. "We'll talk about this later."

"What a witch," Johnny said after she had left the tiny cubicle.

The old man actually smiled. "She sure is. That's Rochelle, my boss."

The woman with the pouf hair poked her head over the cubicle wall. "Who is this fine young man?"

"My nephew," Old John answered.

She narrowed her eyes and studied Young Johnny's face. "Which high school do you go to?"

Johnny was insulted to be taken for a high school student, but Old John didn't give his younger self a chance to answer. "He is visiting from out of town."

She smirked. "Since a lot of us brought our kids in, we're going to take extra time for lunch."

Old John sighed again. "We have a lot of deadlines, and without Bill, I'm afraid I can't authorize that."

"It'll be fine. We'll make it up later. We can't expect these kids to have the same attention span we do."

Old John put his hand on his forehead and rested his elbow on the glowing desktop. "Alright."

The poufy-haired woman smiled and sauntered off.

Johnny watched his older self type on the keyboard, then stick a headset over his ear and start talking aloud, "Did you find those packages yet?" and after a short pause, "Bill's not here. They have to be there somewhere. I know you are busy with current shipments, but the company made a promise... I know you looked yesterday, but I have a good feeling if you just look again... Alright. Keep me posted."

Old John released a frustrated breath and looked to his younger self. "I ought to go down to the warehouse, but I can't very well leave you here."

"I'll be fine," Young Johnny said, hoping for a chance to explore without his alleged counterpart.

The conversation throughout the office got louder and exploded in an outburst of laughter outside the cubicle.

Old John jumped up from his seat and called beyond the fabric walls, "Jen! Jen, can you go to the warehouse for me and look for that lost shipment?"

The poufy-haired woman, leader of the revelry, scowled. "That's supposed to be Bill's job. I've got my daughter with me today. Why don't you do it?"

"I've got my own work to do."

"Fine, I'll do it after lunch."

"I need it done now."

"I'll do it after lunch," she said. "Relax, it will get done."

Old John slumped in his chair and retrieved an antacid from his desk drawer.

All at once the office silenced. Johnny peeked around the cubicle wall. "Where did everyone go?"

Old John looked at his watch. "Lunch. Ten minutes early, and they'll be back 30 to 40 minutes late."

Could Johnny grow up to become the office joke? "How did you end up in a job like this? I'm going to be an artist."

Old John shook his head. "Sammie and I needed cash. I hired on here. It was supposed to be temporary, but when they offered me the promotion... I couldn't turn down the money. Sammie started introducing me to people with my job title, like my job is who I am."

"Come on," Old John finally said. "Let's go home."

"Won't you get into trouble?"

"It doesn't matter anymore."

Old John drove through the McDonald's drive-thru on the way home. Johnny ordered a burger, fries and a shake. Old John began to order a salad, but then smiled, copying his younger self.

The car hummed quietly into the suburban garage. "First time in months I've been home before dark," Old John said. "What did you think? This has been my life, six days a week for the last ten years."

In the living room, a photo of a woman sat on the mantle. Her jowls had begun to sag slightly, but she was still beautiful. "Where's Sammie?" Johnny asked.

"She's not here."

"Still at work?"

Old John shook his head and chugged a beer. "She took the kids a year ago. Has an apartment on the west side." He half laughed. "She's dating an artist."

Johnny's heart sank into his gut. He finally realized how desperate his pitiful counterpart was. This was no hoax. "You stole those components from your work."

"Borrowed," Old John admitted. "I used Chronocorp's time scoop to yank you into your future." He looked at his watch. "You will start pulling back soon.

"Like a rubber band? Snapping me back to my present?" Young Johnny finally felt awake and for the first time that day became nervous.

"It won't be an immediate transition, not like a rubber band, more like falling, like gravity, pulling you faster and faster through your future, into my past."

Johnny didn't know what to expect, but Old John's description didn't sound pleasant. The world took on a blue tint, and a gentle tug pulled Johnny backwards.

"I screwed everything up," Old John said. "But it doesn't have to be this way. You can change it! You don't have to be me." He pointed to the bedroom and begged with sagging eyes. "There's the door. Save me," he implored. "Save us."

Young Johnny turned away in disgust and headed for the bedroom door, resolved not to become this pitiful man. Johnny anticipated the harsh light of the dormitory bathroom, or the long wide hallway on his floor, maybe even his own dorm room with his roommate at his little desk.

The smell of old pizza and musty clothes greeted Johnny ten times more intensely than in his dorm. Cold night air seeped through the thin glass of large-paneled windows. A skeletal man sprawled diagonally on a twin-size bed, and his scraggly hair hung over the mattress. Spots of paint covered the walls and floor. A blank canvas sat on an easel, and on a workbench rested a bottle of wine next to a bottle of sleeping pills.

Young Johnny's mind was alert now. He half understood what his older counterpart had meant. The journey back would not be immediate. He still felt the tug pulling at him, but he had become stuck again, still in his future. He resisted the tug in order to get a glimpse of the man on the bed.

This new John was thin, an improvement, Johnny supposed, over the tubby vision that had greeted him that morning, but long, stringy hair couldn't disguise the growing bald spot. Bags sat under his eyes, and the flesh under his cheek bones shrank inward like a cadaver.

"Hey." The man stirred. "What do you want? You new in the building?"

"No," Johnny said. "I'm you."

"Oh." Old John didn't show any surprise as he sat up and held his head. "I guess it is about that time. Not quite twenty years ago I met old me. Here we are again."

"Where's the rest of your place?" Johnny asked, looking around the studio.

"This is it. There's a kitchenette off to the side in case you want some tea or something."

"Where's Sammie?"

"Sammie? Oh, right, my college girlfriend. I haven't seen her in years. We broke up shortly before graduation. I hear she's married to some middle manager with two point five kids. You know the type. After her, I went out with Jen for a couple years. Do yourself a favor and stay away from her."

"Oh crap!" Old John said, looking at the oversized digital clock next to his bed. "I've got to get to the gallery."

A gallery full of Johnny's future works. Now this would be more like it. Young Johnny hadn't done anything yet, but he would, and the changes had already taken place for this future self. He followed Old John out the door and into an exterior hallway littered with trash. Grime streaked the chipped walls.

In the cold alley, Old John squeaked open the door of a dented up car. After several attempts the car finally choked to life, and they rolled out onto the city street.

"What a piece of crap," Johnny said about the car.

"Yeah," Old John agreed, "but it works."

The gallery was everything Young Johnny had imagined—wine and cheese, track lighting, men and women in impeccable dress. The pieces were in completely different styles and media, a testament to future Johnny's versatility. His work would really evolve.

Johnny's blood chilled when he saw Rochelle, his boss in the other timeline, talking and laughing with his older self. She signed a check and gave it to Old John.

After she walked away, Johnny asked, "What are you doing talking to her?"

"That nice woman bought my painting," he said, gesturing behind him to a picture of dogs playing poker. "700 bucks."

"700 dollars just for this one!"

Old John was beaming. "Now that I've sold one, the gallery might allow me to hang a couple more."

"What do you mean, a couple more?"

"I've been trying to get in here for years, and they finally let me hang one of my paintings this weekend."

Johnny looked at the many great works surrounding him, then at the piece behind his older self. "That's it?" he said. "This is the only painting that's yours?"

"Yes, what do you think?"

Young Johnny scowled. "It's dogs playing poker."

"Exactly."

Johnny just stared into the sallow face of his older self who said, "It's meant to be ironic."

"What's ironic about it?"

Old John dismissed his younger counterpart. "You just don't get it."

Johnny had thought the whole show had been devoted to his older self. "700 dollars is a lot of money though."

"Sure is. I can pay the rest of last month's rent and this month's electric bill."

"What else are you going to do with it?"

"What do you mean, what else? It's only 700 dollars, and the gallery takes their cut first."

The owner of the gallery congratulated Old John and took the check from him. Johnny turned away in disgust. Young Johnny had changed or would change his future. Instead of an incompetent middle manager, he would turn himself into an almost destitute hack artist.

What could he do? He had tried everything. No hope remained. He pushed open the gallery door, but instead of the chilly night air and the neon signs, sunlight blinded him. Rows of stone markers dotted the green hills surrounding him. Johnny read the untended marker below him, seeing his name, date of birth, and the date he had gotten out of bed, the day he had been pulled into the future.

He fell to his knees. The future had seemed so bright, but no matter what path he took, he would always be a failure. He had thought there would always be time to fulfill his potential, but perhaps there was no potential to be fulfilled. Young Johnny had taken, would take, the only road left.

Suicide.

A gasp from behind startled him. He stood, turning to see that older version of Sammie he had seen in Old John's photograph.

"I'm sorry," she said. "It's just...you look so much like him." She held flowers in her hand.

"You still visit my...uncle's grave?"

"I visit whenever I'm back in town, but it's been a couple years." She looked down at the gravestone. "He was an artist."

Johnny spied the wedding band on her finger. "You're married?"

She nodded.

"Is he nice?"

She paused, studying Johnny before answering. "I suppose."

"You suppose?"

"He is nice, but lately he's become a bit self-absorbed. I think he's having a midlife crisis."

"What does he do?"

"He's a middle manager at a shipping company. He's done it for years and gotten bored with it. Sometimes I think he blames me for pushing him into that job. A few months ago he started shutting me and the kids out. He just doesn't talk to us like he used to. I... don't know why I'm telling you all this."

Johnny shook his head. "Middle management. A paper pusher. Don't you think he should have done more with his life?"

A fire passed over her eyes. "That paper pushing provided for our family for seventeen years!" She collected herself. "I'm sorry. You sound so much like your uncle used to. You'll understand when you're older. People have to make sacrifices... compromises. I guess he thought he sacrificed too much."

There was so much Johnny could read in the tone of her voice and the look in her eyes. "You love him. You left him because you thought he didn't love you anymore."

She stared at Young Johnny, mouth wide and brow furrowed. "I did leave him, just last night. That's why I'm back in town. How did you know?"

Johnny had been referring to his older self, not Sammie's husband in this timeline. "Patterns repeat. He loves you. I know he does." Johnny looked down at his own grave. "Someone just needs to talk some sense into him."

"You're pretty wise for a kid."

"I've grown a lot today."

She followed his gaze to the grave, and Johnny surrendered to the pull. He turned to walk under a tree and into a studio warmed by golden radiance. Sunlight shone through a bay window and onto cushiony couches built into the wall.

A little, sandy-haired boy brandished a toy ray gun and chased a small girl through the studio. They circled Old John at his easel before screaming out of the room again.

Old John looked at his younger self and shook his head. "They didn't even take notice of you. I used to say the kids weren't allowed in here, but that didn't last long." He stabbed at the canvas with his brush. "The chaos inspires me."

Old John dressed casually. His hair was a little longer around his balding head than the first time they had met, but his face was full.

"You aren't surprised to see me?" Johnny asked.

"I figured I'd be seeing you soon. It's been around twelve years since I was you."

Twelve years. The trip back to his present was increasing in speed.

Johnny circled around the canvas to see what his older self was working on. "Oh no!"

Old John smiled. "Oh Yes! It's a commission for some friends of mine in a local band. The name of their new CD will be Dogs Playing Poker. I'm not charging much since they are friends, and it will be good exposure for me. There's no way I could make it with this as my only source of income."

The brushstrokes were much more playful than in the other timeline. "Do you ever wish you could paint full time?"

Old John shrugged. "Honestly, I think I would get bored doing this eight hours a day. Painting is my escape. I can't imagine forcing myself to do it as a job. My work and my family are my inspiration."

On a wall hung a large portrait of the kids. On approaching, sharp edges became fuzzy and indistinct, but crystallized into a perfect likeness when viewed from further away.

"John," a woman called from the other room. Sammie held the phone in her hand as she entered. "It's Jen from the office—" Sammie paused at the sight of Young Johnny. "Who is this?"

Old John smiled. "Don't you recognize me?"

Sammie studied the stranger, and then a smile spread across her face. "Oh! It's that time!" She seemed to want to reach out to Johnny and grab him, but stopped herself and put her hand to her mouth. "Will you be here long? Can I make you a snack?"

Johnny looked to his older counterpart. "You told her?"

"Of course. Why wouldn't I?"

"Oh!" Sammie remembered the phone in her hand and held it out to Old John. "It's Jen from work. She wants you to come in today."

Johnny wondered if it was the same poufy-haired Jen from the other timeline.

"Tell her no," Old John said as he serenely moved his brush along the canvas.

"I did. She says it's important."

Old John sighed and took the phone from his wife. "It's my day off," he said into the receiver. After a short pause he smiled and winked at his younger self. "No, I'm not doing anything in particular today, but it's my day off." He clicked off the phone, tossed it aside, and looked to his younger self. "It's just that easy."

Johnny liked thinking of his older counterpart giving poufy-haired Jen a hard time.

"You've got to learn to say no," Old John said. "Take time to enjoy the now."

Sammie continued staring at Johnny. "I'd forgotten how young we used to be." She then looked to her husband and they kissed, gently and sweetly. It made Johnny queasy, as though he were watching his parents.

"When that promotion came up a few years ago," Sammie said, "John said no. The money would have been nice, but we get by."

"And I did sell a painting last week."

"Yes, he did," Sammie said. "And the gallery wants to hang another."

This man's life wasn't so different from the first Old John he had met, but this man was happy. The only real difference was his attitude.

Old John and Sammie seemed to recede, and Johnny felt himself being pulled away.

"You won't be here long." Old John said. "Just remember, anything is possible. The present is what you make it."

"I want to see more!" Although Johnny felt like he was screaming, he only heard a whisper as he struggled against the pull.

Young Johnny fell on his butt in the doorway to the dormitory bathroom.

A burly jock in a towel looked down at him. "Excuse me."

Johnny rolled aside, apologizing as he stood.

"Nice clothes," the jock said as he pushed through the bathroom door.

Johnny still wore Old John's clothes from the future. He pulled at the fabric, and it fell apart, disintegrating in his hands. "Crap!"

Johnny raced across the hallway and banged on the door to his dorm room. His robe, towel, and bathroom supplies were all gone. This embarrassment could have seemed like the end of the world, but he knew it wasn't.

Tom finally opened the door and saw Johnny wearing a layer of dust. "What happened to you?"

"It's a long story," Johnny said. "At least 20 years long."

Upon entering the room, Johnny immediately picked up the phone and dialed Sammie. Things would be different. If they weren't, he would deal with it. They would deal with it together.

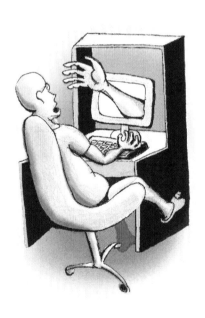

THE IMMORTAL WRITER

I changed a few words, removed a comma, then continued scrolling through the document. The story was good, possibly the best thing I had ever written, but it had to be perfect.

In the past, I'd let myself be hindered by guilt. I was reluctant to throw such vile situations at the characters I loved, but stories only thrive with conflict. Without conflict, my stories wouldn't sell, and if they didn't sell... my characters would never truly live.

This was the story of a single mother and her daughter on the trail of a giant snow beast in Alaska. But the creature was not working alone. My heart raced re-reading my own story, even though I had written it and reread it many times, as the woman found a tunnel in the snow which led to the mastermind's lair.

I had invested so much into to this story, breathed life into these characters like I had never done before, but if the first page didn't grab the editor, if I change verb tenses anywhere in the story, even if the introduction had one too many stealthily hidden adverbs, the editor might toss it aside without a second thought, not even finish reading it. Passive voice had to be avoided at all costs!

I had a hard drive full of stories. A few of them were as good as what I had read in the fiction magazines... Okay, perhaps only one or two were really that good... or maybe... maybe one... But *this one!* This story deserved to live!

Submission editors were bombarded with unsolicited slush. The quicker an editor could reject my story, the sooner they could move to the next one, the easier their job was.

There was nothing to distinguish my fiction from the rest of the unsolicited manuscripts in their pile. I had no following, no network, no name recognition or fans. I didn't get into writing to bring attention to myself. I did it for *them*.

I had sacrificed much to bring life to these stories. I'd refused lucrative promotions, and my friends didn't understand why I was always turning down their invitations. They were insulted to think that I would rather sit alone in my den than have fun with them.

My characters were my friends now.

A loud boom shook the house. The image on my screen flickered, and I whispered a tiny prayer while trying to remember what changes I had made since the last time the document had been saved.

The computer was fine, and I did a quick save. The stairs creaked behind me, and a woman's voice said, "What is this place?"

My heart caught in my throat. No one had been in the house with me since my ex left a year ago. Life with an unknown writer was not the life she had planned for herself.

I swiveled from my desk and saw a tall, lean woman in a ski suit. She lifted her goggles, revealing sparkling blue eyes. Blonde curls spilled from under her hat. She unzipped her coat, and snow fell from her shoulders, even though it was a hot July afternoon.

"What is this place?" she demanded again. "Who are you?" Her voice was light and every syllable clear, like a news anchor.

I was speechless. Shouldn't *I* be the one asking questions of this intruder? She came closer now, the smell of cold on her, and studied me.

I became self-conscious. I had not showered in 48 hours and was wearing an old, stained track suit. Even through her padded ski outfit, I could see the proportions of a model. She was impossibly familiar. I had to be dreaming.

She looked at the monitor over my shoulder. "This is about me! Have you been following us?" She looked me up and down, evidently assessed me as harmless, and reached over me, scrolling thought the document. "What has the monster done with my daughter?"

Rene was mere inches from me, this beautiful woman who I had created. Was this a practical joke? She was too real to be a hallucination. Would this turn into some writer's wet dream? With her as my muse, there was nothing I couldn't accomplish!

"Your daughter is fine!" I said. "I promise. Nothing alienates readers like harming a child."

She raised a hand to her mouth. "Bruce was there!" Her eyes became wet. "The love of my life was there the whole time, in the same town, *the same camp,* and I never knew!"

I began to stutter. "It increases tension."

Her eyes burned into me.

I tried to explain. "That's what elevates this beyond a simple adventure story! The reader wants the two of you to get back together. They see you are so close, just yards from each other. The reader will be rooting for you the whole time, but—"

Another crash boomed outside, and a look of disgust crossed her face. My wet dream became a distant fantasy.

"And the monster dies I suppose?"

"Perhaps. I might want to bring him back for a future story."

"So you can torture him again! Do you think you are God?" she said. "Playing with our lives like we are characters in some story?"

I didn't know what to say. They were characters in my story.

A clawed hand crashed though the wall beside my desk. Long arms covered in white woolly hair knocked wooden boards and cinderblocks aside. I was in a bi-level house, my office half underground. Dirt spilled over the carpet. I turned and fell from my chair.

Rene wasn't the only character in my story who had come to life.

The computer lay on its side, but my story had been saved. With it safe, I turned my attention to Rene. I had to get her out of here!

To my surprise, she was smiling. "You are the real monster in this story! You will never hurt anyone again."

I had never hurt a real person in my life! These were supposed to be *fictional characters.* How many of them had I tortured or killed off for the sake of a good story?

A clawed and heavily padded foot stamped the carpet beside me, a foot as long as my whole arm. Dirt clung to white fur on the massive calf muscle supporting it. Fingers wrapped around my head like it was an apple.

"How do *you* like being toyed with, writer?"

My characters couldn't do this to me! "I gave you life!" I tried to think of some way to escape, some flaw I could give the beast, but fear paralyzed my mind.

The beast took a step as it lifted me by my head. The pads of its enormous feet left a dark, dirty stain on my carpet, every toe printed on the fibers. I looked to the end of the room and the box of unpublished stories and rejection slips.

No publisher had any reason to single my stories out. No reader was demanding to know more about my writing. No one knew or cared who I was.

My head hit the ceiling, and I thought about what people would find the next morning: collapsed walls, giant footprints, and a hard drive full of unpublished manuscripts.

"What are you laughing about?" Rene asked.

"You've just made me—"

The floor came up, carpet slamming into my head before I could finish the sentence... *immortal.*

The apparitions wafted away as my life left me, but my characters would live on without me. Together we would now live forever on the printed page and in the minds of readers all across the globe.

REBRANDED

Faces crowded over Brand as he lay on the table in the humid room. Candles from the Christian altar behind the table lit them in soft light, while harsh light from a narrow window accentuated sharp angles and creased skin. A sickly old man ran his hand over Brand's spiky head. Angelo admonished the man and urged the other patients to back away. Perhaps these Filipinos had never seen hair as red as Brand's before. Strawberry-blond body hair was barely visible on his splotchy, pink chest, and blond now peppered his temples where the color had faded.

Felipe Reyes spoke as he spread water over Brand's naked belly. Angelo repeated the words in English, "The blood is poison. Felipe will remove the toxic blood from the spleen."

Brand closed his eyes and rested his head on the flat pillow. Felipe had gotten that much correct—Brand's blood *was* poison. Perhaps the healer could really do what he claimed.

Brand grunted as Felipe pushed his thumb hard against his abdomen. The healer left one hand on the skin and splashed more water before wiggling his digits into Brand's torso. Blood oozed around his fingers, and Brand smiled. He barely felt a thing as Felipe pulled out long, bloody pieces of his corrupted body and discarded them in a bowl. Much of the diseased flesh looked like pieces of liver, clots, or perhaps actual pieces of his toxic spleen, but Felipe also pulled out a tangle of black hair, and Brand furrowed his brow, wondering how that had gotten in there.

Felipe moved his hand to splash more water, but it wasn't just water he picked up. Brand caught a glimpse of something round and pink. More blood oozed over Brand's skin, but he now doubted it was his as more painless strips of animal meat came out from under Felipe's hand. The next time Felipe moved his hand away and gathered more water, Brand grabbed his wrist, hard, and sat up. A bladder of blood and more pieces of meat fell from Felipe's hand, causing quite a commotion.

"What are you doing?" Angelo asked, and Felipe was yelling too, although Brand couldn't understand the words. "He was helping you!"

Brand looked out at the angry faces. "This is fraud!"

One of the other patients yanked Brand from the table.

"Tell them!" Brand yelled.

Angelo shoved Brand toward the door. Brand whirled on him. "Are you in on it?" The force of his fist on Angelo's chin tingled, causing him to momentarily forget about the itching pain in his fingers, but he was already breathing hard, and his heart strained to beat the toxic sludge though his arteries as he exerted himself. More hands pulled him away, and more men fell beneath Brand's fist, but then he paused, seeing the faces of the other patients shoving him toward the door. They were frail men and women. Some were young, but most were over twice Brand's age. "You don't understand!" Brand implored, pointing at the table and alter. "They are taking advantage of you!"

He allowed them to push him out into the open air, although outdoors was as muggy as inside, and the atmosphere smelled of car exhaust. Brand sucked in gasps of air and leaned against the brick wall, cursing the ooze which passed for blood within him.

His red shirt flew out the door and landed on the sidewalk. One of the many patients still lined up outside picked it up and handed it to him. The old man asked, "You okay?"

"They couldn't understand me!" Brand pointed at the doorway, relieved to hear English. "Felipe is stealing from you!"

The man shook his head, and his eyes softened with pity. "They understood you. You could have been cured, but your western outlook couldn't accept the help Felipe was giving you. What you can't understand, you ridicule."

Brand stood erect and wavered on his feet. "I saw him grab bloody meat from a bowl and claim it came from me. It's sleight of hand, a magic trick!"

A young woman in line with the man spoke next. "We've been coming here every week, hoping to get in, and every week Felipe runs out of time. Your money gets you ahead of the line and you cause this delay! Here we are at the front, but we may not get in again! She put a hand on the man's shoulder. "Grandpa may not have another week."

"But—" Brand didn't have the strength to argue anymore. He turned and wobbled away as though drunk. Less than a block away, he slid his back down a wall and brought his knees to his chest, trying to slow his breathing. The line of patients was watching him, but he didn't have the luxury of embarrassment. If he didn't get his heart rate down, he might have a heart attack.

Brand concentrated on his breathing, taking in slow deep breaths punctuated by sudden gasps. His fingers itched and he could feel the bruise forming on his stomach, even though Felipe had barely touched him during the alleged *psychic surgery.*

A few weeks ago, Brand could have torn that place apart with his bare hands, broken Angelo's arm and snapped Felipe's neck without breaking a sweat. But what good would that have done? Even with the evidence right in front of them, the patients still kept coming. They saw Brand as the villain, not the men who were stealing from them.

"You need a doctor?" A young pair of eyes came into focus.

Brand shook his head. "Cab?"

The boy nodded eagerly and waved down a car on the clogged street. He then helped Brand stand up and opened the door for him. Brand handed the kid a dollar and the child gave a happy, "Salamat po!" in thanks.

On the military base, Brand got himself checked in to the clinic. Plastic tubing drained red sludge from his arm into a bag. The nurse lifted her eyebrows. "I've never seen blood flow this slowly before!"

"Polycythemia vera," Brand explained. "It's very rare, means I make too much blood."

"Oh, I know, Corporal," she said. "I see it all the time with vets."

"You do?"

"Yeah. Maybe something you were exposed to caused it. I've never seen it this thick though. When was your last therapeutic phlebotomy?"

"Less than three weeks ago." Brand remembered the burning oil wells, the blowing sand, the burn pits, and wondered if any of that could have caused his illness. "Why am I only now hearing this could be service related?"

She lowered the bag to the floor, and gravity helped the blood flow more freely. "It's not something the government likes to advertise."

Brand stared at the ooze draining out of him and remembered the red-tinted water at Felipe's altar. "Phlebotomies are only a temporary fix. Take all you want; I just make more. At some point, this is going to kill me."

"I heard of a guy who was cured once."

Brand perked up. "You did?"

"Yeah, visited some fire priest in… South America somewhere."

Brand deflated again. "I've spent money on faith healers all over the world. None of their cures are real. Then they blame me for not having enough faith while their customers keep throwing money at them. Even when they die a few weeks after being *cured*, they never stop believing."

"Perhaps they at least feel better for a little while, even if it doesn't keep them from dying."

"Maybe, but at what cost? Some of them spend their entire life savings, or even their kids' savings!"

"Well, this one is supposed to be legit. My friend's friend went into total remission."

Brand grimaced. It was always the friend of a friend of a friend… "Well, I've been everywhere else. What's one more?"

* * *

Customs was a madhouse. The crowd of people and disorganized lines made Brand jumpy.

"What branch were you in? Marines?"

Brand turned to see a brown-haired man in black carrying a canvas duffle almost identical to his own. "How did you know?"

He raised a fist and bumped Brand's. "I was Navy. Saw the buzzed hair, the hyper-alert nervousness." He motioned to the black man and broad-shouldered woman near him. Brand recognized them from the same plane that had taken him here from Panama. "We'll watch your back. Line goes quick. Where were you stationed?"

"I spent most of my term in northern Iraq."

The man became excited. "Oh, wow! Fallujah saw some heavy fighting!" He extended his hand. "Rick Braydon."

Brand returned the gesture. "Bobby Brand."

Well, Bobby Brand, what brings you to Paraguay?"

"You'll think it's dumb."

"Try me."

"I'm visiting a healer out in Tataguigua."

Rick's eyes swelled. "Well, isn't that a coincidence? That's where we're headed!"

"You need a faith healer?"

Rick chuckled. "No, we're private security. You have transportation out there?"

"I was planning to catch a bus."

"That will take you a few days. Why don't you hitch a ride with us?"

"You've got room?"

"Sure!"

Once Brand was through customs, he awaited his new companions as passengers came and went. Despite being an international airport, the land outside was flat, rural scrubland. Brand slung his jacket over his shoulder. Only a few wispy clouds dotted the clear blue sky above, and the sun beamed its heat down on him.

A black van waited along the curb. The driver hefted their duffels in back, and Brand sat in the middle row. He was grateful to have enough room to shift his legs and prevent blood clots. Sitting in one position for too long could literally kill him. "You all work private security?"

"Yeah," Rick said. "Sweet gig. We get paid way better than Uncle Sam used to pay us. You look pretty tough, maybe you could join us?"

Brand shook his head. "I did a short stint with Strateegis before I got sick. I'm afraid I wouldn't be much good to you now."

The woman in back looked Brand up and down. "I heard Strateegis only took the best. Maybe I heard wrong."

The black man leaned against the window. Even relaxed, his muscles threatened to burst from his shirt. "Ignore Torrez. She just needs to get laid."

"That's not what your momma said when I left her bed this morning."

"You're just bitter 'cause *your* momma took one look at your ugly face when you were born and tried to take you out."

"Shows what you know, Wilson. I was almost twelve before my momma tried to kill me the first time."

Rick smiled and shook his head. "They're always like this."

"I get transportation *and* a show? I miss this kind of camaraderie. Ever since I got sick, I don't get out much."

"That's too bad," Rick said. "You hungry? We're stopping at Rodeio Sabor. We tried it last time we were out. They have the best asado. You have never had steak this good!"

Wilson beamed a bright white grin. "I'm getting ribs this time!"

Torrez added, "You better enjoy some good food now. Once we get out of this town, there is nothing but a whole lot of nothing."

Brand felt relieved they hadn't asked about his illness. He was so sick of explaining polycythemia to everyone he met. "This town already seems pretty empty."

"This is a metropolis compared to where we're going."

The prices on the menu made Brand balk, even with the currency conversion, but Rick said, "This one's on us!"

"You sure?"

"Yeah, but you have to try Chinchulín."

"No!" Wilson said. "You don't have to—"

"I'm game."

Torrez rolled her eyes. "It's cow intestines."

Brand shrugged and closed the menu. "Life is short. Why not?"

The Chinchulín was crisp and a little salty, reminding Brand of calamari. "Not so bad." The intestines were forgotten once he tasted the steak. "You were right! This is the best meat I have ever tasted."

Rick chuckled. "Told you."

Forty minutes later, Brand waddled to the van and plopped into the seat with a satisfied sigh.

The narrow dirt road took them north into the Chaco region of Paraguay. Rick pointed out construction equipment tearing through trees and compacting earth. "This trip will be much faster once the highway is finished."

The driver stopped for gas, allowing them time to use the restroom and stretch their legs. Rick pointed out the convenience store. "Helpful hint: pick up some candy. The kids in Tataguigua love candy. Quickest way to their parents' hearts is through their kids' stomachs."

"Thanks. Are you getting some?"

"No need. We're fully stocked with American candy bars." Rick winked. "They go nuts over the imported stuff."

At last the van pulled up to a hotel which resembled an old-school hacienda. "You're on your own from here," Rick said. "The van can take you to the edge of the village and come back for us tomorrow."

"Wow, that's very generous. Thank you."

It felt good to stretch out even more once they were gone, but the empty van was lonely. The narrow dirt roads were deserted. Dark brown mountains rose on the distant horizon. The vehicle passed tilled rows of soybeans and pale cows grazing on stubby grasses. Here and there, wooden sheds dotted the pastures. Poles supported big plastic basins of water near the roads and on hilltops.

The van finally pulled up to a row of buildings, and the doors hissed open. Six kids huddled outside the door shouting and smiling. They wore shorts or jeans and t-shirts, not that different than the kids in the States. As instructed, Brand gave them the little candies. They waited and peeked into the doorway behind Brand as though expecting more visitors. The driver left Brand's bag on the ground and zipped off the way he had come.

"I'm looking for a healer," Brand said, but the kids chased each other, ignoring him now that his candies were gone.

"Welcome to Tataguigua," a man said. He wore a button-down shirt and a cowboy hat. "You aren't with Hesperion?"

The man didn't pronounce the *H,* and Brand didn't understand the reference, but didn't much care. "I'm Bobby Brand. I heard a healer lives here. I'm hoping perhaps he can help me."

He took Brand's hand. "Cesar Alfredo. They call me *Mayor,* although my actual title is intendant. So, you are sick? A hopeless case?"

Brand nodded.

"Sepe Guerrero may be able to help you. We don't get many visitors outside of festival, and even then…"

Cesar escorted Brand between buildings. It looked like someone had taken the center of a Spanish town and plopped it in the middle of nowhere, just the town plaza and the buildings around it. In the middle of the square rose a ring of ancient bricks stacked three feet high and three feet wide. It resembled a well, but instead of water, flames waved a foot or more above the old stones. Children ran past the bricks and raced around the fire, which didn't seem too inviting in the day's heat.

"He will be here for evening prayer," Cesar said. "In the meantime, you will need lodging and food. Milka can help you." He called across the plaza. "Oscar!"

One of the children, a tall boy, perhaps fifteen or so, skidded to a halt, and his smile collapsed.

"Oscar!"Cesar called. "Take this man's bag."

Brand and Cesar followed the boy. On one side of the plaza sat a square, one-story office labeled *government center.* Across from it, clay tiles decorated the roof of a bright yellow, three-story adobe building with balconies on every side, the tallest structure in the plaza. Once through the archway, Cesar rang a bell in an outdoor courtyard containing tables and chairs, a deserted restaurant. The levels overlooking the courtyard contained rooms to rent. The boy plopped the bag on the tile floor and disappeared into the rooms within.

After some shouting, a young woman with curly black hair rushed out. Her red skirt trailed behind her as she moved. A white blouse poofed over her breasts and narrowed at her waist. "I'm sorry. We don't see many visitors outside of festival season. You're not with Hesperion?"

Cesar answered for Brand. "No. He's looking for Sepe Guerrero."

Her face softened. "Ah, you need a healer."

Brand nodded, a bit embarrassed to admit his weakness. "Yes. I heard he helped someone with a similar condition, a friend of a friend."

"You can meet him at the ceremony tonight. You must be tired from your trip. I'll set you up in a room. There is a shared bathroom here on the ground floor. Are you hungry?"

"I ate on the way here."

"Oscar, take his bag upstairs."

Brand asked, "What time is this ceremony?"

"After sundown. You'll hear it." She left Brand alone in a basic room with a small cot and a basin of water.

Brand removed his shirt and splashed water over his face. For some reason, water, especially very hot water, made his fingers itch, another side effect of the polycythemia. Even this lukewarm water, which should have been refreshing, irritated his splotchy skin. Minor itching intensified the more he scratched, so he scraped harder, until his hands bled.

Milka broke the cycle when she entered with a plate of browned, yellow cake. Brand's face flushed as though caught doing something wrong. "Thank you," he said, even though he had told her he wasn't hungry.

After a short nap, he finally tried the cake. It was like cornbread but filled with onions and cheese.

That night, the smell of roasted meat and corn wafted into Brand's window. About 150 townsfolk had gathered in the square and conversed in small huddles. The town flame was more dramatic now that the sun had gone down, and the temperature was comfortable, like being inside a climate-controlled room.

Behind Sepe Guerrero sat a one-story chapel with a bell on top. Even the rambunctious kids stopped playing and watched in awe as a well-dressed couple carried their infant to the healer waiting next to the town fire. Beads hung from Sepe's neck over a cotton shirt. He was short, and his cheeks were smooth, giving the appearance of youth, but deep lines formed around his eyes and mouth when he smiled at the child. He placed his arm within the flames, and flickering light danced over his hand when he pulled it out. He held his glowing hand over the child and said something that might have been a blessing. The flame immediately died out when he touched the baby.

Brand had seen tricks like this before. You could cover your hand in a volatile gel which would burn for a short time while keeping the skin underneath cool. The magician never kept his skin in the flames long enough to get burned.

The villagers cheered and began to dance while two men played guitar. Milka cast a brief smile at Brand as she twirled and her long red skirt drifted around her. A narrow gap between her two front teeth added to the charm of her wide, white grin.

Cesar introduced Brand to the healer. Along with the beads, a wooden crucifix also hung around Sepe's neck. Like the Philippines, here too native spiritualism mixed with the

Christianity of the colonizers. "Hello," Brand said. "Thank you for meeting me."

Sepe smiled broadly and responded in a language that did not sound anything like Spanish.

"Sepe speaks a Guarani language, from before the Spanish came. He is asking, *Do you see fire?*"

Brand could feel the warmth from the city's flame, though there was no smell of smoke or gas. "Of course."

Cesar continued to translate. "That is not fire. It is belief." As if to demonstrate, the healer stuck his open hand above the flames. Brand's pupils narrowed with anxiety. He knew the man had his tricks, but Sepe Guerrero slowly turned his glowing hand like a scoop. Orange light streaked up from his fingertips and lines of smoke wriggled up through the air. A wave of heat threatened to singe Brand's eyebrows off.

Brand couldn't take it any longer and pulled the man's hand away, scorching his own arm hair in the process. The music stopped, and villagers froze, staring at them in stunned silence. Brand turned Sepe's hand over in his, but saw no burns or blisters. The skin felt cool to the touch.

Sepe chuckled. The villagers laughed and the music began again. "You see," he said with his own voice in broken English. "Not fire."

Brand felt as though he were being tricked. "Can you help me or not?"

Cesar translated for him again. "Not yet. You don't believe." Sepe turned away and greeted a couple who gave him a plate of food.

"Wait! What do you mean?" Brand turned to Cesar. "What does he mean? He won't help me?"

"He did not say that, exactly. He said you aren't ready."

Brand furrowed his brow and sighed. He could feel his heart struggling against the thick sludge in his veins. If Sepe Guerrero expected blind belief like Felipe Reyes had expected from his patients, that wasn't going to happen. All this time, effort and expense would be for nothing, and there was no place nearby for another therapeutic phlebotomy. Brand might die here in this village.

His thoughts drifted to his son. Brand had spent more time with fake healers than his own child, who he would never know and who would never know him. His ex would continue to raise the boy alone.

The hand on his shoulder surprised him. "Dance with me!" Milka said.

"I don't much feel like dancing."

She pulled his arm forward, moved in, pulled out again, then spun around. "It seems you are doing it anyway!"

Brand smiled and let her lead him into the plaza. If he was going to die here, he might as well live while he could. He had always been stiff on the dance floor and let her do most of the work, which she seemed happy to do.

"Sepe Guerrero likes you," she said.

"That was how he shows he likes me?"

"I read him better than most," Milka said. "He is my uncle."

Brand lifted his eyebrows. "Milka… Guerrero?"

She confirmed her last name with a smile. "Yes."

"Can he really cure me?"

"It is possible," she said as she spun around him. "He can't regrow a limb or anything like that, but I've seen him burn toxins and cancers from the body."

He watched her move, wondering if the people she had seen were really cured, or just believed they were and went home to die.

The tempo sped up. Even with Milka doing most of the work, Brand felt the euphoria of movement, and began to laugh until he fell on his butt. Milka leaned over him. "Are you all right? I shouldn't have pushed."

Brand caught his breath. "No! That was fun." He grabbed her hand and closed his eyes. "I just need a moment." She knelt next to him. He opened his eyes and stared into her deep brown irises in the flickering light. "Thank you for pulling me out of my head." He struggled to stand, and Milka supported his arm. "I feel like an old man."

She led him to his room, and he sat on the cot. "You aren't old."

"How old are you?"

Her lip twitched, and she looked away. "Twenty-four. I am considered an old maid in Tataguigua, but it's not like there are a lot of prospects here. The young men who don't own land move south for work. Local landowners are selling to corporate farms and leaving. I stay to take care of my mama. She owns the inn."

"You don't have to defend yourself to me! You don't need a man to complete you."

"Maybe not, but here, it is expected."

"Screw expectation! Are you happy?"

"Of course! This is my home."

"Then that's all that matters!"

"You are such a strange man!"

He chuckled awkwardly. "Thank you?"

"It is a compliment. The white men who come here all want something."

"In that, I guess I'm no different. I came to be healed."

She sat next to him. "But you talk to me like a person. You ask. You don't take."

Brand felt a little guilty. If he could force this cure from them, he might. "How could I steal the cure if I wanted to? *The fire that is not fire?*"

"The flame was here before we were and will be here when we are gone. What we see as fire is left over from creation. When God said, *Let there be light,* He left a little of himself behind. All things are made of fire."

He raised his eyebrows skeptically. "I don't remember learning that in Sunday school."

She touched his chest. "You will see. The fire is in here. It is in all of us."

He held her hand and stared into her eyes. He wanted to kiss her, to take her, but he could not please her. How could she love this helpless creature he had become?

She touched his face, and her finger came away wet. "What is it?"

He turned away so she couldn't see his tears. Men aren't supposed to cry. "I'm fine. I'll see you in the morning, Milka."

The cot creaked as she stood. "Hasta Mañana, Señor Brand."

* * *

Feminine yelling interrupted Brand's sleep. "Milka?" Brand rose stiffly and massaged his legs before attempting a step.

Milka marched into the morning light. A short, tubby man lowered a cable into the town fire and scanned readings on the tablet in his hands. He wasn't wearing a suit jacket, but the tie still seemed out of place in this heat.

"This land is not for sale!" Milka yelled.

"You do not understand what we are offering. We are not *buying,* we are *leasing.* You will still have the land and be rich on top of that. You merely grant us permission to study your flame and tap the energy."

Cesar added, "Just hear Dr. Truman out, Milka. Hesperion could bring economic development and resources."

Young Oscar looked up at Milka with wide eyes. "We could have what the rest of the world has—jobs, cars, internet."

"We don't need anything they have to offer!"

Brand finally caught up to her. "It's true. Those things just bring impatience and stress. They don't bring happiness."

The stranger, Dr. Truman, blinked, studying Brand. "You are new, Mr....?"

Brand didn't answer, and Milka folded her arms over her chest.

"These readings are remarkable," Truman said. "Pure energy! There is no reason to fight. If we could harness it, we could bring cheap, nearly limitless power from the heart of the earth to benefit this entire region… and beyond! What are you using it for now? To look pretty and dance around?"

Brand folded his arms too. He may have been a skeptic, but even Brand found that offensive. "It sounds like they don't want you here."

"Hey, Bobby! You made it!"

Brand turned to see Rick striding forward with an M4 assault rifle slung around his chest and a Sig pistol holstered to his hip. Children darted around him stuffing miniature Snickers into their mouths and discarding the wrappers on the ground. On the opposite street, in front of the chapel, his partners kept a watchful eye over the pedestrians and guarded the same van that had brought Brand here. Wilson raised a hand, saying, "Hey, B.B.," while Torrez gave a nod.

"Rick?" Brand said. "You're with this guy?"

"Dr. Truman signs our checks. You find that cure you were after?"

Brand could barely speak as he took everything in. "Not yet."

Milka looked to Brand, then to Cesar. "Sepe Guerrero will never let them pollute the flame."

Cesar's head hung low. "He may not have a choice."

There was nothing obviously wrong with the way Truman smiled and blinked again, but it still felt artificial somehow, overly deliberate. "That is correct. The government of Paraguay already signed off on this. The highway is coming. It will connect you to Asunción, the capital, bring the world to your door. Your cooperation would make things easier. You could have input on our plans. I have a contract for you to sign. We can minimize our presence, and the infrastructure will bring jobs, money…"

"It won't be the same," Milka whispered.

Brand was torn. Nothing stays the same forever. Was it just nostalgia that offended Milka so much? She'd grown up here. Perhaps she just didn't want her little restaurant to compete with a McDonald's opening across the plaza.

"How do we even know you will honor this contract?" Milka asked.

"You have my word." Truman's smile was as crooked as the independent contractors Brand had worked with in the Marines, men who agreed to fix a country, but pocketed most of the money for themselves.

Cesar nodded. "Give us time to talk it over, Dr. Truman."

"You have 24 hours to sign our contract and reap the rewards. The highway is coming. Nothing can stop it."

Rick waited for the rest of his group to board the van, before backing through the door. "Good seeing you again, Bobby." He gave a quick salute. "See you around."

Brand gave a half-hearted salute back to his friend. Sepe Guerrero's sudden voice startled him. How had he snuck up so quietly?

"I know, Cesar said, but what choice do we have?"

"What did he say?" Brand asked.

Milka answered, "We can't let them control the fire."

Brand struggled to keep up with her as she returned to the inn, pouting. "I don't understand," Brand said.

Milka didn't stop walking. "The fire is not good or evil. It takes on the personality of the person who wields it."

Brand didn't believe the fire was magic, but her words held some truth. Nature didn't give a crap about humans, but humans could manipulate nature for good or ill. Truman claimed the fire was a natural phenomenon, like a volcanic vent. If that was the case, maybe it really had been here since creation. Brand had assumed Sepe tended the fire, keeping it lit, but perhaps the fire had been here first, and the village built around it. Brand had read about priests in other cultures breathing in volcanic gas to go into trances or produce hallucinations. Brand didn't smell gas here, but it could be scentless…

Brand pondered aloud. "For someone who says he doesn't need your permission, this Truman guy seems awfully intent on getting the town to sign off. The land they are building the highway on must belong to someone too. They can't just take it."

Milka finally stopped and faced him. "Governments have been taking land and pushing my people out of the way for over 300 hundred years."

"Then why aren't the police or the Paraguayan army here instead of Rick and his mercenaries? We need time to figure this out."

"You heard Truman! We don't have more time!"

"They can't do anything more until that highway comes through. Do you have a truck and a map?"

A faint smile appeared on her troubled face. "I do!"

* * *

Milka insisted on driving, and Brand was glad she did. She left the dirt road and steered the white pickup without headlights over tilled farmland and grazing pasture. "When I was little," she said, "this was all forest." It didn't take long to spot bright white lights casting narrow trees into black silhouettes as they neared the growling machinery.

"They've made so much progress!" Brand exclaimed. "Truman wasn't exaggerating! They must be working 'round the clock. I expected they'd be shut down, their equipment just sitting out here abandoned."

"We are here now. You can't back out!"

Brand popped a couple of aspirin. "I didn't say I was backing out." He got out of the truck, and as he used a machete to hack through tangled branches, he wondered why he was doing this. Was it just to impress this girl whom he barely knew? He crept closer to the massive machines ripping roots from the earth while others mashed the earth flat behind them. Clouds of insects swarmed in the brilliant lights which lit their work. Even when Brand had been healthy, it would be difficult to take out four workers unarmed, and nearly impossible without seriously hurting any of them. A flashlight shone directly in Brand's eyes.

"Quien es?"

Brand raised his hands in submission. It wasn't too late to talk his way out of this. Perhaps he could get a clearer idea of what was really going on.

The flashlight fell, and the man holding it groaned. When Brand's vision cleared, he could see Milka bashing the man in the head with the back of a shovel. The man caught her hands in his. There really was no turning back now. Brand's knuckles itched around the machete as he bashed the blunt hilt into the back of the guy's head.

The other men hadn't heard the scuffle over the sound of their machines. The driver of the machine in the rear nearly had a heart attack when Brand leapt into the driver seat with him. Brand switched the machine off. "We don't want to hurt you."

The poor man didn't understand Brand's words and saw the machete. He fell to the ground, where Milka met him with ropes to tie him up. These skinny men were no threat. They were just doing their jobs. The man in the lead machine turned off his engine and lifted his hands in surrender while Milka spoke to him. He allowed her to tie him up with the others.

"What did he say?" Brand asked.

"He says Hesperion will just hire more guys tomorrow."

"He's right. We aren't after the workers."

Brand groaned as he lifted himself into the driver's seat and drove one massive machine into another, knocking it onto its side. He stuck another in a ditch. He and Milka did as much damage as they could to the engines before Brand fell over with exhaustion. Milka did not tire so easily and took her anger out on the machines, using the machete to hack apart hoses and belts and bash gears.

When at last she seemed sated, Brand went to untie the men, but they resisted him.

"They don't want to be untied," Milka said. "They will be in trouble if they run away... and in more trouble if Hesperion thinks they are sympathetic to us."

"We can't leave them tied up all night!"

One of the men spoke, and Milka said, "The next shift will be here soon."

Brand nodded and led the way back to the truck. He collapsed in the seat as Milka drove through the darkness. The truck bounced, and Milka hooted with exhilaration. Brand laughed and held her hand.

* * *

Brand heard heavy feet and slamming doors, but his muscles refused to move. His eyes finally shot open when his own door burst inward. Wilson pulled him out of bed. "I found him!"

Brand beat his fists meekly against Wilson's bulging shoulders. Wilson smiled, saying, "That all you got?" before tossing him against the wall, knocking over a table and the water basin on the way down. Brand could already see multiple bruises spreading over his pink skin. For Brand, a bruise could kill.

Wilson swept his arm around Brand's neck and lifted him from behind. "I thought you were one of us, *ginger*." Brand hated that word. No one referred to Brand by that term when they weren't trying to hurt him, but he could barely breathe, let alone protest as Wilson shoved him out the door.

He didn't resist as he was marched down the stairs. Sepe Guerrero sat tied up in the plaza. The eternal flame flickered behind him as it always did. Wilson shoved Brand to his knees next to the healer. A cut graced Sepe's mouth.

"Sepe had nothing to do with this!" Milka shrieked. Brand locked eyes with her and shook his head, willing her not to incriminate herself. Chauvinism had so few advantages. If they believed a girl wasn't capable of sabotage, let them.

"What have you done?" Cesar shouted down at Brand. "You can leave here any time you want! We will be the ones to suffer the consequences of your actions!" He turned to Rick. "It wasn't us! The American acted alone. Do not hurt Sepe!"

Kids and adults surrounded the plaza, watching their healer with helpless terror.

Rick sneered. "Sepe Guerrero is the spiritual leader here. Without him, the rest of you will fall in line. If you want to keep your precious healer safe, all you have to do is sign the contract."

It was hard for Brand to recognize Rick, the affable travel companion, as the same person threatening Sepe. "You have to be bluffing!" Brand said. "You wouldn't execute someone in cold blood, especially in front of all these witnesses!"

Rick winked. "I do whatever it takes to complete a mission. We tried offering the carrot… Don't get all moral now, Bobby. The violence where you were stationed—you can't tell me you never hurt anyone. If we encounter an obstacle…" He focused on Sepe and then the crowd. "We remove it."

If Brand paused to think, he might realize how true Rick's words were, and that's not something he wanted to consider. Brand stood on shaky legs and charged in sudden rage. He had hurt people, killed people who got in his way, mostly very bad people, but some innocents got caught in the crossfire. Milka and Cesar had treated Brand like he was worthy of friendship, but was he really that different than Rick?

Wilson shouted warning, and Torrez targeted Brand with her gun, but too late to prevent impact. Rick was momentarily pushed toward the crowd, who reeled back from the fighting men.

Rick turned and swung a fist into Brand's jaw, laying him out on the grass. "What is wrong with you, Bobby?"

Brand felt incredulous. *What is wrong with me?* As Brand attempted to lift himself up, he wanted to ask, *What is wrong with you? Threatening an innocent man's life?* but he collapsed, unable to catch his breath. He'd spent most of his life trying to solve problems with his fists. As a civilian, it rarely worked out, but the Marines had harnessed that rage, sharpened it into a weapon. Now that he was sick, that wouldn't work anymore. He needed to learn a new way.

Rick stared down at Brand's impotence and shook his head with pity and perhaps a touch of disappointment at the betrayal of their nascent friendship.

Truman blinked and paced back and forth in front of them. "You do not seem to understand, we don't need to offer you anything. We could drill into this hallowed ground, dig a pit in the middle of your town for our pipes. The contract ensures that we will find less obtrusive ways. Everyone will get what they want!"

When Truman blinked again, Brand realized it had been exactly four seconds, which seemed about right on average, but with Truman there was no variation. He blinked every four seconds like clockwork.

The crowd whispered and pointed. The town flame, allegedly eternal, died down to nothing. Sepe Guerrero, arms still tied next to an armed Torrez, knelt and whispered with eyes clenched shut.

Rick pointed his gun at Sepe. "What are you doing?"

Before anyone could answer, fire exploded out of the well, cracking the old bricks and shooting high above the buildings. Truman shielded his eyes as flames engulfed Sepe and Torrez. A sizzling wave washed over Brand and knocked Rick over. A blanket of fire fell over Brand and scorched his lungs as he sucked in flaming air.

Fingers encircled Brand's weakened limbs. The explosion only lasted a moment. While men dragged Brand's limp body away, he glimpsed the darkened, empty well with one side blown outward. Wilson swatted Torrez's smoking scalp with his hands. Reality and dreams blurred as he drifted off.

Sunlight penetrated gaps in the twigs which made up this shack, one of numerous little structures that dotted the area farms. Sepe Guerrero smiled down at Brand from a chair next to the cot.

Brand sat up. "How did we get here?"

Sepe raised a finger to his lips.

"They're hunting for us?"

Sepe nodded, and a child entered with a cup of tea. Brand downed it. He felt so cooped up. The bitter green liquid tingled on the way down, and a burst of energy shot through him. His boots and jacket somehow lay near the cot. "I can't just sit here."

Sepe shook his head and pointed at Brand.

"I know," Brand said, tying the shoelaces. "It's my fault. If I hadn't interfered, maybe the flame would still be there. Even if you relight it, you'll always know it's just ordinary fire now, not eternal."

Sepe shook his head adamantly and shoved a finger into Brand's chest. He then picked up a pitcher of water and poured it into Brand's empty teacup.

"Thank you. I am pretty parched."

Sepe kept pouring until the entire pitcher was empty, but not a drop spilled from the tiny cup. He handed it to Brand and smiled.

Brand sipped it. "Is this really the best time for a magic trick?"

An excited kid ran in with a broken drone in her hands. Brand grabbed the drone from her. "They know we are here!"

He pulled Sepe toward the door. "We have to get you out of here!"

Wilson's broad shoulders and long gun completely filled the doorway. He sneered and pointed his rifle at Sepe. "We don't need the healer, but Rick will want to talk to you, ginger."

Brand shoved his way between them and socked Wilson in the nose. The big man staggered back, and Brand grabbed the rifle in both hands. Wilson roared like a beast and shoved Brand further into the shack, knocking over table and chair. Brand gritted his teeth and pivoted, slamming Wilson's head through the brittle wall and pressing the horizontal gun into Wilson's throat.

Wilson laughed. "Looks like you got some fire in you after all!"

Brand didn't feel the least bit winded, and his heart beat slow and steady despite the adrenaline coursing through his body. He looked to Sepe. "What was in that tea?" He was certain he would pay for this exertion later.

"Rick welcomed you like one of us," Wilson said, "and this is how you treat us?" He effortlessly shoved Brand to the dirt floor.

Without the element of surprise, even with this newfound vigor, size mattered. Frustration boiled and seethed within Brand, and his hands clenched into fists on the ground. Wilson raised his gun at Sepe, and the air thickened. When Brand raised his open hand in protest, the tension escaped. The dry walls around Wilson blazed into blinding fire. The big man howled and rushed for the doorway, but tripped over the toppled chair and bumped the wall instead. He turned, and the fragile roof collapsed over him. Flames leapt into the sky through the hole.

Brand shielded his eyes. The heat wasn't as intense as he feared, even in such close quarters. "Sepe!" he shouted, but the magician was nowhere to be seen.

Brand found Wilson below the smoke and shoved fiery debris from his back. He then dragged the big man through the flaming doorway. Once safely outside, Brand fell on his butt and watched the building collapse in a pillar of black smoke.

"Damn it, Bobby! You burned another of my men!"

Brand looked up to see Rick and Torrez along with an armed local. There were almost always locals you could recruit for the right price, usually far cheaper than bringing in your own people. Torrez's head was wrapped in gauze, burned by the explosion at the plaza, but she held her gun steady at Sepe.

Rick narrowed his eyes. "This is starting to feel personal."

"Not for me," Brand said, motioning his chin at the surrounding farms. "It's personal for them. This is their land."

"Not anymore it isn't!" Rick dropped to Wilson's side. "Can you walk?"

The big man nodded, stood, but then collapsed in a coughing fit. His shirt and face were stained with soot, making it impossible to see how badly his skin was burned underneath.

"A little help!" Rick demanded. "We need to move him."

Some farmers loaded Wilson into a wheelbarrow. In spite of the pain the mercenaries were causing, when the farmers saw a wounded human being, they helped. Rick pointed at Brand and then at the wheelbarrow. "Start walking!"

Brand pushed, and the single wheel bounced over uneven turf, causing Wilson to groan. Despite the heat, the giant was shivering. Brand paused, removed the jacket from his sweaty frame and draped it over Wilson, who was probably in shock.

"Keep moving!" Rick ordered. As they walked, Rick looked to his fallen teammate. "You good?"

Wilson extended a thumb into the air. "We stay… until the mission is done."

Rick smirked and looked to Brand. "You see that, Bobby? Loyalty— to the mission, to the unit... your friends."

"Loyalty has a flipside— when you see your friends hurting people and you don't say anything..."

Townsfolk who had once filled the plaza now sat concentrated along one sidewalk. A few of the kids cried, and Cesar tried to comfort them. He looked up when Rick rounded the building. "Sepe!"

The townsfolk murmured and pointed. They seemed to be staring at Brand more so than their own healer. Brand's face became warm, and the daytime temperature almost unbearable, making him want to move, to dash away from their gaze into the shade, but any sudden motion might get him shot.

Above, one mercenary watched with his rifle next to the chapel bell. Another stood on the top tier of Milka's inn. Milka raised a hand to her mouth in the archway, and Brand couldn't help but smile when he saw her.

Rick left them in the plaza and wheeled Wilson into the inn where Milka helped him carry the big man inside.

Truman lowered probes into the empty well which once contained the town fire. He looked up from a laptop balanced on the darkened bricks and glared at Sepe. "Where did the fire go?" After a few seconds he asked in slow, annunciated Spanish, "Donde… esta… el fuego?"

Sepe gave a narrow smile and puffed out his chest as he met Truman's eyes and spoke four terse syllables.

"What did he say?" Truman asked. "Frida?"

"It wasn't Spanish," Torrez said.

Brand explained, "He doesn't speak English or Spanish." As Brand said it, he wondered how much the healer understood. Sepe reacted as though he comprehended what everyone was saying.

"Well," Truman said. "What *does* he speak?"

"Some native language."

Truman looked to the laptop again. "That fire was one end of an axis of flame which extends through the core of the planet. The other end of the axis is inaccessible, but this…" He waved at the empty well. "…should have been simple. If it's not emerging here, it must have found a different path, a new outlet to the surface, but the satellites aren't picking up any new activity on the ground or underneath. The infrared glow shone like a beacon from space, but now it's vanished! It is my name on all the expense reports. We are not leaving without something to show for the money Hesperion is spending!"

A tall boy, still dressed in his ill-fitting festival vest, tugged Truman's sleeve. "I know where it is."

Cesar shouted, "Oscar! No!"

"Where?" Truman demanded.

The heat rose inside Brand as Oscar pointed. "In him."

Truman narrowed his eyes. "That's not possible." He approached Brand but halted suddenly with one hand in front of him. He then retrieved what looked like a flat-faced camera mounted to a gun handle, a portable infrared detector. "You're burning up!" He turned to Torrez. "Take him inside!"

Brand felt even more restrained in Torrez's grip. He twisted, causing her to grab his shoulders more forcefully. She suddenly yelled and let go.

Brand didn't waste time asking questions. He spun, punched her, and yanked away her rifle.

Brand sprinted down the street while bullets rained down from the chapel. Bricks in the well shattered in the hail of projectiles. Truman grabbed his face as it was hit by stone fragments. Unnatural, green smoke rose from the shallow wounds.

Brand pointed his newly acquired M4. His bullets chimed against the bell, and the gunmen recoiled from splintering wood. The man above the inn fired a couple shots but was too far away.

By now, however, Torres was on her feet and Rick charged out of the inn. Torrez gritted her teeth and held the grip of her Sig in a loose two-handed grasp like an amateur, which was odd because

Brand knew her to be highly trained. Brand ducked between the government building and the chapel.

Torrez shouted to Rick, "Wait! What's wrong with Truman?"

Brand peeked out. Truman had fallen to one knee. He gurgled and panted as though he couldn't catch his breath, but the punctures looked superficial. Green mist continued to wisp between his fingers, which were firmly planted over the tiny wounds. Cesar made the sign of the cross. Even Sepe backed away with furrowed brow and gaping mouth.

In a wet, croaking voice, Truman shouted, "Get me inside!"

Rick had paused, but now took aim at Brand with his rifle. Brand ducked, and the stucco where his head had been turned to powder. Rick wasn't taking prisoners anymore. Brand sped around the corner, shocked to note he still wasn't out of breath, even with all the day's exertion. He'd heard that people about to die sometimes got one last gasp of energy. Perhaps he was so sick that his body had stopped sending pain signals to his brain. If that was the case, he didn't mind. It was better to go out feeling like this than lying on a bed in constant pain.

A back door to the chapel swung open, and Brand pointed the rifle. Oscar lifted his empty hands and waved him inside.

Brand whispered, "You could have been shot, Oscar! I'm so glad to see you!"

The darkness within was overwhelming after the bright sunlight. Heavy footsteps thumped on the stairs above, and Brand took shelter between the long wooden pews.

"Have you figured it out yet?" Oscar asked.

"What?"

"Look at your sleeves."

Brand looked at his short sleeves and saw perfect, black handprints where Torrez had grabbed him. They smelled like smoke.

The child shook his head. "You really are a waste." He then popped up and ran. "Here! He's here!"

The gunman who had been on the roof was now at the front doorway and took aim.

Brand took in a gasp of air and raised his rifle, but before either could fire, a rush of glowing, orange air lit the room and blew the man out the chapel doorway. The townsfolk outside cheered.

Rick appeared in the sunlight framed by flames in the doorway, and their eyes met. His radio crackled with Torrez's voice. "Chief, we've got orders. We'll get him later!"

Rick's lip curled, and he stepped out of frame. Sepe and Cesar filled the gap and rushed to Brand's side.

Brand sat in a pew. "What the hell is going on?"

"You were supposed to leave," Cesar explained. "To take the flame away for safekeeping, but now they know where it is."

"You can't put volcanic fire inside a human being!"

Sepe tilted his head and raised his eyebrows. He grabbed Brand's hand and positioned it palm up. He then held his own hand the same way. Flames flickered across Brand's palm. Brand sat straight up, waving his flaming hand frantically through the air, but that just fed the flames. "Put it out! Put it out!"

The two men laughed, and Brand realized the fire did not hurt him. In fact, he felt more alive than he ever had.

Sepe held his hand palm up and took in exaggerated breaths.

"Follow Sepe's example," Cesar said. "You need to calm down."

Brand held out his palm, watching the fire dance over his hand. He hadn't realized how labored and shallow his breathing had become since the diagnosis until now when he could fill his lungs to full capacity once again. "What did you do to me?"

Sepe closed his hand, and Brand followed, extinguishing the fire. He slowly opened his hand and examined the intact skin. "Why not put the fire in one of you?"

"That's the first place they would look," Cesar explained. "You were supposed to take it away from here."

A question burned on Brand's lips, but he was too afraid to ask. *Was he cured?* If so, would he remain cured when the fire left him? "You want it back?"

Sepe closed his eyes and slowly shook his head.

"Not yet," Cesar said. "The town is still in danger, and that thing… Truman. Something was inside of him."

"Inside?"

"You didn't see?"

"I saw green smoke. You looked pretty freaked out."

Cesar fondled his own face where Truman had been wounded. "Something… moved inside his wounds."

Sepe nodded. "Demon."

Cesar crossed himself again.

With all the hectic action, Brand assumed they must have misinterpreted something. There was no such thing as demons, was there? Brand again examined his undamaged hand. Before a few minutes ago, he hadn't believed in magic fire either.

Rick and his soldiers had taken Truman and fallen back to the inn. One mercenary still stood watch on the top level while Torrez guarded the entrance. Brand felt bad seeing the gauze wrapped around her hands and the yellow scarf covering her burned scalp. He told himself it wasn't his fault. She'd brought that on herself.

The inn might as well have been a fortress. They could spot anyone approaching.

"We've got to get Milka out of there," Brand said.

"She refuses to leave," Cesar said. "Her mom is mostly bed-ridden. Milka can't abandon her, but she is safe for now. Oscar has been inside—"

"That damn kid almost got me killed!"

"He would not let them hurt his sister."

Brand scowled, hoping that was true. "What about Wilson?"

"In shock, but alive. Milka is looking after him."

* * *

Work had restarted on the new highway. Heavy equipment tore through tangled root networks and flattened earth behind them, but now a man stood guard with a rifle.

A fireball sprang from the new road behind into the engine of a steamroller. The driver leapt to the ground and rolled in the dirt. The guard took aim at the redheaded man standing on the flattened earth, but had to dodge a barrage of bullets from Brand's stolen rifle.

An inferno swelled inside Brand, threatening to pop his sweaty body like a boiling blister, as though all his extra blood from the polycythemia had turned to fire. The rifle fell from his hand, and convection currents rose off his body, tickling his short, red hair. He reached out his hand, and another flaming ball shot into the second engine, relieving the pressure inside him.

The guard and workers ran from the flames, abandoning their work. Cesar and Sepe joined Brand.

"You've turned me into a weapon again."

Sepe shook his head vigorously, and Cesar explained, "Fire doesn't only destroy. It… changes, it purifies, transforms wood into heat and smoke, meat into food."

A child ran out of the trees. Oscar stopped short when he saw Brand.

"You tried to get me killed!" Brand yelled.

"I didn't know they were going to shoot at you!"

"What else did you think they would do?"

"This is important!" Oscar said. "They are going to drop dynamite into the well trying to get to the fire below."

"There is no fire below."

"They don't know that. They've detected a hollow space underground. They are ordering us to evacuate the plaza before two o'clock this afternoon."

Cesar's eyebrows lifted. "We can't let them destroy the whole town!"

Brand closed his eyes. "They know we will try to stop them. It's a trap. They'll pick us off from the roofs." Cesar and Oscar waited, staring at Brand.

Now that Brand was cured, he could abandon them any time, perhaps finally become a real father to his son. But his son wouldn't even recognize him, and what if Brand accidentally burned him someday? All Brand had to teach him was destruction. Brand was a stranger to his son, and he owed Sepe and the others his life.

Brand had been a perfect soldier, a living bullet who would execute a plan with precision and accuracy, improvising when necessary, but he had never been expected to *make* the plan. How could he stop or delay Rick without someone being hurt or killed? "They can't possibly have permits to implode the whole plaza!"

"What they are planning is certainly illegal," Cesar said, "but my phone calls are still being ignored. I have no doubt the government would eventually side with us, but by then the plaza will be gone, and our town with it! Hesperion money talks louder than I can."

"Truman figures it's easier to ask the government's forgiveness later than for permission now… By then it will be too late." Brand felt like he was living in an old western, with authorities too far to help and justice in their own hands. "Do you have weapons?"

"A few shotguns," Cesar said, "for hunting and shooting jaguars who get too close to our cattle."

"Not much against automatic rifles on rooftops…" Brand removed the cowboy hat from Cesar's thinning hair and placed it on his own head. "Our only chance is trickery. From the roof, I can look like any other farmer." He sketched the plaza in the dirt with a stick. "If you gather a big group and march into town between the government building and the chapel, that will draw all their attention. I'll sneak in from the opposite direction. Hopefully I'll be able to stop them from dropping the dynamite before anyone gets hurt."

* * *

Milka spotted Brand climbing over the second story balcony with the rifle dangling from a strap, and he held his finger to his lips. Old gloves barely protected his hands from the course rope.

A single shot echoed from the opposite side of the building, and Brand hoped Cesar was alright. Brand was gambling that Truman would want Brand taken alive since he contained the magic fire they were after. If they thought Cesar was Brand, they shouldn't kill him, at least not right away. Now that the guards had spread across the plaza, the one remaining guard atop the inn couldn't look every direction at once, and they were all watching for Brand on the plaza-side of the inn.

"You alright?" Brand asked.

"I'm fine, but the man, Wilson, I'm worried he could be septic. He is doped on painkillers, watching from the third story."

Brand nodded. "You couldn't by any chance barricade the stairs, could you?"

"I don't see how."

Brand had already known the answer. There was no way to effectively close off the wide, open stairwells. He wanted to also ask if Rick had stashed any extra bullets nearby, but this distraction wouldn't last long. "Where is Truman?"

She escorted him to one of the rooms. Truman lay in bed, staring at the ceiling with unblinking eyes.

Brand leaned in, examining what appeared to be a hairline crack in his cornea. "Is he…?"

Still without blinking, Truman tilted his head and sucked a long inhalation of gas from a soda can sized canister. Fog formed inside his eyes, and faint wisps of green wafted from his nostrils. "You were supposed to be in the plaza."

Brand yanked Truman up by the collar and held the barrel of the gun to his ribs. Blisters of uneven, mismatched skin glistened atop Truman's facial wounds. "Seems your spy got it wrong," Brand said, referring to Oscar. Brand had known the kid couldn't be trusted and had changed the plan as soon as he left.

Brand dragged Truman plaza-side and propped him against the balcony with the gun trained on him. "Stand down!" Brand shouted.

The plaza was abandoned except for Rick, who held a now hatless Cesar by the shoulder and gestured with his pistol. Bundled sticks of dynamite sat near the well with blasting caps a few feet away.

Light glinted off Rick's silver, heat reflective suit, the kind used to investigate volcanic vents. He looked up to the balcony. "You won't kill Truman! You don't have it in you!" He thrust his pistol against Cesar's temple. "But *I* do!"

Rick was calling his bluff, and Brand was frighteningly low on ammunition. "I don't have to *kill* Truman," Brand said. He lifted a hand, and orange light flickered along Truman's unblinking face. His irises didn't even contract from the light, but he stiffened.

Milka held a walkie-talkie to Truman's lips, and Brand used his shoulder to shove him hard against the railing. Sulfurous smoke leaked around the fleshy sealant on his face.

Truman blurted into the radio, "Drop your weapons!"

The guard atop the government building and Torrez on the chapel looked at each other, and their rifles fell to the ground below. Farmers with shotguns and farm implements marched in and surrounded the plaza. Brand thought this might actually work out more easily than he had feared, but that hope didn't last long.

Rick grimaced and fired his pistol up at Brand. Brand released Truman and pulled Milka out of sight below the popping clay tiles above them. She yelped and recoiled from Brand's touch. Her upper arm reddened and blistered before their eyes.

"I'm so sorry!" Brand cried.

More bullets popped around them, and one even erupted from the floor beneath them. Truman crouched with his hands covering his head. Brand rose, and his anger exploded in a ball from his hand which hit Rick square in the chest. Rick staggered back, but immediately fired back, protected by his suit.

A stream of fire rained down from Brand's hand. The wind carried it a little off mark, and he swiveled his arm back and forth. It felt like he was exhaling through his hand, pushing air out until it hurt. Rick lowered the suit's silver hood over his face and dropped his pistol. Bullets burst from his M4 at Brand's head. Rick was really going to kill him!

Brand retreated into the interior and found Wilson wobbling unsteadily down the stairs with rifle drawn, forcing Brand to hide in the archway. Ashy skin peeked out from Wilson's gauze bandages, which were clean and white on the edges, but stained yellow with pus in the centers. Wilson could barely keep upright, but didn't need to be steady to kill someone with that M4, and likely not just who he was aiming for. He might hit Truman or Milka by mistake.

Milka and Truman huddled on the balcony. "The fire is not fire," Milka said. "It burns within us all, fueled by belief, not oxygen."

Brand furrowed his brow. Why would she pick now of all times to give him stupid riddles? Smiling farmers stared at him from the fringes of the plaza. He felt the heat of their intense gaze, and convection currents once again rose off his body. He collected the warmth into a tiny flame, no bigger than a match head, which hovered in his cupped hand.

Rick paused when it hit his chest and then cackled madly when it disappeared. "Running out of fuel?"

Brand stood frozen with his throwing arm outstretched. He was shocked nothing had happened, but could still feel the spark growing, like a child who had left the nest.

Rick raised the rifle, but his chest heaved up and down, and smoke puffed out where the hood met his neck. He screamed and hurled the hood away as he fell panting to the ground. Steam wheezed from his mouth.

Brand clung to the wall, startled by what he had done.

Rick looked over his shoulder as he crawled away, but he wasn't retreating. He reached for the dynamite lying near the well. Brand narrowed his eyes and let the fire stream down. Rick shielded his face, and Cesar ducked with his hands over his head as the paper wrapping the explosive sticks blackened and peeled away, but the dynamite burned harmlessly without a charge to detonate it.

The blasting caps intended for that purpose lay a few feet away. Truman was feeling his way up the wall to a standing position when the fire reached them. The popping caps caused him to stumble while damaged eyes darted all around.

Milka grabbed him, trying to calm him, but he frantically pushed her and swung against her grip. He pulled loose and ran full speed to the edge of the balcony. His waist stopped abruptly when it bumped the railing, but his head toppled over. Milka screamed and grasped at the air, but Truman fell out of reach.

Silence hung over the plaza. It wasn't a long fall, and, with luck, he might only break a limb, but Truman had already been injured. His leg now twisted under him. For a moment, he lay still. A finger twitched. Then his shoulder spasmed, and he flipped onto his back, which arched upward while a high-pitched grating squealed from his mouth, along with a fresh puff of green smoke. The body collapsed, and two green tentacles shot out of his mouth and flailed in the air. Another quaking appendage joined them, and they all stiffened. No one spoke until the tentacles wilted and collapsed.

Rick was back on his feet, holding his side and staring down at his boss. The blank look on Rick's face suddenly turned to fury as he looked up at Brand on the balcony. "You're dead!"

"Come on, Rick." Wilson's voice was tired and raspy next to Milka. "Truman's gone… and I… need a…." Wilson collapsed.

"Wilson!" Rick called.

Brand squatted over the fallen giant but feared his burning hands would hurt Wilson even worse.

Milka knelt across from Brand on the other side of Wilson. "The fire that is not fire…"

Brand nodded and grabbed both of Wilson's hands. The mercenary howled in pain, and his wounds sizzled. Steam rose from the gauze.

Brand almost pulled away, but Milka urged, "That's it! Keep going!"

"Brand!" Torrez's voice crackled over the radio. "Leave Wilson alone!"

By the time Torres thumped onto the balcony, Brand leaned against the wall, exhausted. Torrez took aim, but Wilson stopped her.

"Don't." Without the bandages, his raw, pink skin glistened. "I'm ok. It just… really hurts."

Milka squared her shoulders and stood between the men and Torrez. "Bobby burned away the painkillers and the sepsis, but infection will set in again if Wilson doesn't get to a hospital."

Torrez looked past Milka at Wilson in open-mouth confusion. The radio crackled again with Rick's voice. "The natives have phones… with cameras."

Torrez narrowed her eyes and fled. "Priority orders! Get Truman out of sight!" Wilson grimaced and followed.

Milka looked Brand in the eyes. "How do you feel?"

His eyebrows lifted. "Better than I have in a long time. I think… I didn't just destroy stuff. I did some good… Are they leaving?"

"I think so."

Rick reluctantly lowered his rifle and dragged the body to the door by its arms. Wilson and Torrez joined him, and they hauled Truman to his old room, ignoring Brand and Milka.

While Wilson and Oscar packed up gear, Brand found Rick and Torrez staring quietly down at Truman. Slender tubules still protruded out of the lifeless mouth and ruptured cheek. The room stank like rotten eggs.

Rick wore a heavy jacket despite the heat, and his skin had taken on an orange tinge. Every breath wheezed from his lungs. Brand's flame had burned him from the inside. "It appears I'm the sick one now, Bobby."

I'm sorry, Rick. I didn't mean to—"

Rick whispered, "It was war, Bobby. You won."

Torrez added, "Without the town fire, we have no reason to stay. The highway is no longer worth all the money Hesperion was sinking into it."

Brand looked down at the body. "What was he?"

Rick tapped Truman's open eye, and it clinked like glass against his finger. "Hell if I know, but his checks cleared. Our last order is to destroy Truman's body."

"You can't!" Brand said. "This body is evidence of something way stranger than property rights and energy."

"We follow orders, Bobby. Loyalty still means something to us."

Torrez looked up. "Maybe he's right, Rick. This isn't normal!"

Rick's face flushed crimson as he lifted a can of gasoline. "I'm still in charge here! Finish loading the van!"

She glanced at Brand.

"Now!" He demanded. She left, leaving Rick to drizzle gasoline over the body, covering the foul corpse with volatile fumes.

Brand rushed forward to grab the can. "You don't have to! Without Truman, there is no reason for us to fight! Don't you want to know what he really is?"

He shoved the can into Brand's chest and then smacked him in the face with it, spilling noxious gas over the floor. "We failed our primary objectives. We aren't going to screw this last task up."

Brand backed off, holding his chin, and the thermometer rose. "Please, think about this. We were friends!"

"We might have been, before you betrayed us, burned my crew, sabotaged the mission. Wilson claims you helped him, but without you, he wouldn't have been burned in the first place!" Sweat dripped from Rick's face. He dropped the can and drew his pistol. "Is that what a friend does?"

"You can't!"

Rick cocked the gun, but instead of firing, pivoted out of the room. Brand's fear ignited the fumes around him. Fire licked over the floor and engulfed Truman's body. Tentacles twisted and writhed, spiraling up and down their lengths as they blackened like black snake fireworks on Fourth of July.

Rick cackled beyond the doorway. "Thanks for the light, Bobby!"

Brand cursed himself for letting Rick trick him like that. Milka raised her hand over her face at the door. The curtains blackened to ash in an instant, and flames curled around the table and desk. A decorative plant curled and blackened, much like Truman's bizarre tentacles.

"Stay back!" Brand shouted. "We need water!"

"We used all the water treating Wilson!" Milka shouted.

Brand tried to inhale but coughed on the smoke. After finally experiencing clear lungs, it was doubly traumatic to have his breath cut off, and his eyes watered from the fumes.

"Get out of there!" Milka shouted.

He dropped to his knees, under the smoke. With one hand, he lifted his shirt over his mouth and nose. He extended the other into the flickering light. "The flames don't hurt me." He closed his fist, and the flames around it died down but didn't go away. He extended both arms, palms up, and felt the heat outside his body. It was nothing compared to the furnace within. He opened his arms until he felt the stretch in his joints, then slowly pulled them inward and wrapped them around his torso. He closed his eyes, and when he opened them, the fire was out. Truman's body, however, was now smoldering ash stuck to the blackened mattress.

Milka rushed into the room and stopped short. An unneeded fire extinguisher dangled from one hand.

Brand escaped the thick air and leaned against the wall, releasing a few coughs. Milka held her hand against his back.

"I'm... sorry about the room," Brand said, eying the big bandage on her arm where he had burned her.

"The rest of the inn survived," Milka said. "With a new coat of paint, the room will be good as new."

He spied ash that had once been Truman. "And a new bed."

Wilson was already aboard the van with his head propped against the window. Torrez finished loading it up while Rick guarded its door. He nodded at Brand and Milka as they marched into the fresh air. "I knew you'd be alright, Bobby. Fire doesn't bother you anymore, does it?"

Oscar stepped into the van carrying a small bag.

Milka screamed, "Oscar, where are you going?"

"I love you, Milka, and I appreciate everything you've done for me, but there is nothing for me here. The modern world will never come to Tataguigua, so I must go to it."

"With them?" Milka cast a side-glance at Rick. "They are criminals! I forbid it!"

Rick scanned the plaza with narrow eyes. Farmers with shotguns stood watch, and one held a discarded M4. "Come on, little man. Bus is leaving with or without you."

Oscar turned away from his sister and stepped aboard. Milka shrieked while Cesar held her shoulders. Rick backed into the van with one hand on a metal rail. The other held the trigger of his rifle as the van hissed away.

Sepe and Cesar each put a hand on one of Milka's shoulders as she kneeled in the dust.

"Oscar must seek his own path," Cesar said. "He may find his way back once he has his fill of the city."

Sepe nodded. "I did."

Brand did a double take, staring open-mouthed at the healer. "You spoke English this whole time?"

The corner of Sepe's mouth lifted. "A little. My Spanish is better."

"You could have just told me—"

Cesar interrupted. "Words get in the way of simple truth."

"I suppose you want the fire back."

Cesar nodded, but Sepe shook his head. "If the fire returns, so will the demons. The fire cannot stay."

"If the fire is in me…" Brand waited, but no one completed his statement for him. "I have to leave."

"If you stay, the demons will return."

For the first time since leaving the Marines, Brand had felt like he belonged. Now they were kicking him out. He understood their reasoning, though, and his mind turned to the enemy. "A monster working at an American company... chasing the magic fire... I wonder how many more there are... Is this something from your mythology?"

Cesar gave Brand a sideways glance, and Milka finally turned her head away from the road. "Our stories are not mythology to us."

"Sorry."

"No," Sepe continued, "Not exactly like any of our stories, but it is..." He paused with a word Brand didn't recognize. "Evil seeks power."

Cesar clarified, "Universal."

Brand raised an eyebrow. "The same everywhere, I suppose. And whether they believe it to be magic or volcanic gas, the fire is power."

Sepe nodded.

"Perhaps I could..." Brand was filled with doubt, but Sepe's eyes widened with anticipation. "Find the monsters?"

Sepe nodded his head. "Yes! Let the fire use you! Protect Tataguigua by hunting the demons. Once they are gone, the fire can return."

Brand's heart filled with resolve, and white-hot flame glowed between his fingers. He felt invincible. His body hadn't been the only thing sick. He had needed purpose, a mission. Now he had one. Demons beware. Brand is coming for you.

THE LIFTED VEIL

Originally published in *And the Dead Shall Sleep No More: Volume I* on October 31, 2021 by Input/Output Enterprises.

This tale took place about 250 years ago in the tiny central European village Ombra. The village sat at the foot of a big hill, and on top of that hill sat a ruined castle. Looking at the crumbling towers, you might think it abandoned, but at night, a light appeared in a single window.

Count Renaud kept to himself, but on rare occasions, he would appear in the village at twilight to buy supplies. Merchants didn't object to his money, but villagers crossed the street to avoid passing next to him. Being such a recluse, it was natural for the villagers to spread rumors about him. Every time a sheep died or a woman miscarried, they blamed it on Count Renaud.

Mae was a lovely villager of sixteen years with curly black hair and rosy cheeks. Her mother had died in childbirth. Her father adored Mae as though she were the most precious thing in the universe. With her older sister already married off, Mae took care of their little cottage. She did the laundry, cooked the meals, all the duties that a wife would usually do.

One evening, her chores all done, Mae strolled over cobblestone streets to the market in the center of town. She stopped to sniff blood red roses at a merchant's cubicle. She had a few extra coins and thought they might make the house smell nice. She didn't notice when a horse up the street got spooked and took off at a full gallop, dragging an empty cart behind him. Villagers scattered as the cart swung to the side and crashed through a vendor's booth. The world seemed to stop as the cart careened toward Mae. The wheels squeaked, and the vendor reached out to her helplessly. If the cart didn't kill her, it would tear her clothes and break her bones when it hit.

A strong hand caught the rein and a man in a velvet coat took the impact of the cart, stopping it inches from Mae's face. You can imagine Mae's surprise when she looked up into Renaud's pale blue eyes. His wavy blond locks bounced when he turned his head, seeming to fall around his face in slow motion. White lace rose from his velvet coat and hugged his neck.

He glared as he handed the reins over to the owner of the horse. "You should be more careful!" Then he turned to Mae. "Are you hurt?"

Mae's heart raced as she tried to catch her breath. "You saved me, sir!"

"It would be a shame to see something so beautiful trampled."

She nodded. "The flowers are lovely."

"I was talking about you."

Mae's cheeks blushed as red as the roses. No one had ever talked to her like that before.

"Allow me to see you safely home."

As they walked, Mae talked to Renaud about her family and the other kids in the village. Renaud told Mae how life had changed in the village over the years, how his family had all left and how lonely life was in his castle. Other teenagers turned their heads and whispered as they passed. The attention made Mae feel special. At sixteen, she was considered almost an old maid, but none of the village boys were as fascinating as Count Renaud.

They continued talking in front of her simple cottage until Mae's father finally called to her.

Renaud took Mae's hand and kissed it, sending a tingle through her young body.

"I wish there was some way I could thank you for saving me," she said.

"There is," he said. "Allow me to walk you home again tomorrow night."

When Mae left the house to get water the next morning, she found a single red rose tucked into the doorframe.

Night after night, Renaud regaled her with amazing stories, describing life in the village as it used to be.

Her Papa and older sister warned Mae to stay away. "Nobles have no use for commoners," Papa said. "You are just a plaything to him."

Mae shook her head. "Renaud cares for me. If you could see the way he looks at me with those amazing blue eyes, you'd understand!"

Papa folded his arms. "He looks at you like I look at my lunch! Stay away!"

"What about the rumours?" her sister whispered. "That he has lived in the castle forever. That he is the reason our animals and children get sick and die."

Papa implored, "I have a sister in the city where Renaud won't find you. She can look after you."

"Why can't you be on my side?" Mae said. "Don't you think I'm good enough for a man like Renaud?"

"We are on your side!" Papa said. "We are always Team Mae."

Mae clenched her fists at her waist. "Being Team Mae means being Team Renaud too!" She slammed the door and sulked in the garden. They couldn't possibly understand how she felt. Papa had been alone ever since mother died, and Mae's sister, only seventeen, bickered with her husband like an old woman. That wasn't love.

Renaud walked her home again that evening. "What's wrong?" he asked.

"My family doesn't approve," she said. "They say that you're…" She hesitated.

"Different?" he asked.

She nodded.

"Why don't they say this to my face?"

"They're afraid you will bite off their heads."

A smile crept across Renaud's face, and he began to chuckle. "I am known for my temper. I would never hurt you Mae, never raise my voice to you." He grabbed her hands in his. "But they are right. I am different. You've noticed how I only meet you at night, how I never share a meal with you."

Mae's heart thundered in her chest. "I don't care. I love you, Renaud."

His face lit up. "I love you too, Mae." They shared their first gentle kiss.

They continued their nightly walks until the morning Mae did not return home. In those days, when a woman moved in with a man, they were considered married, and Mae became lady of the castle. They softened the stone walls in two upper-level rooms with curtains and couches. Lanterns and a blazing fireplace bathed the rooms with warm light, and her bed was covered with quilts.

They made love for the first time early the next morning. The cock didn't crow until the first rays of sun peeked over the horizon, and Mae was spent. Her fingers lightly danced across Renaud's flawless cheek. He smiled and pulled away.

"Where are you going?" she asked.

"I must return to my crypt by day. You have the run of the castle while I am asleep, but be careful. The building is old and can be treacherous."

She grabbed his arms. "Can't I come with you?"

He shook his head. "That is not possible. You must promise never to come to me while I am sleeping."

"But—"

Renaud raised his voice to Mae for the first and only time "Promise!"

Mae nodded, and Renaud kissed her on the forehead. "The day will pass quickly. I will see you tonight."

Renaud had not been exaggerating about the state of the castle. The rough walls were bare, and furniture rotted. Only Mae's rooms were warm and furnished. After the long night, Mae slept the day away in her big, comfy bed.

Renaud pushed in a wheeled table with roasted quail and potatoes. It smelled and tasted wonderful. While Mae ate, Renaud went out for supplies. When he returned, they made love again, and again, he pulled away to sleep alone.

Night after night, the pattern repeated. Renaud brought Mae food, kissed her gently, and made love to her in the morning before retiring to sleep alone.

Mae spent her days sleeping and exploring. She mapped the castle. Down in the depths of the fortress, even at noon, no sunlight reached her. She carried a lantern down the narrow, twisting stairs. Decades of dust covered the floor, but there was a clear spot in front of an arched door where it would swivel if opened. She tugged at the door, but found it locked. She knew the sun would be setting soon and returned to her bed.

The smell of bacon and eggs woke her, and she discovered Renaud smiling down at her.

"You were sleeping so soundly," Renaud said. "I let you sleep in."

They exchanged the gentle evening kiss as they always did. She was hungry, but not for bacon. She pulled him over her.

"Your breakfast is getting cold," he said.

"But I'm all warm." For a moment Renaud seemed overcome with passion. He pulled her close, almost devouring her lips, and she didn't care if he did. She wanted to be consumed in body as she was in spirit.

But he pulled away, as he always did when night began.

"I must go into the village to gather supplies."

"Not yet."

"I must." Renaud leapt to the window and turned to her, saying "I'll be back as soon as I can," before leaping into the night.

Mae ran to the window and gazed out at the stars. Far below in one of the flickering windows, her family was sitting down to dinner.

Mae ate her bacon and picked at the cold eggs before falling asleep with her plate only half empty.

Cold hands slithered under the sheets and pulled her close. She embraced her lord without completely waking. Renaud had returned. Normally they would make love, but she was so tired. She merely turned and latched onto him. She didn't awaken until he pulled away again.

"You just got here," she said.

"I've been lying with you for hours."

"Make love to me," she begged.

"It's too late now. Tomorrow."

"But I want you now!"

He gave her a gentle kiss. When Mae opened her eyes, she was alone.

She lay pouting for a time, but she had a plan. The next night began the same as always. Renaud prepared her meal and went out to run errands.

Mae followed the twisting path down into the depths of the castle. She found the old door and discovered, as she had hoped, that it was unlocked. She nearly gagged on the stale air within the musty room, but amid the dust was the lidless coffin she hoped to find.

Renaud returned and made love to her like he always did, but there was something even more special about it tonight. When he pulled away, she did not resist. She turned an hourglass over and waited... and waited.

The sand was not even halfway through when she descended the stairs once again.

The old door creaked open. The wax she had placed in the lock had done the trick. How surprised Renaud would be when he found her in the coffin with him the next morning. He would see that there was no harm in it, and from then on, they would be together night and day.

She brought her lantern over the coffin and saw the familiar velvet jacket, but the hands were not the smooth hands she was accustomed to. The fingers were long, and the nails like dirty razors. A bloated stomach bulged though the buttons of the faded velvet, while the rest of the body within was nearly a skeleton. A few wisps of blond hair graced a dry brown scalp. Above the moth-eaten collar, thick lips curled into a circle like a suction cup lined with concentric rows of tiny, sharp, white teeth.

This wasn't Renaud! It couldn't be!

Mae ran from the room. The echoing clang of the door made her heart jump for fear the ghoul would awaken and chase her up the steps to the warm refuge above.

She threw another log on the fire and huddled under the quilts.

It couldn't have been Renaud. She must have gotten the wrong room. When evening came, there would be some reasonable explanation, and they would both laugh.

It was no surprise when the cart rattled and Renaud's graceful steps crept into the room. She wanted to be reassured by his handsome face, but she couldn't bring herself to lift the blanket. Rough hands slid under the sheets and caressed her. It was the same familiar touch, but she had never realized how cold and dry his hands had felt before. The velvet arms of his jacket wrapped around her, and he exhaled a cold breath smelling of moldy meat. Mae clenched her eyes shut and pretended to sleep.

At last the arms retreated, but Mae remained frozen in the bed for some time before she finally turned around. A sumptuous feast sat before her, but she was not hungry.

When Renaud appeared in the window, skin stretched over his gut like a balloon ready to burst. Long fingers reached for Mae. His glistening red lips pulsated with a wet, slurping sound as he moved in for a kiss.

"Why do you pull away?" Renaud asked.

Mae's mouth quivered. She could not answer.

His dry, skeletal face cracked with sadness. "You went to the crypt, didn't you? Why? I told you not to."

She finally managed to stutter out, "What happened to you?"

He looked away from her horrified gaze. "This is the real me, Mae. What you saw before was a glamour, an illusion."

Tears dripped from Mae's eyes. "Bring it back!"

Renaud shook his head. "I'm sorry, Mae. You can't unsee what you have seen. I really do love you, Mae. I wish it didn't have to end like this."

Mae sniffled and stared into the undead face. "I love you too, Renaud. I don't want it to end."

"Can you really love this face?" Renaud moved closer. Mae leaned toward the pulsating lips and rows of sharp teeth. These were the same lips that had been kissing her all these months. Those wisps of blond hair had formed the same golden mane she had caressed when they made love. As their faces neared, she closed her eyes, wanting to let the tiny teeth caress her lips as they always had before, but at the last moment she turned away.

Renaud raised his hands into the air and howled like a dying animal. A burst of cold air blew out all the torches and candles in the bright cheery room, plunging them into darkness.

That morning, Mae appeared on her father's stoop with a suitcase. No one asked her what had happened, and she never talked about it. Any gossip about the castle's lord hushed when Mae appeared.

She sometimes gazed longingly at the castle on the hill, but the window remained dark.

Mae was still young and beautiful, but sadness now tainted her big eyes. The boys never came around, but she didn't mind. No one could ever match the illusion of love she had felt with Renaud. She dreamed about kissing Renaud as she first saw him, but when she pulled away, she faced rows of teeth and throbbing wet lips on a dry, lifeless face. She wished she would have had the strength to kiss that dead face and embrace those skeletal arms, wished he had never discovered she could see the real him.

When Papa died, Mae moved in with her sister. She doted over her nieces and nephews, and they loved her very much. Her nieces and nephews had kids of their own, and they doted over Mae. She was a graceful old woman, but no one lives forever… well almost no one.

The family cried at the funeral, but they understood the nature of life and death. A handsome man in a velvet coat watched the funeral from a distance. When the crowd dispersed, Renaud dropped a single red rose onto the grave.

"Did you know Great-aunt Mae?"

Renaud gasped when he saw the rosy cheeked girl and her curly, dark hair. "You look just like her!"

The girl chuckled. "That's silly. She was an old lady."

"We were all young once. Your aunt was a remarkable woman. What is your name, young lady?"

"Amelia."

"I am Renaud, lord of the castle."

Amelia gazed at the lifeless ruin on the hill. "No one lives in the castle."

Renaud nodded. "No one has truly lived there for many years."

"You're funny," she said.

Renaud smiled for the first time in decades. "Allow me to walk you home."

DISCOVER THE SECRET ORIGIN OF HARMONY IN *HARMONY UNBOUND*

DISCORD

Red wax dug into my fingernails, and my knuckle scraped raw against the wall. I finally dropped the fragment to the floor and picked up another crayon, but it was only a nub itself. I'd pilfered every red crayon from the tub in the craft room, glad that my denim skirt had big pockets, but it might still not be enough. I continued flattening the crayon against the wall in the dim, yellow light from the lamp by the little twin bed. I had to make her real, even if it was just a picture. No one else remembered her, but she existed, and together we had saved the town.

Where did you go, Harmony? Why won't you talk to me? Or is it the pills that make me unable to hear you?

The crayon rubbed back and forth, hypnotizing me. I forgot where I was and what I was missing while the outside world moved on without me. Only the layering of color mattered. I was so engrossed that I didn't hear the footsteps outside my room until it was too late.

"Lights out!" It was Jerry, the orderly, in dark blue scrubs.

I leapt into bed with the wax nub still in my hand and switched off the lamp. I thought if I didn't look up, he wouldn't see me or my picture, but white fluorescence poured over the room, blinding me even through my eyelids.

"Victoria," Jerry said. "You're fifteen years old. You know better than to draw on the walls." He picked up the crayon nubs from the floor. I'd hoped to squish them together to get a little more out of them. "Is this all there is?" he asked.

"Yes," I squeaked.

He cocked his head, waiting. When I didn't say anything more, he opened the drawers by the bed and pulled out the flattened yellow. I was done with that though. I'd had plenty of yellow, and her boots and chest were done.

He gazed at me again. I averted my eyes like a child. Was he reading my mind, or was I just that predictable?

He yanked the sheet from my bed, saw my clenched fist, and held his hand out. "Give it to me."

My whole body quaked, but I shook my head. I couldn't let him stop me from making her real. I needed her.

Jerry grabbed my hand and began prying my fingers loose, one by one.

"Stop it!" I used my other hand to cover the crayon, but it was no use. He burrowed his fingers into my fist. I only had one weapon left.

I'd never bitten anyone before, at least not since I was a toddler.

Jerry jerked his arm back with a curse and raised his hand, but instead of striking me, he left the room.

 I looked to my mural and cried, "Help me!"

I was no artist. The inconsistent, grainy scribbles looked like something a five-year-old would do. The crayon picked up the texture of the wall, leaving the recessed areas without color. Geometric shapes formed a flattened human outline. Yellow graced her wrists, chest, and long boots. God, I loved those boots. And when she wore them, I wore them, because we were one.

But if we were one, how could she be gone?

I didn't have a flesh-colored crayon, so her face and hands were just outlines, and her wild hair was only yellow. I needed to add some red or orange to get it the right shade. I pawed my own hair—straight, brown, oily. Had I washed it since coming here? I couldn't even remember for sure how long ago that was.

I was about to start adding color to Harmony's hair when Jerry returned with another orderly. The nurse with bright red hair and pink scrubs, Cranston, stood by the door and watched as they held me down. When I saw the straps, I screamed.

If they strapped me to the bed, I'd be helpless when the demon came.

There was nothing I could do to stop Jerry from taking the crayon. "I'll be good!" I shouted.

I pulled against the padded leather straps. The light flipped off, and I was alone. Well, not completely alone. I looked to my drawing and noticed light reflecting where her eyes should be. I stared for over an hour, trying to tell if it was a trick of the light, or if she was really crying.

My heartbeat and breathing sounded loud, like I was in a box or under water. With every breath, the room seemed to throb around me, closing in and out in time to my breath.

Something blocked the window in the door. Back and forth, it passed before the tiny square of light like a pendulum. When it stopped, two orange eyes stared in at me. The door didn't lock. It could get in, and I could get out… if my wrists weren't restrained.

The head sank below the window, and something clicked along the tile floor, getting louder and louder until it suddenly stopped. I brought my feet up under the sheets as much as I could and pulled at my restraints. If Harmony were here, she could snap these bonds like tissue paper, bust through the wall like it was Styrofoam and fly away.

I looked to my static drawing on the wall and called, "Help me!"

The shadowy head rose at the foot of the bed, peering at me with those bright orange eyes. Silhouetted by the dim light from the door, it appeared to have two horns sprouting from the back of its head. I didn't believe in demons, but a week ago, I hadn't believed in superheroes either.

If my hands were free, I could bury my face in the pillow, but all I could do was clench my eyes shut. The sheet moved slowly down across my body. A plaintive moan echoed through the room, and it took a moment to realize it was coming from my lips.

The sheet jerked away, and ice-cold fingers grabbed my ankle. The ring on its index finger burned as though it had been sitting in fire.

I screamed, loud and long. I took a deep breath and shrieked again.

The lights clicked on, and I opened my eyes. Jerry and Nurse Cranston hovered over me.

"You're disturbing the other patients," Jerry said.

"It grabbed me!" I said.

Cranston's voice was rough and raspy. "It was just a nightmare."

"You look uncomfortable," Jerry said. "If we untie your wrists, are you going to behave?"

I nodded.

They undid my wrists, and as they left, I asked, "Can you leave the light on?"

Jerry smiled and nodded his head. I hadn't even used a nightlight since I was ten. I felt like such a baby. I gathered the sheets up over me and looked at my childish, lifeless drawing in the bright fluorescent light.

* * *

The sun shone through a window by the bed. The strong glass in the window was frozen shut. They didn't want any of us crazies getting out that way. In the light of day, my grainy scribbles looked even more childish.

The corner of the bed sank when Bohman sat his big butt down. A rim of white hair formed a crescent around his chubby, bald head. Dr. Bohman was the new guidance counselor at school. He somehow started all of this, had me committed to this place.

"I hear you had a rough night, Victoria." Bohman said.

"How long have I been here?" I asked.

"A few weeks."

"That's not possible! I was just at school, and you called me into your office." If I was really missing this much school, I might end up needing to repeat the whole ninth grade!

"I met with every single student. You have all experienced a great trauma."

I almost laughed as I remembered. "Yes. The school was attacked, but we..." I looked at my primitive drawing on the wall. "She saved us. She saved the school, the town… the entire country!"

Bohman stood and examined the drawing. "Indeed? She must be quite remarkable. Tell me about this… Harmony."

"You must have seen her on the news. She's strong, fast…"

"And she can fly?"

"Of course! Oh, to fly and be free! The wind in your face, houses shrinking beneath you and speeding by. It's the most wonderful feeling!" I had to pull back some of my enthusiasm. "I mean, I imagine it would be pretty cool." He couldn't learn how Harmony and I shared our existence. That would ruin our secret identity.

"You sound like you speak from personal experience."

"You've never imagined flying?"

A corner of his mouth lifted. "Oh, yes. I've imagined quite a few things."

He gazed at me a moment before continuing. "Tell me, who do you think attacked the school?"

"A robot," I said. "An evil robot."

"Really?"

I nodded. "You must have seen it on the news."

He shook his head. "I must have missed that."

I furrowed my brow. "Then why were you at the school? What was the trauma you keep talking about?"

"A student with a gun."

My mouth hung open. "That could never happen in our little town. Who…?"

"A troubled young man named Daniel MaCavoy."

I shook my head. "No. No! Danny is my friend! He would never!"

"He fit the profile. Loner, kept to himself, picked on, wore black."

"Wearing black doesn't make you a killer! And we're freshmen. We all get picked on."

"That's why you two became friends, wasn't it? You both got picked on by the popular kids."

"No! Danny was nice! Why are you using past tense? Where is Danny now? Is he here too?"

As Dr. Bohman told me about Danny, a distant voice whispered. I could barely hear her, but when I looked to my drawing, I could make out her words. "The boy is not dead. Everything this doctor says is a lie. You must escape this place. Set us free!"

"Victoria?" Dr. Bohman followed my gaze to the wall. "We'll pick this up later. It's time for breakfast."

About a dozen patients gathered around the main desk. Locked double doors separated us from the elevator. Like passing through the airlock on a spaceship, you had to wait to be let in or out. The wing was a little over half capacity, with several rooms empty. Only one patient in the ward was younger than me— a twelve-year-old boy named Jacob. A few patients already ate at little tables across from the ping pong table.

An old woman with leathery skin and only three front teeth shouted at me. "There she is! She got the Devil in her!"

Jerry, the orderly, interrupted her tirade. "Eat your breakfast, Eleanor. Victoria's not bothering you."

Eleanor had been nice to me the night before. She kept demonstrating how to say *I love you* in sign language, over and over again, like it was new every time. She had treated me like a child, but I didn't mind. I was short and skinny, and she had probably assumed I was younger than I was.

"She's always looking at me," Eleanor said. "She thinks she's fooling us by being all quiet. She thinks she's better than me, but she's not!"

I shook my head. "I don't!"

"I was like you," Eleanor said. "Good in school. Had me some friends. Then I went into the hospitals. In and out. Nobody understands, but God has plans for me. I'm special. He looks after me, and he's better than any devil you got!"

I wondered if she knew something about the nightmare and the demonic apparition. The other patients all stared at us. I shook my head again. "I'm just here temporarily. I'll be out soon."

Eleanor cackled like a Halloween witch. "Is that what the Devil whispers in your ear, young lady?"

Jerry physically got between us. "Eat your breakfast, Eleanor."

Eleanor harrumphed. "Forget breakfast. Get me a cigarette!" She continued talking as she wandered down the hall, even though no one was there to listen."

Jerry looked down at me. "She didn't mean anything personal. She's just having an episode. You'll be her best friend by lunchtime."

"Thank you." I noticed the square bandage on his forearm. "I'm sorry about your arm."

"Get your breakfast before they take the cart away."

Before Nurse Cranston would give me my plastic tray, she handed me a little medicine cup with two pills, one blue and one yellow.

"What are they?" I asked.

"Something to help you relax," she rasped.

I popped them in my mouth and took a sip of the water she offered.

"Open your mouth and lift your tongue," Nurse Cranston commanded.

"Why?"

"Are you trying to make trouble like you did last night?"

"No."

"Then show me."

I swallowed the pills hidden under my tongue and opened my mouth.

"Good girl," she said.

Before I took my tray, I asked, "Can I have some ketchup?"

She pulled two condiment packets from a drawer and tossed them on my tray.

"That's not enough," I said.

She glowered and threw two additional packets on my tray. I thanked her and set my tray on one of the little tables, but instead of sitting I headed down the hall.

Jerry the orderly hovered with his arms crossed. "Eat first."

I stared at the bandage on his arm. "But I really need to go to the bathroom. You want me to pee my pants?"

"Your eggs will get cold. Take a few bites, swallow, then you can go."

I sat down and started eating. The little mound of scrambled eggs was indeed already getting cold. Jerry wasn't watching anymore, but I knew there was no point in going to the bathroom now. Too much food sat on top of the pills for me to puke them up.

Jacob tugged on my sleeve. With me sitting, he stood about eye level with me. "Do you want to play a game?"

"Sure. Ping pong?"

He shook his head and pointed at the television in the lounge with the ancient videogame console.

I shrugged and he set the game up. The words *Harmony Unbound* blinked on the screen in mono-color glory.

"I go first!" he said.

Digitized fanfare played as a pixilated, 4-bit woman in red and yellow flew across a one-dimensional city skyline. Despite her movement, her hair remained a frozen, orange zigzag on her head.

"What year is this from?" I wondered aloud. A pen and ink rendition of the superhero on my wall grinned at me from the box. This artist had all the colors right, even the strawberry blonde hair and white reflections on the metallic yellow. Her legs flew back, and she threw one fist forward as though she were popping right off the box, like one of my dad's Jack Kirby comic characters.

The illustration was a far cry from the low-resolution woman on the screen. Robots came at the woman, and she smashed them to pixels, one by one. But more robots piled on, speeding faster and faster. She punched one final robot, but a dozen more took its place. Jacob jumped and squealed as he twisted the joystick. The robots overwhelmed her, and she blipped out of existence with a frowny face and digital whine.

"Oh, man!" Jacob handed me the controller. "I can never get past level one. Show me how it's done!"

"I was never much of a gamer. Computers and games are Danny's thing."

"What do you mean? You've played this with me lots of times."

I wanted to question him, but the game started. Like Jacob, I was able to punch my way through the robots by moving the joystick and hitting the red button. When they sped up, a few got some punches in before I was able to dance away. I waited until the screen was full and they were about to pounce, then cleared the entire screen with a single punch.

"Power Punch function!" I shouted.

Jacob cheered. I turned to him, but the boy I high-fived was my height, with dark bangs combed forward. I backed away, eyes wide.

"What's wrong?" Jacob asked. It wasn't Danny. Had never been Danny. Why had I seen him so vividly?

I tried to smile. Jacob thought I was cool. He was like the little brother I never had. I didn't want him knowing how troubled I really was.

Jacob asked, "You think she's real, don't you?"

"Who?"

He motioned at the screen. "Harmony. I heard you talking to Dr. Bohman."

My face flushed. "No."

"I wish she was real."

"You do?"

"That would be so cool!" He gazed at the monitor. "Where do you think she goes when she's not saving the town?"

My heart beat like thunder. He might actually understand. He was my only friend in here, and I wanted to tell him our secret so badly. But I realized that if he understood, it was because only a child could understand something so silly. "I don't know."

"Vicky," Jerry called. "Your mom is here."

We weren't a touchy-feely family, but I flung my arms around my mom, hugging her tighter than I ever had before. Jerry took Jacob to the other side of the room, and they started playing ping pong.

"Mom!" I said. "You've got to get me out of this place!"

Paddles on the other side of the room popped the ball back and forth.

"I'm sorry, Vicky. You still have issues to work though."

I pulled back, hurt. "Issues?"

"These fantasies."

"You don't remember Harmony either?"

She sat at one of the tables, and I joined her. "Dr. Bohman says you created her to make yourself feel strong."

"You never liked her! Where's Dad?"

"He's seeing the new owner of the factory, hoping to get a job. Besides…"

"What?"

"Since your breakdown, he doesn't know what to say to you or how to act around you."

Dad's eyes used to sparkle when he looked at me like I was the most amazing person in the entire world. The thought of him not wanting to see me broke my heart. I shook my head. "The only thing giving me a breakdown is this place!"

Mom touched my hand, but I pulled away. Her forehead creased under her glasses. "Dr. Bohman says you can break free of the fantasy by becoming strong on your own."

I folded my arms over my chest.

Mom's mouth formed a tight line. "Tell me about her."

"What?"

"Tell me about Harmony. Where does she live? Where does she go?"

"Why does it matter if she's not even real?"

"Please, Vicky, I want to understand."

DISCORD
DISCORD   251

Something nagged the back of my mind, and I couldn't concentrate. My stomach tied in knots. A tiny whisper buzzed in my brain, crying, "Help me!"

I ran from the table and spotted the janitor's cart outside my room.

"No, no, no, no!"

I got there just as a cleaning woman started rubbing the sponge over Harmony's arm. Red and yellow smudged together. It would have been the perfect color for her hair.

"Stop!" I shouted, jumping between the janitor and my art.

Mom panted in the doorway. "What's going on, Vicky?"

My drawing stood only a head taller than me, not like the real Harmony... if she was real. My art was disproportionate— head too big, legs too short. I was as ashamed of my art as of my behavior.

Mom regarded the drawing. "Is this her?"

I nodded.

The janitor glowered at us both. "I have orders to clean this wall. Do I need to call someone?"

Dr. Bohman appeared. He took the sponge from the janitor and presented it to me. "No. If anyone should clean this wall, it should be you, Victoria. This is your fantasy— your delusion. Only you can make it go away. You needed it because you felt weak and helpless, but you don't need it anymore. You can be strong on your own."

Soapy water dripped over my hand from the wet sponge. My brain buzzed as Mom and Dr. Bohman waited.

"Do you want out of here?" Bohman asked. "Freedom is right in front of you. All you need to do is clean the wall."

The buzzing got more intense as I brought the sponge closer to Harmony, like a thousand bees crawling through my honeycombed head. Where the drawing's eyes should be was only a flat wall and a dark stain where a tear might fall.

I dropped the sponge and hid my face in my hands. "I can't! I'm sorry."

Bohman put a hand on my shoulder, and Mom wrapped me in her arms.

"It's alright," Bohman said. "You aren't ready yet, but you will be."

The janitor picked the sponge up off the floor. Under her breath, she muttered, "I hate this floor," as her cart squeaked away.

"Don't worry," Mom said. "We will figure this out. I'll be back tomorrow."

I hugged her again as I realized what a sacrifice she was making to visit me. Our town was too small to have a facility like this. She was driving an hour and a half one way for this short visit, and she still needed to go to work today. Until Dad found another job, she was the only breadwinner.

I wiped my eye as I watched her disappear out the locked double doors and wished I was descending the elevator with her.

I rinsed my face over the sink with soap and water. When I arose, the face in the mirror wasn't mine. Orange eyes stared back at me. The demonic face was well-lit this time. Those weren't horns in back of his skinny head. It was a crescent of white hair combed back and up. His lips stretched into a grin so wide it threatened to split his face in two. I backed away from the mirror and clenched my eyes shut. When I opened them, my own pimpled face and bloodshot eyes stared back at me. I shook my head and looked back at my drawing on the wall.

Maybe it was all in my head— seeing things, hearing voices, being the hero in my fantasy. Perhaps I was as crazy as old Eleanor. I ran my hand along the drawing, feeling the wax under my fingers. I seemed to hear a distant whisper, but I couldn't make out a voice. Maybe the drugs were working. Maybe I needed more.

I looked at my face in the mirror again and thought of the demon. "If Harmony is my desire for strength, then who are you?"

I nearly jumped when Jerry called me from the doorway. "It's time for arts and crafts."

"I'm coming." I wondered if Jerry ever went home from this place.

DISCORD

Patients gathered around a table in the craft room while Ms. Garcia instructed them how to make friendship bracelets out of tiny rubber bands. I took the empty seat next to Jacob. Thankfully, Eleanor wasn't there.

Two patients flicked rubber bands at each other across the table. While Ms. Garcia was occupied with them, I found the tub of crayons on a shelf and ran my hand through them.

"Vicky!" Garcia shouted. "We aren't using the crayons today."

"Sorry." There weren't any more red ones anyway, but I had to check.

On my way back to my chair, I passed a wall covered in drawings and paintings. One child-like drawing stopped me in my tracks. A thin man with green, scalloped half cape and white, pointed hair stared out at me with fluorescent orange eyes. Fire scribbled out of a ring on his finger.

The demon man had to be real, and he was haunting another patient besides me!

"Ms. Garcia!" I shouted.

"Yes?"

"Who drew this?"

Garcia furrowed her brow. "You did, Vicky. Two days ago."

I looked at the drawing again. It had the same amateur quality of the drawing on my wall. I didn't remember being a patient here at all two days ago, but Bohman said I'd been here weeks.

"Vicky?" Garcia called. "Are you alright?"

"I'm fine." I couldn't disguise the worry in my eyes, but I grinned and returned to my seat. If they knew how addled my brain was, I'd never get out of here.

Jacob handed me a friendship bracelet. He'd made it with red and yellow for me. I quickly finished mine to give to him while he started another.

Then it was time for lunch: turkey sandwich with fruit cup and a side of potato chips. Cranston thought it was weird that I wanted to put ketchup on my chips— Like that was the weirdest thing she'd seen in this place.

Patients gathered around the television while Jacob and I played ping pong, and then it was time for dinner and more pills. One day blurred into another. There weren't even any clocks on the walls, and it was easy to see how weeks could go by without feeling it.

Dinner meant soon it would be time for bed, and another visitation from my demon.

A pool table sat next to the ping pong. I had never played before, and Jacob had gone to bed, so I practiced hitting the balls by myself.

Dr. Bohman interrupted me and motioned for me to sit. "It's past lights out, Victoria. Are you avoiding going to bed?"

I shrugged.

"I've instructed Nurse Cranston to get some pills to help you sleep. You won't even dream tonight."

I shook my head. "No. I'm fine. I'll sleep on my own."

"But you look exhausted. Why not take the pills?" Bohman spoke in a calm monotone. If anything could make me tired, his voice could. "Is this something to do with your fantasy?"

"If the demon isn't real, I have nothing to fear. If he is, I need to be awake to face him." My leg felt cold where he'd grabbed me the previous night. A red bump, like an insect bite, swelled where his ring had made contact. If he could touch me, then I could fight him. At least I could try.

Bohman didn't seem fazed at all at the mention of a demon. "And what of Harmony? Do you still think she is real?"

"I don't know anymore."

"What seems more plausible, Victoria? Where does she hide? If she is real, why isn't she here?"

"I'm tired," I said.

Bohman escorted me to my room and circled my bed. "There is nowhere in this room anyone could hide, and no one could sneak by the staff. You are safe." A bucket of warm, soapy water and a sponge sat on a table next to my artwork on the wall.

"In case you can't sleep, you can wipe away your pain at any time. If you want to get out of here, all you need to do is clean the wall. All this could be over."

I nodded.

"Good night, Victoria."

The door creaked and clicked shut. Dim light from the hallway drifted in the little square window. The only sound was my own, irregular wheezing.

I counted the ceiling tiles, waiting.

Perhaps the demon wasn't coming. Perhaps the drugs had done their job.

I clicked on the reading lamp. The closet didn't have a door, and the corners were well-lit by the lamp and the window in the door. My drawing looked so foolish in the pale light. The soapy water was still warm. I brushed her hair as if it was real. It was still the wrong shade. I pulled out a packet and squirted some ketchup onto my fingers.

The red smudged into the yellow, producing the perfect shade. Then I smeared ketchup over her arm and torso. It took quite a bit to fill it in, and I never got a completely solid color.

I sat on the bed, licking my fingers and admiring my work. My breathing paused, but the wheezing continued. I held my breath, listening. There was still one place in the room where someone could hide. I slowly let my head dangle below the bed frame. Two orange pinpricks stared back at me.

I pulled back onto the mattress, as though that were somehow safe. A hand sprang from under the bed. I recoiled, only to be harassed by another hand on the other side of the bed.

The hands retreated, and the demon slithered up from the shadows. He raised his hands and towered over me, grinning like a shark.

"Help me!" I shouted, turning to the wall, but my drawing was gone!

The apparition reached for me, but stopped moving forward. I followed its gaze downward. My grainy drawing now graced the tile floor, and the demon's boot sat in its flat hand. The drawing slid backward and dragged the demon with it until he slammed into the corner. The demon's ring flashed with lightning, blasting the floor into chunks.

I held my hands to my face, worried Harmony was lost forever. Jerry and Cranston peeked in the little window. The door handle rattled, but despite not having locks, the door wouldn't budge.

The wall beside the demon stretched into a fist and pounded his jaw. Another fist struck from the other side. Being drawn in the corner gave Harmony new depth. Scribbled hands held the demon, but his ring flashed again, and the wall crumbled. He then aimed at the floor as waxy red and yellow streaked toward me. The tiles cracked and split on a path to the bed. I leapt from the mattress as it sparked ablaze.

The demon loomed larger. Briefly shielded by the bed frame, my drawing reached out to me, straining against the floor as though it were a thick membrane. I reached out to her but stopped when I saw Jacob's friendship bracelet dangling from my wrist.

"Don't do it!" Jerry called from the doorway.

"Don't retreat further into the fantasy!" Bohman shouted.

"We can help you!" Cranston rasped.

The demon swelled in my peripheral vision.

Like the ceiling of the Sistine Chapel, I touched my drawing's hand.

A bright, white flash engulfed the room as though a camera bulb exploded where our fingers touched.

I stood up straight and tall in the guidance counselor's office. Golden sunlight poured through the blinds, and sulfurous smoke rose from a flat video monitor behind the desk. Dr. Bohman had fallen out of his chair. A metal tinker toy contraption smoldered around his head. I reached into my wild, strawberry-blonde hair and found an identical contraption on my own head. The door opened, but instead of a tall superhero, Principal Small found plain Victoria Bond standing over the fallen counselor.

"Good Lord!" Principal Small said. "What happened here?"

I presented the brain probe to the principal. "Dr. Bohman put this thing on my head, but something went wrong with it."

"That is not school approved equipment!" Principal Small crouched over Dr. Bohman and shook him. The doctor moaned but didn't awaken. Small looked up at me. "Are you alright?"

I nodded.

"Send the school nurse and return to class."

"Yes, Sir."

The clock read 1:30 pm. I'd been in there less than 30 minutes, but those weeks in the mental hospital had felt so real. I reached for the door, and my wrist felt light without fake Jacob's fake friendship bracelet.

A powerful female voice echoed in my head. "Dr. Bohman knew most of our appearances centered around the school. He was interrogating all the students, hoping one of them knew our secret. But his brain probe wasn't designed to handle someone with *two minds*."

"Did he find out anything?"

"I don't know, but at least for now he is in no condition to share his knowledge."

I took a deep breath. "I escaped. You set me free."

"No, Victoria. Yet again, you set me free. You have no idea how terrifying it was to be trapped in your mind, unable to act. No matter how I screamed, you would not hear me. I feared you were going to forget me and lock me away forever!"

As I walked down the hall talking to the voice in my head, I remembered old Eleanor and wondered if I had broken free of my mental prison or fled deeper into my delusion. But I smiled. Either way, I had escaped to a better life. Danny sat by me in my next class, Dad waited for me at home, and I… was a superhero.

SANTA'S CLAWS
(or SURVIVING A WHOLE HOLY NIGHT)

Christmas Eve, the house locked tight
Terror building this snowy night
Children cringed awake in their beds
Blankets pulled up over their heads
The fireplace dark behind a gate
If Santa came, no escape from our fate
He'd diced up the neighbors just last year
365 days later, we lived in fear
The killer in red didn't fear laws
He'd kill us with those bloody claws
He'd laugh "Ho ho," the killer in red
Saving baby for last, wishing for dead
So to save her the grief we placed pillow on face
To let her die with a little more grace
Lifeless lips dropped sugarplum
I kissed baby sister, feeling numb
A thump on the roof let us know he was here
Daddy pointed shotgun, mommy guarded rear
Like a bowl full of jelly, Santa's gut blew apart
But it takes more than that to silence his heart
Laughing with cheer while mommy ran
Daddy's screams didn't sound like a man
Mommy's feet fell, jerked away
I called her name, begging, "Please stay!"
He hovered over us, I pulled out our rations
Milk and cookies were his passions
He shoved milk-sopped treats into his maw
While sister snuck up with a chainsaw

Claws sparked against the chain
Our efforts alas were all in vain
The cock finally crowed, sun arisen
He winked, pinched his nose, and left unbidden
Night over, I had survived
My statement, officer, is not contrived
Arrest me if you think I'm the killer
But next year Santa will eat YOU for dinner

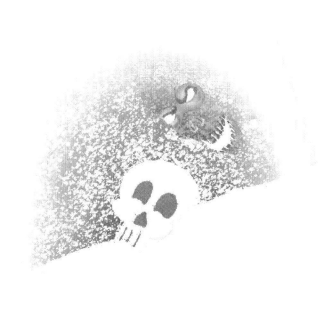

THE LONGEST NIGHT

Originally published in *Gifts of the Magi* from the Speculative Fiction Guild October 31, 2014. Note: this story takes place after *Valora* and before *Brute: Chasing Shadows*.

Tears filled Mother's eyes when she pulled the fur hat down over my ears. I was tall for my age, and she had to look up at me. Normally there would be nothing to do but sit by the fire eating stored food, but the supply of firewood was dwindling fast. We hadn't seen a winter like that in my lifetime. I was only twelve, granted, but twelve years is a long time.

It wasn't the cold that scared Mother so.

I said goodbye to little Elsa, who lay on her cot facing a wall of mismatched stones and pine timbers. When she turned to me, terror filled her big brown eyes, and she shrieked like a banshee.

Mother pushed me aside and grabbed the child in her arms. "Oscar!" she scolded, "what were you thinking?"

In all those layers, I must have looked like a bear. I never thought what kind of an effect that could have. Only five nights earlier, a monster had burrowed right through the thatched roof of Elsa's cottage and killed her family. Elsa was too young to understand. She still begged to see her parents before she went to bed at night.

We were Elsa's family now.

Every night that week, a villager had been killed. These attacks were like nothing I had seen. I know; I was only twelve and hadn't seen much, but this beast didn't just attack people out in the woods. It burrowed into people's homes and sliced families apart.

I was sweating under my layers and glad when Father called me. I was tall, but my father towered over me. He really did look like a bear in all those furs. Someday I will be as tall and broad-shouldered as him.

We slung axes over our shoulders and headed outside.

Father scowled at the evergreen wreath hanging on our door and tossed it to the ground.

"Mother hung that up after Elsa came," I said. "She says it keeps the Night Monster out."

Father harrumphed. "I have more faith in the slate tiles on our roof. No monster is getting in here."

I hoped Father was right. I didn't see the harm in a little extra precaution.

The eastern mountains cast long shadows over our valley.

Father and I joined red-faced Bilbee and his son, Josa, in the village square. We called it a square, but it was just a flat, grassless area between the trading post and the Chief's house.

Josa lowered his scarf, stuck out his tongue, and crossed his eyes. He was my age, but much shorter of course. I would have returned the gesture, but Father scowled. Father didn't like to joke around. Bilbee seemed much more fun.

Lumes and his Sun prophets gathered around a metal sculpture called a *sundial*. It was supposed to tell time using shadows, but the mountain cast a larger shadow than it ever could.

Lumes shouted to all who would listen, and those who didn't want to listen were forced to hear him as well. "The days grow shorter! Night is winning!" His words came out in long clouds of condensed moisture. The tall, slender prophet wore orange robes and a yellow sash over his furs. A thick, yellow cap graced his balding head.

Even the Sun's emissaries weren't immune to the cold.

Lumes and his two assistants had accompanied the king's men into the village last fall. We only heard from the king at harvest time when he collected a percentage of our produce. That was the only time anyone came from the lowlands. Father said it was easier to give them what they wanted so they would leave.

The king's men left, but the prophets stayed.

"Tonight is the line!" Lumes continued. "If the days grow any shorter, Darkness will win. Night will consume all our days forever! But you can turn the tide against the forces of death!"

One of the prophets, a short, pudgy man, slipped a necklace around my neck. A golden disk dangled from the chord. "You must wear a sun disk if you are going into the woods! Only three Histerns."

Father pushed the pudgy prophet away and threw the disk back at him. "Keep your trinket and keep your hands off my son!"

Lumes interceded. "The sun disk will ward off the monster."

Father's voice was flat. "For only three Histerns. What a bargain."

"Indeed!" Lumes said. "A small price for the Sun's protection."

"The mountain provides all we need," Father said.

"Look around!" Lumes shouted for all to hear. "This mountain is dead. Only through the Sun can there be resurrection."

Father turned and walked away.

Lumes shouted, "It is one thing to reject the Sun's blessing for yourself, but think of your child!"

Father's mouth narrowed into a firm line. I thought he was going to turn around and punch Lumes. Josa acted instead. He lifted a stone from the ground and slung it into Lumes' face.

Lumes' two allies doted after his bleeding head, but the prophet pushed them away.

"Night is eating Day!" Lumes shouted. "Make your offerings to the Sun. Put a wreath on your door to show you are his…"

Lumes' ravings faded as we made our way from the village. In less than an hour the western mountains would cast their shadow over the valley.

"What if Lumes is right?" I asked.

Father took a deep breath. "The sun doesn't care if we have a wreath on our door."

"But the nights *are* getting longer."

"The nights always get longer this time of year."

I didn't remember anything getting longer or shorter. I remembered it getting cold, but never this cold. This year was different.

The trees in the outskirts of the pine forest were saplings. We went deep into the woods where the firs were large and thick.

We started chopping. My breath crystallized on my scarf, and my nose ran uncontrollably. I couldn't stop to wipe it without breaking rhythm. Two of us drove our blades forward as the others pulled away. The rhythm made the work easier.

At last one of the trunks creaked and we stopped to watch it fall.

The shadows were deep, and the sun hidden.

Bilbee called to us before we could begin again. A man lay in the snow! The fur cloak over his blue tunic offered meager protection from a mountain winter.

Father examined the stranger's fingers. "He looks like a southerner." He raised his voice and addressed the stranger, "What are you doing up here this time of year? Are there others?"

The stranger spoke an unfamiliar language, but we understood a few common words. "...all dead."

"Idiots!" Father said. "Coming up here this time of year. We have to get him indoors."

Young Josa argued, "If we leave now, we'll have to start all over tomorrow."

"We have no choice," Father said. "He may lose those fingers as it is."

We loaded the stranger onto the sled intended to carry firewood for the village. The sun sank lower as we made our way back.

Something flapped in the trees above. It was the first animal sound I had heard all day. I looked up, but saw nothing through the thick pine needles. Something landed in the tree to the left of us. I caught a glimpse of movement. The branches moved aside. Two eyes glowed like the setting sun.

"Father!" I called. "The monster!"

A thin body dropped from above. Leathery wings slowed its descent, and the monster's boots landed silently in the snow. The skeletal creature wore clothing like a man! No chilled breath emerged from the monster's mouth. It was Death coming to claim us for Night, just as the prophets had warned.

I ran.

I ran until the shouts disappeared. I didn't look back, but imagined the gray face grinning like a skull behind me.

I tripped over a tree root and rolled down the slope. Snow dug into my sleeves and boots. I finally came to a stop, half buried.

My breathing finally slowed, and the world stopped spinning. I awaited the sounds of pursuit, but none came.

I don't know how long I remained. I could no longer ignore the cold moving through my body. If I didn't move, this pile of snow would be my grave until the spring thaw. I remembered Lumes' words. If Night won its battle with the Sun, there would *be* no spring thaw.

Powdery snow reflected moon and stars, casting a gloomy gray over the forest.

I tried to crawl up the slope, but slid back down. More snow found its way into my coat. Calling out might bring the monster, and I had no idea if Father or Bilbee were alive to hear my cries.

I had run like a coward while they faced the monster.

I removed one of my boots and dumped out the snow. My thick socks were wet... useless. I needed to get indoors, or I would be no better off than that foreigner we had found. I replaced the boot and followed the bear constellation. That would hopefully get me close to home before I froze to death.

My toes burned as though on fire. I imagined myself dead and heard Mother scolding Father for not putting a disk around my neck. Then I remembered Father might be dead as well and saw Mother and Elsa alone in our cabin.

Snot froze to my face.

I collapsed. I just needed to rest for a moment...

I almost dozed off. A moment's rest could become an eternity frozen on the mountain slope.

A faint light shone in the distance. I forced my stiff limbs into action. The cave of the prophets was ahead of me. I could almost feel the warm fire within.

Tribute of dried meat and bread sat on the ground outside the cave— gifts from fearful villagers who thought the prophets could protect them. For me, the prophets really were salvation.

"Hello?" I called as I entered. Being away from the wind offered some relief, but I needed to get those wet boots off.

A giant gold disk hung on the wall. The fire glowed upon the gold, accentuating the friendly, paternal face engraved on it. Barrels sat along the opposite side. Crates formed a wall in the back of the cave.

"Hello?" I said again. I appeared to be alone.

I stripped before the fire and placed my outer garments flat on the cold dirt. I sat on my coat and huddled as close as I could to the flames without getting burned. I rubbed my feet until they started to feel again.

My coat became a makeshift blanket.

The flames blew back in a gust of wind and dust. I awoke, and my breath once again froze.

Bat wings framed the corpse-like monster in the cave entrance.

This was a place the Night Monster shouldn't be able to go. The giant disk was an altar to the Sun, far more powerful than a necklace.

The monster pulled its wings inward. It leaned forward on its toes as it marched closer, and my heart pounded with every step it took. Needle-claws jutted through the thing's boots. Those boots wouldn't be much use in the cold, but the monster didn't seem concerned with cold. Its clothing was much too thin for life in the mountains. Its pleated doublet could have been that of a rich lord if not so torn and stained. Pine needles stuck in the monster's straggly, black hair.

Its slow march became a rushing charge, and my thundering heart seized.

The monster suddenly turned from me and plowed into the stack of crates. I marveled at the food which spilled out over the floor. The villagers took good care of these prophets.

A child-like giggling echoed from the cave entrance. The Night-Monster gnashed its teeth and followed the laughter. Its wings almost spanned the width of the cave. The monster gasped, and its leathery wings shriveled. Pinkness dawned over its gray cheeks, and it fell forward. The wheezing monster hammered its fist into the dirt.

The flames wafted toward me, and the embers threatened to die. A hawk-nosed face stared at me from the flames, then faded as it moved forward. A frigid draft chilled me to the bone.

The feminine voice came from my left. "Who have we here?" Then she was on my right. "A chance for some fun?"

Then she spoke from across the room again. "Hide, you stupid boy!"

My breathing came in short bursts. I moved behind the toppled crates. My clothes tumbled after me as though pushed by a great wind, and I pulled them behind the crates with me.

I had no time to ponder these strange events. Lumes was here.

His two prophets dragged the monster deep into the cave and manacled him. His chains were staked to the rock wall by a metal spike. I still called him a monster, but he was now just a scrawny, dirty man.

"Ariel!" Lumes called. "Where are you?"

"Here, Prophet," came the mischievous voice.

Lumes continued to look around, evidently as disoriented by her movements as I.

"We must be going," Ariel said. "This was a fun distraction, but our master calls."

"Your work is done," Lumes said. "Tonight was the longest night. After tonight, one way or another, we are done with your monster."

The pudgy prophet interrupted. "The sun is rising, Master. Villagers are already arriving with tribute."

Lumes grinned. "Excellent!"

The prophets left the cave. I shivered behind the crates for a time.

The raggedy man-monster called to me in a raspy whisper. Tangled black hair hung over his eyes. His chains rattled as he scooted a bowl of half-eaten scraps toward me. I think he was offering me food.

"You attacked us last night," I said.

I couldn't understand his quiet pleas. I'm told our mountain language is unlike any in the lowlands.

He gave up on communication and rested his face in his hands.

I couldn't believe this pitiful man was the same monster who attacked us last night. The same monster who killed little Elsa's family. Gaping tears remained in the back of his doublet where leather wings once carried him through the night.

Lumes' preaching was a distant whisper at the cave entrance.

Ariel startled me. "Well, boy? What are you still doing here?"

I recoiled from the voice. "Are you the prophet's servant?"

"No one controls me. Much." Her voice circled the room. "The master wants the monster, so I am bringing the monster, but travelling is so tedious. The prophets offered me entertainment, so I agreed to play by their rules. The monster is theirs until the longest night is over."

She must have seen my face trying to follow her voice.

"Are you looking for me?" Her voice jumped to the other side of the room. "Am I here?" then jumped again. "Am I there?"

Ariel cackled and the man-monster withdrew into the corner, as frightened as I was.

"If you are going to go, now is the time." Ariel's voice was now by the entrance. "Follow me."

My clothes were still damp, but at least they weren't frozen anymore.

"Come on!" The voice was behind me again and moved through me like a frigid wind.

Once dressed, I kneeled by the cave mouth. Ariel directed me to stop behind a pile of evergreen wreaths and stay close to the mountain wall.

The rising sun stained the valley red. Someone from every family in the village gazed up at Lumes. Lumes and his prophets had their backs to me as they looked upon the flock.

"Another of the unfaithful has died at the hands of Night," Lumes said. "But this shall be the last! Through your faith, the Day is reborn! The long night is over!"

The wind stole the warmth from my damp clothes. Only one villager looked my way, but I ignored her and continued away from the crowd. I was in a hurry to get home, and running kept me from thinking about the cold. My stomach cramped, and my breath came in rapid clouds. The village was in sight, but I had to stop for a moment.

"Ariel?" I called. She didn't answer, but I had no way of knowing if the spirit was really gone.

The cold permeated my clothes, and I forced myself onward. All the homes had wreaths on their doors.

Mother shrieked and embraced me. She stripped me and hung my clothes next to the fire. Even reserved little Elsa gave me a warm hug. Dazed and exhausted, I sluggishly returned the gesture.

Other clothes hung by the fire. The foreigner lay near the crackling warmth. Bandages covered his hands. I could see two fingers on one hand and one finger on the other had been removed. I could not see his toes, but I knew some of them would be gone as well. The remaining digits were gray in color. Once a digit froze solid, it would poison the rest of the body unless removed.

Mother gave me a bowl, and I spooned warm, salty broth into my mouth. I reclined by the fire while Mother rubbed my icy toes with her calloused hands.

I awoke when Father came in. He had narrow, deep cuts in his arm.

"I looked for you all day!" he said. "We were back in the village before we saw you weren't with us."

"You're alive!" I exclaimed.

He nodded but was grim. "Josa wasn't so lucky."

Thankfully, Father didn't mention my cowardice. It was hard to believe Josa would never make faces at me again. I had run. He had stayed.

"I took shelter in the prophet's cave," I said. "The prophets keep the monster like a pet!"

The foreigner suddenly became excited. "You saw? In daytime?" He was better with our language than the man-monster, but still hard to understand. "What was he like?"

The stranger's sudden intensity scared me, but I tried to answer. "He's not what you expect. He is a man. The prophets use a spirit to control him."

The foreigner covered his face with his mutilated hands and rocked back and forth. I'd never seen a grown man cry.

The foreigner tried to explain. "I was sent to return him to Valora. He never stayed in one place more than one night until now." The foreigner looked at his hands. "I've finally caught up to him, but there is nothing I can do."

"Oscar," Father said. "Are you sure the monster is in the prophet's cave?"

"Yes! I was just there."

Father slung an ax over his shoulder and headed for the door.

"Please," the foreigner pleaded. "Don't hurt him. He is harmless in daytime."

Father turned briefly. "I make no promises."

I dressed in dry clothes. Mother tried to stop me from going into the cold again, but I wasn't about to stay home. Not going would be the same as running away again.

Smiling villagers parted before Father.

"Why so grim?" someone asked. "The long night is over!"

Lumes and one assistant smiled at the cave entrance. "Enough of you showed faith," Lumes announced. "Enough of you gave offerings, hung wreaths on your doors. The Sun is pleased! The Day is reborn! If we remain faithful, the days will grow longer once again. If we remain faithful, this land shall be resurrected!"

"It was the prophets all along!" Father announced. "They control the monster!"

The villagers closed around Father, making it impossible to get any closer to Lumes.

Bilbee appeared amid the crowd. His eyes were dim and puffy. "We were wrong. There is hope now. Josa can be the last to die."

"Go home!" another shouted. "The Sun is the way to salvation! Embrace the Sun or leave!"

"You never liked Sun worshippers." Bilbee said. "Josa's death was as much your fault as the monster's!"

The entire village had turned against us. These people had been our friends yesterday. Every person here owed Father a favor.

"I saw it!" I shouted, but the crowd drowned out my tiny voice.

Father stared into Lumes' face. "If the prophets are not responsible... Lumes will not mind if we look inside."

The crowd quieted for a time. Father never took his eyes off Lumes.

Lumes narrowed his eyes. "Be our guest, but remember: this is sacred ground. Do not offend the Sun on his special day."

Father pushed past Lumes. I was close behind, followed by Bilbee and three other villagers.

The great, gold disk caught light from outside, and the paternal face seemed to be scowling. I led Father back by the crates and the untended fire.

There was a chink in the wall where the metal stake had been, but the chains were gone.

"He was here!" I insisted.

Father tried to push behind the crates, but Bilbee held him back.

"You have seen inside," Bilbee said.

They ignored me, and I moved ahead. All I could see in the darkness were mats for sleeping and a small table. The rear of the cave wasn't big enough to hide anyone.

"Are you happy?" Bilbee asked. "They had no obligation to let you look."

"Go home!" someone shouted. "You will ruin everything!"

Father and I started homeward.

"I'm sorry," I said. "I swear he was in there this morning."

I could see my tracks in the snow from when I had hugged the rocks that morning. Other tracks now marred my own. Two others had followed a similar path. One of them had stumbled and fallen.

Once away from the crowd, I told Father about the tracks. "Did you notice Lumes only had one assistant with him this afternoon?"

Father continued homeward, as though I hadn't said a thing.

"I swear, Father! The monster was there this morning!"

He stopped and let out a long sigh. We headed back up the mountain but veered north of the cave so we would not confront the villagers again. We came upon a set of tracks in the snow. Now there was only one set of footprints and the two shallow divots of a sled.

We followed the tracks for a time, but we weren't dressed for a long trek. My fingers were numb, and I couldn't feel my nose. Father stopped.

"Just a little further," I begged.

"It isn't worth dying over. Night is almost here. You almost froze to death last night."

Father didn't believe me anymore.

I gazed in the direction of the tracks. Something moved up the slope. A pudgy man in orange robes dragged a sled.

"Look!" I shouted.

"He is far ahead of us. I don't see any monster with him."

The man lying on the sled was too distant to make out clearly. Perhaps Father didn't see him. "The monster is on the sled. He is just a man in the daytime!"

Father still hesitated.

"We can catch him!" I insisted.

Father pressed on, and I followed. We were not burdened by a sled like the pudgy prophet, and he grew larger as we came closer.

The shadows became longer.

The pudgy prophet saw us and sped up for a time, but he must have known he could not outpace us as the slope became steeper. He pulled his prisoner from the sled and unchained his manacles. The man-monster fell into the snow. The prophet kicked him in the ribs, but the man just lay there. The prophet left the man and approached us.

A cold breeze circled us, and I heard a whisper in my ear. "About time you showed up."

With the increase in elevation, we didn't have the mountain shadow to warn us night had arrived.

The raggedy man rose on his arms. His eyes glowed pale orange.

"Father!" I yelled. "The Night Monster!"

The prophet looked at the lumbering man-monster behind him. The monster's face shrank over his skull. Leather wings shot from his back.

The prophet looked to us and smiled. "You are too late." He brandished the disk around his neck. "Did you forget your necklaces?"

The monster pounced on the prophet, who stumbled and tried to regain his footing.

"Ariel!" the prophet shouted. "Ariel! Your monster is attacking the wrong man!"

Childlike laughter echoed in the dusk.

"Lead him away!" the prophet screamed.

"You are not our master," came the girlish voice. "The longest night is over, and so is our game."

The monster sliced through the prophet's yellow robes and fat stomach.

The prophet's screams suddenly stopped. The monster gnashed its skeletal teeth at us and leapt. Its winged shadow fell upon us.

Ariel's girlish giggling came again.

A frigid wind blew down from the monsters flapping wings, and he shot past us. His wings blew the snow beneath him, and he circled back.

"Come along," Ariel said. "Our true master awaits."

The monster rose into the night and soared over the northern peaks.

Father and I exchanged amazed looks, then turned our attention to the dead prophet at our feet. Steam rose from his fresh wounds. We loaded the body onto the sled and turned homeward.

A halo over the distant village surprised us. I feared the village was on fire. With a few kicks we got the sled moving and didn't need to kick off again for several feet, which sped our return quite a bit.

The outskirts of the village were dark and deserted, so we hauled our dead cargo to the center of town. A stack of dry pine trees burned in the town square. Children danced around the blaze singing.

Lumes wore a tall hat and handed out candied fruit. The prophets must have brought the sweet treats from the lowlands. When Lumes saw the sled, the color drained from his face.

Everyone looked in our direction.

Lumes ran. His remaining assistant stood stunned for a moment before following.

Father began to pursue them, but Bilbee blocked our path.

"The monster killed this prophet," Father said.

"Just now," I added. "*After* the longest night was over. The prophets were leading the monster away now that they were done with him."

Bilbee scowled. "More likely *you* killed him! You never liked Sun Prophets!"

A crowd was forming around us, and my breath caught in my throat. "How could you think that?" I asked.

"Look at the body!" Father demanded. "Did *we* do that?"

The men of the village looked the body over. I was frustrated by their lack of urgency. The long, narrow cuts were obviously the work of the monster.

"It can't be," Bilbee finally said. "That would mean…"

Father put a hand on Bilbee's shoulder, as though that could dam up the emotion within him.

The veins pulsed in Bilbee's forehead. "The prophets killed Josa."

Bilbee charged out of the crowd, and we chased after him. A few of the other men followed behind us with torches.

We found the prophets outside their cave with a hastily loaded sled. When Lumes saw us, they abandoned their cargo. It amused me to see the prophets raise their long robes in an attempt to run on the icy slope. Bilbee charged into them and knocked them down.

Bilbee panted, unable to speak.

"You don't understand!" Lumes said. "We saved you!"

Father lifted Lumes by the neck of his robe.

"We trapped the monster last night," Lumes said. "Our brother led it north, back to Winter's realm."

Bilbee looked confused for a moment. I feared he would believe their latest lie, but instead, he punched Lumes in the chin, knocking him back to the ground.

"Then why did you run from us?" Bilbee screamed. "You killed Josa!"

"No!" Lumes pleaded, but Bilbee kicked him in the chin before he could say another word.

Father held Bilbee back.

"Throw them on the fire!" Bilbee said.

"No," Father said. "Let them go."

Everyone turned to Father. Even the two prophets looked doubtfully up at him. I wanted to see those Sun prophets burn as much as Bilbee did. I wanted them to suffer for what they did to Josa and to Elsa's family.

Father said, "Let the mountain decide their fate."

The crowd seemed to relax a little. Lumes and his assistant took up their sled. With a last, fearful look over their shoulders, they started down the mountain.

Bilbee's body was tense, and tears filled his eyes. "Why?" he asked. "They killed my boy!"

"Do you think we let them off?" Father asked. "Two soft men like that travelling the mountain passes this time of year? They will have a worse time out there than they would in our fire."

Bilbee stormed off alone.

We returned to the town square. The children were singing a song of Sun's triumph over Night. I protested the lyrics, but Father said, "It doesn't matter."

"But—"

Father held my shoulder in his big hand. "It doesn't matter. Let them be happy."

Mother greeted us and gave Father a warm kiss. I wasn't accustomed to seeing my parents so affectionate. Someone handed me a cup of spiced cider. The warmth felt good against my raw throat.

Elsa gnawed on a piece of candied fruit. She was too little to join the other children around the fire, so she began dancing around us instead. It was the first time I had seen her smile since her parents had died. It was impossible to stay angry when looking into those joyous eyes.

The entire village was here. No one was afraid to be out tonight. We broke open the stores of food, faithful spring would arrive in a few months and our supplies would be replenished.

Father was right. The people were happy.

The days would grow long, and spring's resurrection was on its way. The long night was finally over…

At least until next year.

ABOUT THE AUTHOR

Matthew Barron was raised by a dog in the cornfields of southern Indiana. His biological parents coaxed him back into the house with television and comic books. He still has a healthy distrust of humans, who are much scarier than anything in his stories.

In addition to two indispensable creative writing classes, Matthew got a degree in Clinical Laboratory Science from Indiana State University and became a medical technologist in Indianapolis, Indiana.

Matthew's diverse stories have appeared in several magazines and anthologies such as *Generation X-ed, And the Dead Shall Sleep No More, Ill-Considered Expeditions,* and many more. In addition to his prose books and short stories, he's produced two of his plays—*I'm Not Gay* (2015) and *Phantom of Fountain Square* (2019)—and released three graphic novels: *Temple of Secrets, The Brute: Chasing Shadows* and *Harmony Unbound.* In 2021 he released a paranormal mystery called *Buried Curses,* a follow-up to 2020's *Waking Terror.* His sword sorcery book *Valora,* dystopian novella *Secular City Limits,* and children's book *The Lonely Princess* are also available.

For more information, visit
matthewbarron.com
or
submatterpress.com

THE WORLDS OF MATTHEW BARRON

GRAPHIC NOVELS

PARANORMAL MYSTERY

KID'S FICTION

FANTASY

DYSTOPIAN

AND MORE

Made in the USA
Columbia, SC
31 August 2024

40798426R00154